PRAISE FOR

A Lady's Guide to Mischief and Mayhem

'With wicked smart dialogue and incredibly strong characters, Manda Collins reminds me why I love historical romance so much. Witty, intelligent, and hard to put down, you'll love *A Lady's Guide to Mischief and Mayhem*.'
—Rachel Van Dyken, #1 *New York Times* bestselling author

'When I pick up a Manda Collins book, I know I'm in for a treat. With compelling characters and a rich Victorian setting, *A Lady's Guide to Mischief and Mayhem* weaves mystery and romance into one enthralling tale.'
—Tessa Dare, *New York Times* bestselling author

'[Manda] Collins is a delight! I read *A Lady's Guide to Mischief and Mayhem* waaay past my bedtime, absorbed by its spot-on period detail, the well-crafted characters, and, of course, the intriguing mystery. Brava!'
—Elizabeth Hoyt, *New York Times* bestselling author

'Mystery, romance, and an indomitable heroine make for a brisk, compelling read.'
—Madeline Hunter, *New York Times* bestselling author

'Both romance and mystery fans will find this a treat.'
—*Publishers Weekly*

*For Aunt Sue, who probably doesn't know
what murderino means, but is one.*

A Lady's Guide to
Mischief and Mayhem

Prologue

London, 1865

If Sir Horace did not desist from his asinine talk about what constituted appropriate conversation for a lady, she would do one of them an injury, thought Lady Katherine Bascomb, hiding her scowl behind her fan.

She was quite fond of his wife, Millie, who'd been a friend since the two ladies had made their debuts together, but it really was hard work to endure the company of Sir Horace Fairchild as a condition of seeing her friend.

Kate had allowed herself to be persuaded away from the evening she'd had planned of catching up on the latest news of the murderer who was currently roaming the streets of the metropolis, the so-called "Commandments Killer," in order to make up the numbers for Millie's dinner party.

A decision she'd regretted as soon as she was ushered into the Fairchild townhouse on Belgrave Square and saw that the guests were among the most stiff-rumped in London.

She'd suffered through dinner, where she'd politely listened to a member of Parliament drone on about the need for something to be done about the coarseness of language in the English press—it never having occurred to him that she was, herself, owner of one of those newspapers. (Or perhaps it had but he did not care. Men were far less prone to diplomacy in their conversation than ladies, in Kate's experience.)

Then, thinking to find some more sensible conversation when the ladies withdrew to leave the gentlemen to their port, she'd been trapped in a corner of the drawing room with Mrs. Elspeth Symes, who'd talked of nothing but purgatives and remedies for digestive ailments for nearly a quarter hour without pausing for breath.

The reappearance of the gentlemen had given her a chance to escape Mrs. Symes, but no sooner had she accepted a cup of tea and a plate of what looked to be delicious biscuits than Sir Horace began to speak.

If this was what one had to endure to maintain friendships, Kate thought crossly, then really it was better to remain at home alone.

"Not if I do him an injury first," said a voice from beside her. And to her horror, Kate realized she'd spoken aloud.

Turning, she saw that a dark-haired young woman had taken the seat beside her.

"Caroline Hardcastle." She offered her gloved hand. "My friends call me Caro. We met before dinner, but really, anyone who is capable of remembering names after one introduction is not worth knowing, don't you agree?"

Kate blinked. Miss Hardcastle was a tiny creature with

large dark eyes and a pointed chin. She was exactly what Kate's mind would have conjured if she'd tried to imagine a woodland sprite in exquisitely tailored silk.

"These are quite good," Miss Hardcastle continued, biting into a biscuit. "I detect a hint of lemon, but it's not enough to overpower. And the shortbread is exceptional. There's not enough butter, but one can't have everything, I suppose."

"I'm Lady Katherine Bascomb." She felt as if she should say something, and there were so many options that Kate decided to go with the most obvious.

"Oh, I know who you are." Caro discreetly brushed the crumbs from her hands. "I read your column in *The Gazette* religiously. I'm something of a writer myself, but my work is mostly about cookery. I was pleased to learn you would be a guest tonight, so I could meet you."

Kate opened her mouth to demur at the compliment, then Caro's words sank in. "Caroline Hardcastle. You don't mean to say you're C. E. Hardcastle, the cookbook author? I think you're too modest! There's not a housewife in London without one of your recipe books in her home."

But Miss Hardcastle waved away the praise. "It's little more than trial and error coupled with writing down observations. I daresay anyone could do it if they felt the inclination."

It was the sort of modesty that was expected of ladies, but Kate disliked seeing someone as obviously talented as Miss Hardcastle so dismissive of her own talent. "Your books are more than just recipes, though. There are bits of history and cultural notes. I've read all of them, and

I only set foot in the kitchen to give instructions to my cook."

Flags of color appeared in Caro's cheeks. "Thank you. Coming from you, that's praise indeed."

Clearly uncomfortable with the discussion of her own writing, Caro changed the subject. "It seems we were both captured by less than entertaining conversationalists before we found each other." She cast her eyes in the direction of their host, who was speaking to the room at large. "And now we all are forced to listen to this lecture on propriety from a man who is known throughout the *ton* for his affairs."

That was news to Kate. Poor Millie. She'd known Sir Horace was a rotter; she just hadn't realized how much of one he was.

"He is a bit hard to take, isn't he?" Caro said, watching as the man continued his monologue.

"And really, how dare he suggest that any topic should be off-limits for ladies?" Kate scowled. "After all, we ought to know what's going on in the world around us. We are the ones who are most often preyed upon by unscrupulous, and even deadly, men. I, for one, would even go so far as to say that if ladies were encouraged to speak openly about the things that most frightened us, we would all be the safer for it. One cannot protect against a danger that's completely unknown."

As she spoke, Kate's voice rose and, as sometimes happens, did so during a lull in the other discussions in the room.

"I must protest, Lady Katherine," said a portly gentleman with walrus-like whiskers. "Ladies are not constitutionally strong enough to hear about the harshness in our world. It is our job as fathers, brothers, husbands, to protect you from the knowledge of such things. Why, I know of one young lady who went mad from hearing about such awfulness."

Before she could respond to the criticism, Kate heard a sound that was partway between a train coming into the station and a kettle on the boil. To her amusement, it had erupted from Miss Hardcastle's mouth.

"Mr. Symes, please acquit us with some degree of sense. I know very well you're speaking of your niece, Miss Ruby Compton, and everyone knows that she was and is far from mad. She simply chose to fall in love with a fellow neither you nor her parents found smart enough and you had her spirited away to Scotland. The story of her madness and fictitious institutionalization might very well fool some people, but I knew Ruby at school and had the full story from another school friend."

It was quite difficult to watch the man's mouth open and close, rather like a fish removed from a stream, without laughing, so Kate decided to speak instead.

"I agree with Miss Hardcastle. It does no one any good to be wrapped in cotton wool and protected from the things that pose the most danger. I don't suppose you would agree that it was perfectly acceptable to tell your daughter that arsenic is safe to eat, Sir Horace? Or you, Mr. Harrington, would you tell your sister that your prize bull poses no danger to her?"

Not waiting for them to respond, Kate continued, "Only a mile or so from here, there are girls as young as five years old who know more about the dangers posed by the predators of London than a gently raised young lady of eighteen. Why should an accident of birth mean that we should be kept in ignorance?"

"Well said," Caro agreed from beside her.

"I think Katherine's right." Millie's voice was a bit shaky, but she pressed on. "There are dangerous things, and men, in the city and yet you would protect us to such a degree that we wouldn't recognize the devil himself if he crossed our paths."

Kate rather suspected Satan counted disguise as one of his specialties, but refrained from pointing it out.

"An excellent point." Caro gave a smile of encouragement to Millie. "And since Scotland Yard hasn't managed to capture the likes of the Commandments Killer as yet, then we need every tool at our disposal. And knowledge happens to be the most readily available."

At the mention of the murderer whose string of killings across the capital had even the most confident of men looking over their shoulders, a murmur went through the room.

"Now, Miss Hardcastle, you go too far," said Sir Horace. "The superintendent of police is a good friend of mine, and he's got his best man working on the case."

At the mention of the man leading the investigation, Kate couldn't stop her own sound of skepticism. "If you mean Inspector Andrew Eversham, Sir Horace, then I fear your confidence is misplaced. He's been leading the investigation for months now and hasn't brought forth one reliable suspect."

"There was a hint in *The Chronicle* that Eversham was

fixated on the theory that perhaps the killer was a trades-man because he was so easily able to move through the streets," a matronly lady with graying gold hair offered. "But I think perhaps a hansom cab driver could just as easily elude capture."

"What about a servant?" asked Mrs. Araminta Peabody. "They're always around, but one doesn't notice them, does one? Why, you there"—she gestured to a footman who was collecting the tea things—"you might be the Command-ments Killer and we'd never even know it."

"Eversham is a good man, dash it," said Sir Horace, his florid face growing redder. "I won't have his name or that of Superintendent Darrow sullied in this way. This is just the sort of conversation that I was warning against earlier. See what's happened already? The lot of you women have grown overexcited. I daresay you've grown feverish, you're so overcome by all this talk of mischief and mayhem."

"Oh, don't be an ass, Horace," said the man to the left of him. He was a doctor, but Kate couldn't have recalled his name at pistol point. "This talk is no more dangerous for ladies than it is for men." He turned to Kate. "I think the Commandments Killer is a woman, myself. Remember that a posy was found on the body of the second victim. It's possible it was from a man's buttonhole, but I don't know many men who would wear forget-me-nots."

At the doctor's words, the room erupted into chaos.

Under cover of the din, Kate turned to Caro.

"I know we've just met, but I've an idea for my paper and I think you might be interested. What would you think about our writing a column together about this sort of thing?"

"About men trying to stop us from commonsense understanding of the world around us?"

Kate laughed. "Not quite. I had something else in mind. A column about our thoughts on the kind of crimes typified by the Commandments Killer. Two of the victims have been women, after all. These are the sorts of things ladies find of interest but are discouraged from speaking about."

Caro tilted her head, a grin widening on her face.

"A sort of lady's guide to murder, you mean?"

"Yes, but I think we should call it *A Lady's Guide to Mischief and Mayhem*."

"A tribute to Sir Horace?" Caro tittered.

"Exactly right." Kate glanced over to where that gentleman was holding forth on more of his notions of propriety. "He deserves it, don't you think?"

Chapter One

One Week Later

"And this is my office," Kate said, ushering Caro into her refuge at *The London Gazette*.

It was unusual for a woman to spend time in what was generally considered to be a male sphere, even more so for her to carve out space there. But she'd made it clear to the publisher, managers, and editors when she'd assumed ownership after her husband's death that she intended to write for the paper and to give her input when she thought it necessary.

"Have a seat," she continued, gesturing toward an uphol-stered chair, then moving to take her own seat behind the large cherry desk that grounded the room. A thick Aubusson rug covered the floor, and gas lamps abolished the gloom of the fog beyond the window. "My secretary, Flora, will bring us some refreshments in a moment and then we can discuss our ideas for the column."

Caro, who was outfitted in a deep green silk gown with a matching hat perched rakishly atop her dark curls, looked around her with wide-eyed interest. "You've created a refuge for yourself here. I approve."

They'd started the morning with a tour of the premises, moving from the basement, where the printing presses and typesetters were housed, and making their way up to the floor where the executive offices were located. Kate's office was a corner one and offered a view of the city that was unparalleled—or it would have done if the fog ever lifted enough to allow it. "It wasn't without controversy." She leaned back in her chair. "I may have been the new owner, but none of the men in positions of authority were keen on having a lady on the premises day in, day out. But they eventually came around."

She was understating things a bit. The manager and several of the editors had expressed their disapproval of her plans in no uncertain terms. When she'd made it clear that they were welcome to find employment elsewhere, however, these objections had mysteriously evaporated. After a few years they'd all learned to work together, and if the men still had complaints, they at least kept them away from her ears.

"I can only imagine." Caro frowned. "There is little men dislike more than having a woman disrupt what they consider their own personal territory."

Kate removed a notebook from a desk drawer and took up the fountain pen lying on the blotter. "Now, let's talk about our first column. It should be about the Commandments Killer, yes?"

Removing her own notebook from the little purse she carried at her wrist, Caro agreed. "As two of the victims have been women, I think it's more important than ever that we offer a female perspective on the case. Women are frightened. And rightly so."

Deciding they'd better get a handle on the case itself before they wrote about it, Kate asked, "What do we know about the investigation so far?"

"There have been four victims, two men and two women." Caro read the names of the victims from her notebook, where she'd already written them down. "Each has been left in a conspicuous location, with a note bearing one of the Ten Commandments left somewhere at the scene."

"Here." Kate moved to where a slate like those found in most schoolrooms lay propped against the wall. Lifting it, she hung it on a blank bit of wall from a hook on the back. Taking a piece of chalk, she neatly wrote the names of each victim in one column, the location of the body in another, and the Commandment that had been left with each body in the last. "Now, what can we conclude from this list?"

"The Commandments are out of order," Caro said after staring at the list for a moment. "Nate Slade, the first victim, was marked with the Tenth Commandment, 'Thou shalt not covet thy neighbor's goods,' but the second victim, Martha Peters, was left with the Fifth, 'Honor thy father and thy mother.' And so on."

"Good point," Kate said thoughtfully. "I wonder why."

"It's possible the killer selects his victims based on things they've said or done and so chooses the Commandment to fit the victim and not the other way round," Caro said. "I read in an article about Slade that he was known for his jealousy of his brother's boots, which he himself could never have afforded on his wages. He'd complained rather vocally about them in his local pub the day before he was found dead."

"Oh!" Kate began shuffling through a stack of newspapers on her desk. When she found what she was looking for, she said with triumph, "Here it is. The fourth victim, Betsy Creamer, was overheard at a chophouse, near where her body was found, declaring that she'd not been to church in over a year. She was marked with 'Remember to keep holy the Sabbath.'"

It took them some time, but after the two ladies had read through the accumulated stories about the four victims, they found associations between each of the victims and something they'd done or said that went against the Commandments that had been left with their bodies.

"This is important." Kate shook her head in disbelief. "But we've had our best reporters on this story for weeks, and they've heard nothing about Scotland Yard making this connection."

"It's possible they've already come to the same conclusions we have and haven't told the public about it," Caro said. "It's my understanding that they don't especially care for the press."

"But there should be some sort of warning," Kate said. "People are in danger from this killer, and there's been no warning about this."

"To be fair," Caro said, "I wouldn't know how to phrase

such a warning and I've written four books. They were about cookery, mind you, but I'm not unfamiliar with words. Not to mention the fact that a great many people in London break the Commandments on a daily basis."

"I suppose that makes some degree of sense. We don't wish to sound as judgmental as the killer, after all." But Kate still believed the Yard could be doing a better job of getting the word out about the possible motives behind the killings. "And perhaps our column can do something to warn those at risk."

Quickly, they agreed on a basic outline for what they wished to convey in their first foray into writing as a team. Both thought it would be best to give an outline of who had been killed so far, a sketch of their ages and occupations, and whom they'd left behind. Neither wished to dwell on the "sins" that the killer had deemed serious enough to warrant death, so they kept their discussion of the notes and the Commandments to a paragraph at the end, where they issued a general warning that until the culprit was apprehended, the population at large should be very careful about whom they interacted with.

It took them nearly two hours, but finally the two ladies had a sheaf of pages comprising the inaugural *A Lady's Guide to Mischief and Mayhem* column.

"I know it's probably inappropriate to get pleasure from such a dark subject." Caro smiled ruefully. "But that was fun."

"Life is hard enough that I think we must take our pleasure where it is offered," Kate said pragmatically. "Thank you for agreeing to my mad invitation. Not only because this *was* fun but also because I think we can do some real good with our column."

"I hope so." Caro stood and stretched her back. "At the very least we'll be offering a feminine perspective on what has thus far been a very male-centered discussion."

"And if our writing can spur Scotland Yard into doing a better job and perhaps even catching the killer?" Kate asked. "I for one would not mind that in the least."

"Hear, hear." Caro gathered up her things.

"I know it's early to talk about our next column," Kate said, rising from her own chair, "but I think we should do a bit of investigating for it. Perhaps talk to the people at the places where the female victims were last seen."

Caro beamed. "It's never too early to talk about writing. And I think we will get along capitally, because I was just about to make the same suggestion. When shall we start?"

Kate turned back from locking her office door. "Is tomorrow morning too soon?"

"There it is, up ahead," Kate said the next morning as she and Caro, accompanied by Caro's very large footman, made their way through the heart of Spitalfields. "The White Hart."

It was their second stop of the day, which had begun with a trip to The Queen's Arms in Whitechapel, where their questions had been met with blank stares and a decisive reluctance to answer them. Though they'd both donned their oldest, most unfashionable gowns for their errand, their cultured accents marked them as outsiders. That they'd also identified themselves as members of the press only made their task that much harder.

Undaunted, they'd hailed a hansom cab and had him drop them a street away from their destination so that they could get a feel for the neighborhood.

What they'd discovered so far was, in daytime at least, a lively area teeming with people. There were children playing games in the street, a few of whom watched the unfamiliar faces with unashamed curiosity. A beggar, to whom both Kate and Caro gave a few pence each, greeted them as they reached the corner.

There was nothing that marked the area as any better or worse than other locations in the nation's largest metropolis. And yet the body of a murdered woman had been found only yards away last week. Unable to help herself, Kate glanced toward the alley where Betsy Creamer's body, riddled with stab wounds, had been found with a note about keeping the Sabbath day holy propped against her.

"You're to remain out here while we go inside, James," Caro said to the tall young footman who seemed to be more aghast at their surroundings than the ladies he was accompanying.

"But Mrs. Hardcastle made me promise," the young man protested.

"What my mother doesn't know won't hurt her," Caro said sharply. "Besides, I've brought my pistol."

If anything, the man's face turned more alarmed.

Taking pity on him, Kate said, "I'll make sure she doesn't

come to any harm, James. Wait for us here on the corner. We won't be long."

James nodded at her assurance and turned to stand near the corner outside the chophouse.

"Thank you," Caro said in an undertone. "I didn't realize how fastidious he'd become since he was elevated to footman. I used to be able to rely upon him not to take Mama's threats too seriously when he was just a groom."

Kate felt a pang of pity for the young man. He very likely didn't wish to lose his position. And who could blame him?

"Shall we go inside?" she asked Caro instead.

Together they neared the door of the bustling chophouse, where customers brushed against them as they exited the establishment and entering patrons crowded together as they made their way inside.

The smell of grilled meat and unwashed bodies met them as they stepped into the dim interior, lit with gas lamps on the walls. It was clear at once that speaking with the barmaids would be difficult since even at this hour the place was crowded.

But Kate had an idea.

Taking Caro by the arm, she led her toward the back of the room where a door opened into the alley behind the building.

"I was hoping to at least get a chop out of this visit," Caro said as she followed Kate into the lane.

"We were never going to be able to speak to anyone in there." Kate shrugged as she scanned the narrow area for signs of life. Just to their right, a young woman wearing similar clothing to that of the servers inside The White Hart stood leaning against the back wall. "Look," she whispered to Caro.

Her eyes lighting up, Caro followed Kate as she walked toward the woman.

"Is it always this crowded before noon?" Kate asked as they approached.

The girl had obviously been working for some time if the dampness of her hair and the grease stains on the front of her skirt were anything to go by. The cap she wore over her copper-colored hair was slightly askew and her eyes looked as if they'd seen far more in her young life than she should have.

Those same eyes, a watery blue, looked on the two new-comers with suspicion. "Factory shift ends at ten, and today was payday."

"That makes sense," Kate said agreeably. "We're from *The Gazette*. Would it be all right if we asked you a few questions?"

If anything, the girl's eyes narrowed even further. "'Bout what?"

Kate decided to go ahead and ask without preamble. "Were you working the night Betsy Creamer was here?"

"Worked most nights when Betsy was here. She was a regular customer."

"So, you knew her well, Miss—?" Kate left the question dangling in the hopes that the girl would give her name.

She was not disappointed.

"Lizzie Grainger." She frowned. "No 'Miss.' I ain't puttin' on airs."

"And I'm Kate and this is Caro." Kate gestured to her friend, who had taken out her notebook and pencil from some hidden interior pocket of her gown. "Do you mind if we take notes?"

"Suit yourself."

Thanking her, Kate continued her questioning. "So, Lizzie, you said that Betsy ate here frequently? Did you know her well?"

"Well enough. She didn't deserve what happened to her, that's for sure." For the first time, Lizzie's face showed real emotion. "She was a good girl. Who cares if she didn't go to church? Not many around here that does."

"Were you working the night before she was found?" Kate asked again. "It's just that there was a story in one of the other papers that noted she'd said something about not having gone to church on Sunday in over a year?"

"Aye, I were here." Lizzie scowled. "I even saw the fella she left with, though nobody from the police ever asked me about it."

Kate and Caro exchanged a glance. There had been nothing in the papers about Betsy having been seen with a man the evening before her death.

"Can you describe him for me?" Kate asked.

"He was a looker," Lizzie said thoughtfully. "His clothes were fancier than we see around here, too."

She gave a speaking glance toward Kate and Caro's gowns. "Like yours."

So much for their attempts to blend in. Kate realized now how foolish they'd been to think anything from their own closets would work. The gowns were several years out of fashion, but there was no disguising they'd been crafted by London's finest modistes.

"What about his hair?" Caro asked. "Light, dark?"

"It was a bit lighter than yours." Lizzie nodded at Kate. "And he was about as tall as you, too."

"Did he have a beard?" Kate asked. "Or side-whiskers?"

Lizzie shook her head. "No, his face was clean."

Kate asked a few more questions, but it was clear that Lizzie had told them all she knew about the man's appearance.

"So, you said Betsy left with him that evening," she said. "Was there anything unusual about that? Did Betsy often leave with men?"

Lizzie scowled. "She weren't no lightskirt. I told you she was a good girl. You're like all the rest trying to make it sound like she was asking for it."

Kate realized her error and did her best to make amends. "I'm sorry. I didn't mean to imply your friend was asking for what happened to her. I only wish to find out if this was the first time you'd seen her leave with this man."

"It was the first and last time I seen the man at all." Lizzie seemed to accept Kate's apology. "And what worried me about it was the fact that Betsy was almost falling down. I knew that gal for years and I never seen her drink enough to make her that bad off."

Could the man have poisoned Betsy's food or drink?

Tears shone in Lizzie's eyes. "I should have gone after her. I would have if I wasn't up to me ears in customers and I need this job. But still I should have gone after her. If I had, she might be here now."

Kate reached out a hand to touch the girl's shoulder. "You had no way of knowing what would happen. And if you had followed them, he might have killed you, too."

Caro offered the girl her handkerchief and Lizzie blew her nose loudly into it. "Keep it." Caro's tone rose an octave when the barmaid tried to hand the soiled cloth back to her.

"Would it be all right with you if we put this information you've shared in the paper?" Kate asked. She would, of course, give the description of the man Betsy had left with to Scotland Yard. "We won't use your name if you don't want. But it would probably be a good idea for us to give your name to the police so that they can talk to you."

At the mention of the police, Lizzie scowled. "You didn't say you worked for them."

"We don't," Caro explained, "but if they haven't spoken to you before now, it probably means they don't know about the man or what you saw. It might help them find Betsy's killer."

Grudgingly Lizzie nodded. "I s'pose it won't do no harm."

Thanking her, Kate and Caro asked a few more questions about how long Lizzie had worked at the chophouse and some information about her background.

By the time they made their way back through The White Hart and out the front door, they'd been gone for nearly an hour and the look of relief on James's face when they emerged was almost comical.

When he'd gone to hail them a cab, Caro turned to Kate with a gleam in her eye. "How did we find a bigger clue in this case than the Yard has found in all these months?"

"I don't know." Kate shook her head. "But we're going to add this interview with Lizzie to our first column. Even if this man she described isn't the killer, at the very least he was the last person to see Betsy alive. And if he is the killer, then I for one look forward to having something concrete to warn the vulnerable women of London about."

"And if the police object?"

"They missed their chance to interview Lizzie Grainger themselves," Kate said firmly. "We'll give them the information she gave us once we go to print, but they have no authority over me or my newspaper. And if they ask, I'll tell them so."

Chapter Two

"Sir, you'll want to see this."

Andrew Eversham looked up from the witness statement he'd been rereading for the umpteenth time.

There had to be something here that he was missing.

Already there were four dead at the hands of the so-called "Commandments Killer" and he hadn't as yet found a viable suspect.

It was hard to believe that before this incident, he'd been celebrated for his ability to solve cases that left other investigators scratching their heads in confusion. "What is it, Ransom?" He looked up to see the younger man holding up a newspaper. Was it already time for the papers to be out? A glance at the clock on the wall told him it was nearing dawn and he heaved a sigh. He'd been working all night and yet had found nothing in any of the documents that might point him to the killer's identity.

Taking the paper, still wet with newsprint, from Ransom, he read the headline and uttered a curse. "Who the hell is this witness?"

A quick scan of the story revealed that one Lizzie Grainger had seen the latest victim, Betsy Creamer, leave with an unknown man on the night before she was found dead.

After nearly ten years on the job, he knew better than to take one newspaper article at face value, but *The London Gazette* was known for its scrupulous attention to the facts—unlike some broadsheets that invented stories out of whole cloth. The author's name gave him another start. He'd never heard of C. Hardcastle, but if memory served, Bascomb was the surname of the paper's owner.

"We spoke with everybody who was at The White Hart on the night Betsy Creamer disappeared, Mr. Eversham." The chagrin on Paul Ransom's babyish face revealed all. "I don't know how this Grainger woman could have been missed."

Ransom might not know how it had happened, but Eversham did.

He should never have trusted Adolphus Wargrove to conduct the interviews with the employees at the chophouse. He'd known his fellow detective liked to cut corners, but he hadn't believed Dolph would be so sloppy with a case. It was well known within the Yard that his colleague also harbored jealousy over Eversham's successes over the years, but to go so far as endangering lives in an effort to ensure this case went unsolved was too much.

As if conjured by Eversham's thoughts, the man himself strode in.

"Bad break, yer lordship." Wargrove's grin belied his words. "How can you have missed such an important witness?"

The nickname was one that the other man had bestowed upon Eversham as soon as he'd learned that Eversham's father, a country vicar, was a baronet's son. Never mind that the family had long ago disowned the elder Eversham for marrying beneath him. Or that Andrew Eversham had never even met his grandfather or any of his extended family. He'd managed to dispel most of the suspicion from his fellow officers and underlings at the Yard through careful police work and success in some of the more complex cases he'd been trusted with. And yet, Dolph Wargrove, who only saw Eversham's successes through the lens of his own failures, never missed an opportunity to remind Eversham that he didn't quite fit in among his colleagues.

It had taken every one of his years with the Yard to prove himself to those who doubted someone from his background could do the job, but he'd managed it.

And now, Wargrove would do his level best to make sure that this oversight of a key witness in one of the biggest cases Eversham had ever worked would be his downfall.

He would have liked to blame the omission entirely on Wargrove, but Eversham had never been one to shirk responsibility. He'd known damned well when he delegated such an important task to a shoddy investigator like Wargrove he was taking a risk. But with half of his men down with the ague, he'd had no choice. He only hoped Darrow would understand.

Careful not to let his colleague see his rising temper—any sign of upset on his part would only give the man satisfaction, which Eversham was determined not to give him—he said with a calm he didn't feel, "I believe you took care of the interviews at The White Hart, didn't you?"

If he'd hoped for a show of remorse, Eversham was to be sorely mistaken.

"It's a poor craftsman who blames his tools, Eversham," Wargrove said with mock disappointment. "I thought you were the one renowned for your famous deductive skills. Shouldn't you have figured it out and directed your underlings accordingly?"

"Since when have you ever considered yourself anyone's underling, Wargrove?" Eversham couldn't help scoffing at the other man's false humility.

Unable to take any more of Wargrove's vitriol, Eversham rose from his desk. Turning to Ransom, who'd been watching the interplay between his superiors with wide eyes, he said, "Come with me. We're going to speak with Lizzie Grainger before the rest of the papers get to her." What he decidedly did not need was every bit of her encounter with the likely killer plastered across the front page of the afternoon editions before he'd had a chance to glean any new details from her.

"Oh, that won't be necessary, Eversham," Wargrove said coolly. "I'll be doing that in a bit. After you bring me up to date on the details of the case."

Eversham felt alarm prickle at the nape of his neck.

Before he could question Wargrove's words, the man continued, "Darrow's removed you from it altogether."

"Don't be absurd." Eversham spoke before he could stop himself. "Darrow wouldn't do that without informing me first."

"Go and speak to him yourself if you don't believe me." Wargrove shrugged. "And when you're done, I'll need that update as quick as you can. There's a lot of missed ground to cover here, and I'd expect you won't want to delay justice for another minute."

Eversham's jaw ached from how hard he was clenching his teeth. Without a backward glance, he made for the stairs and Chief Superintendent Max Darrow's office.

"It couldn't be helped," his super said even before Eversham could ask. Gesturing him toward a chair, Darrow sighed when Eversham chose to stand. "You know as well as I do that as soon as the people lose confidence in the Met's handling of a case, there's nothing we can do to restore it."

"But, sir, I'm the only one who's been on the Commandments case since the beginning." Eversham tried not to sound aggrieved, but he'd never been taken off a case in his ten-plus years with the Yard. Not only was it a blow to his ego, but more importantly, if he was at fault, he deserved the chance to make things right.

"And that's why it's time for a pair of fresh eyes." The older man's bushy brows lowered. "I didn't want to tell you this, but there have been some inquiries from not only members of Parliament but also the Home Office about this case. They want the Commandments Killer caught, and they aren't willing to continue on with you at the head of the investigation."

At that news, Eversham sat down heavily in the chair he'd earlier declined. He'd heard of other detectives falling victim to the ill winds of political pressure, but he'd naively never expected such a thing to befall him.

The pity in Darrow's eyes was almost his undoing. "I know it's not what you wanted to hear, son, but my job's on the line here, too. You've had a good run. Better than most. Let's see what Wargrove can do with it for the time being."

"But Wargrove?" Eversham didn't try to hide the disgust in his voice. He was no longer concerned about sounding petulant now that he knew there was no way to talk Darrow out of removing him from the case. "Sir, he's the worst kind of investigator. Slipshod and at times dangerously incompetent."

"That's enough, Eversham," Darrow snapped. "My mind is made up, and criticizing your fellows won't keep you from demotion."

He longed to tell Darrow that it had been Wargrove's mistake that had led to the omission of Lizzie Grainger as a witness, but he knew casting blame now would only sound churlish.

There was nothing for it now but to slink off and lick his wounds.

"What do I do in the meantime?" Eversham asked, rising from his chair.

"There's plenty to be done downstairs. Speak to Manton and ask if he's got files that need sorting."

If Darrow had spit in his face, Eversham could not have been more affronted.

And yet, there was nothing to do but take his medicine and wait for the storm to pass.

Ashamed and degraded, he left the superintendent's office. The closing of the door sounded eerily like the click of imaginary leg irons, holding him in place while the investigation went on without him.

"This is the last one, my lady." Flora hoisted the third and final mail bag of the day onto Kate's desk at the newspaper.

In the week since the inaugural run of Kate and Caro's *A Lady's Guide to Mischief and Mayhem* and their subsequent interview with Lizzie Grainger, letters had poured into the newspaper offices from all over the country with suggestions as to the identity of the mystery man with whom Betsy Creamer was last seen.

And much to both Kate and Caro's delight, they'd also received any number of notes from women thanking them for offering a feminine perspective on not only the Commandments killings themselves, but also crime in general. *For make no mistake, even when we aren't the ones what gets murdered*, one Sussex woman had written, *we sure be the ones what has to clean up the mess.*

If the accolades had been peppered with other, not so pleasant, missives whose authors objected to the very notion of women writing about such dark subjects, well, neither Kate nor Caro had been surprised. There were still a great many in England—male and female—who would never look kindly upon progress. Even when it contributed to the public good.

"Thank you so much, Flora," Kate told the bespectacled young woman. "I don't know what I'd do without you."

"I daresay you'd disappear beneath a collapsed pile of newspapers," Flora said wryly.

Glancing around at her office, which was piled high with the last week's editions of various competing newspapers, Kate had to admit her assistant had a point.

"Will you be taking these to Miss Hardcastle's now?" Kate straightened a pile of letters she'd set aside for Caro to look at. "I'll have the next lot ready to go in the morning."

Before Flora could reply, Caro herself burst through the office door, an enormous Siamese cat clutched in her arms.

"I'm sorry to barge in," she said, looking flustered. "But I was walking Ludwig when I heard the news and I came right over."

Upon closer inspection, the cat appeared to be wearing a diamond-studded collar with a leash attached. As if sensing the attention, he began to struggle in his mistress's arms and leapt to the ground.

Turning back to Caro, Kate asked, "What's happened?"

"There's been an arrest in the Commandments case." Caro's brown eyes, which were already large, were positively enormous with excitement. "I saw it on the front of the afternoon edition of *The Times*."

Whatever Kate had been expecting, it wasn't that. "Are you sure?"

Caro reached into the large embroidered bag she used to carry Ludwig when he wasn't on a leash and pulled out a folded newspaper. "Here," she said, "see for yourself."

Taking the paper, Kate saw that just as Caro had declared, one John Clark had been arrested for the murders of Nate Slade, Martha Peters, Leo Burke, and Betsy Creamer. Clark fit the description of the man last seen with Betsy Creamer at The White Hart on the night before her body had been found. There was no further information on how he had been linked to the other murders, but Mr. Adolphus Wargrove of Scotland Yard would be available to take questions that evening at six.

"We did it," Caro said emphatically. "Our interview of Lizzie Grainger led to the arrest of a killer."

But Kate would need to see the man for herself before she would be able to rest easy.

The news that Detective Inspector Eversham had been replaced on the case by Adolphus Wargrove, thanks to their column, had been welcome, but from what Kate had been able to glean from the crime reporters in *The Gazette*'s newsroom, Wargrove wasn't known for his investigative skills. And Kate found it suspicious that Wargrove had made an arrest only a week after he'd taken over the reins of the investigation.

"Maybe." Seeing her friend's frown, she added, "I hope our work led the police to John Clark, but I must admit I won't believe it until I hear more from Inspector Wargrove."

Caro patted her arm. "One of us has to be the skeptical one, I suppose."

Kate laughed in spite of herself. If only Caro had known her before her marriage, when she'd taken everyone at face value. The loss of her naivete had not been easy or painless. But she wouldn't dare go back for anything. She liked to think that her eye wasn't so much jaundiced as discerning.

Even so, she wouldn't be the one to rob Caro of her innocence.

"Come," she said. "Let's go and see what Mr. Wargrove has to say for himself."

She moved to gather her things, and when she turned back around, it was to see that Ludwig was now sleeping peacefully in Flora's lap.

"How extraordinary." Caro shook her head. "Ludwig dislikes most people. But he adores you, Miss Morrison."

"I have this effect on most animals." The young woman shrugged. "I've become so used to it, I forgot to warn you."

"Warn me?" Caro asked. "I'm thrilled. You have no notion how difficult it is to find someone to take care of him when I'm away."

"Are you attempting to abscond with my secretary, Caro?" Kate demanded with amusement.

To her credit, Caro looked rueful. "I won't steal her permanently. Only when you don't have work for her."

"I'll look after him while you go to Scotland Yard," Flora offered.

And with Ludwig's care disposed of for the time being, Kate and Caro set out for Westminster and Scotland Yard.

They were several streets away when the traffic became such that the hansom cab they were traveling in drew to a halt. A glance out the carriage door was enough to show them that the streets were teeming with people.

Clearly they weren't the only ones who'd come out to see what Mr. Wargrove had to say regarding the arrest of the Commandments Killer.

"I wish I'd thought to bring James," Caro said as they disembarked. "I may dislike being reminded of the fact that I'm not as strong as a man, but I'm not so foolish as to think it's not true."

"We should be all right so long as we stick together." Kate looped her arm through Caro's.

It took them nearly half an hour to near the entrance to the Canon Row police station, which housed one of the most prominent divisions of the Metropolitan Police Force. A platform had been erected to one side of the door, which Kate supposed was so Wargrove would be able to be seen above the crowd.

"What a spectacle," she said in disgust. It wasn't that she begrudged the police a moment to declare to the populace that a dangerous killer had been caught. If the man was found guilty at trial, just as much fanfare would go into his hanging. But Kate had never been easy with that sort of gruesome display either.

"I suppose they're thankful it's as well attended as it is,"

Caro said wryly. "I'd hate to think they'd put in all this effort at pageantry only to have no one show up."

As they watched, several men climbed the steps leading up the side of the platform. A portly man with enormous side-whiskers and a world-weary air stepped forward and called for quiet. It took some time for the crowd to settle, but eventually they did.

Finally, the older man introduced himself as Chief Superintendent Max Darrow. He said a few words about how hard his men had worked on the case. How glad he was that they'd finally nabbed the man responsible for the Commandments killings. How he was certain the man would be found guilty by the courts. When he finished, he introduced Inspector Adolphus Wargrove, crediting his quick thinking for the capture of John Clark.

Kate looked on with curiosity at the officer. He was a solidly built man with a barrel chest and wiry red side-whiskers. A receding hairline made him look older than she suspected he truly was. But it was the man's words that she paid the closest attention to.

"I stand before you today, good people of London, as the man who captured the Commandments Killer," he said loudly. And as he'd apparently hoped, the crowd roared with approval. "Others tried before me, but I am the one who succeeded."

"This fellow is proud of himself, isn't he?" Caro shouted from beside her. "It was our interview with Lizzie Grainger that got him a description of the killer. Yet no mention at all of our assistance."

"We didn't do it for the thanks," Kate reminded her. But she, too, was annoyed that Wargrove was behaving as if he had found John Clark all on his own. "Though they would be appreciated."

As Wargrove continued to speak, the crowd began to grow restless. More than once, Kate was bumped from behind, and though she and Caro struggled to remain together, one strong jolt separated them for good.

"Caro," Kate shouted above the din, but before she knew it, her friend had been swallowed up in the maelstrom and she herself was fighting to remain upright.

The feel of a strong arm about her waist had Kate shouting again, though this time with fear. Twisting to get a look at her assailant, she could see only a clean-shaven face and a ruffled head of light brown hair. "Unhand me!"

"Easy there, Mrs. Bascomb," her captor said in the same way one might soothe a startled horse. Before she could ask how he knew her name, he continued, "Besides, if anyone should be concerned here, it's me. I'm the one whose career you've managed to destroy."

This last he said calmly enough, but she could hear the leashed anger in his tone.

"I'm afraid you have the advantage of me, sir," Kate said haughtily. Whoever this man was, he clearly had some quarrel with her and she wished to get away from him with all possible haste. And yet, with the crowd surging around them, it was impossible to move away.

"Stop struggling," he said curtly. "No matter how much I would rather leave you to this mob, I'm still a sworn officer of the law and it's my duty to help you."

His words brought her up short. "Who are you?" But even as she spoke, she knew what he would say.

"Detective Inspector Andrew Eversham," he said, confirming her suspicions. "Now, stop talking so that I can get us out of here."

Chapter Three

He wasn't sure what he'd expected to gain by going to Dolph Wargrove's self-congratulatory assembly, but Eversham most assuredly had not thought to encounter the authors of the infernal interview that Wargrove had used to arrest an innocent man.

One of them—Miss Hardcastle, he supposed, thanks to Mrs. Bascomb calling out to her as Caro—had been swallowed up in the first wave of unruly attendees. If she was lucky, she'd manage to get far enough away to catch a hansom cab. In the meantime, it was taking every ounce of strength and concentration he had to keep the other journalist, Mrs. Bascomb, from being snatched away into the teeming masses.

"I'm Mrs. Bascomb," she said suddenly, as if their current posture would be less improper with introductions.

"Though it sounds as if you'd already guessed that, Mr. Eversham."

He wasn't sure what she expected him to say. Thank you for ruining a reputation it had taken more than a decade to build? It certainly wasn't time for conversation. But despite his impatience with her, Eversham spoke up anyway. "Charmed."

That only made him feel like more of an arse.

"If you don't mind, let's save the small talk for once we're clear of these marauders." That would have to do, he decided as he propelled them forward and toward a side street that would get them to the Embankment, where he could put his charge in a cab.

It took twenty minutes of difficult maneuvering, but finally they managed to get clear of the densest group of bodies, and soon they were able to walk freely side by side.

"I can find my way from here, Mr. Eversham." Stiffly she held out a hand to him.

He wasn't quite sure how she managed it when he was taller than she by several inches, but somehow Mrs. Bascomb was looking down her nose at him.

Eversham stared at her hand for a moment, trying to figure out how it was possible for him to be any angrier with this woman.

He ignored her hand. "What is your given name, please?"

She frowned. "I'm not sure what that has to do with—"

"Ma'am, I just escorted you through a throng of people who were moments away from rioting. The least you can do is humor me by telling me what the 'K' stands for in your pen name."

It was a trivial detail, he knew, but he found himself wanting to know the full name of the woman responsible for his downfall.

"Please don't think I'm ungrateful," she said hastily. "I am truly—"

He cut her off again. "Just tell me your bloody name, please."

Her gray eyes widened at his curse, but she didn't chide him. "Katherine." She licked her lips, then went on. "Katherine Bascomb."

He studied her. He imagined at the beginning of the day her deep blue gown had been clean and her shiny black hair hadn't been falling from its pins. And it went without saying that she'd probably been wearing a hat. And if he hadn't held her responsible for the ruination of a career it had taken him over a decade to build, he might even have found her attractive.

But she was the architect of his downfall, and he most assuredly did not find her attractive.

Not in the least.

"Well, Katherine Bascomb," he said, not bothering to hide his temper from her, "if you don't mind, I'm going to escort you to the Embankment so that I can see you safely into a hansom cab. And then, if there's any justice in this world, I'll never have to lay eyes on you again."

Once again, her eyes widened, and Eversham felt an unwelcome pang of conscience.

"I'm not sure what you believe I've done to you, Mr. Eversham," she said, pulling herself up to her not unimpressive height, "but I can assure you that had you been doing your job as the lead investigator on the Commandments Killer case, then there would have been no need for me to find and interview Lizzie Grainger."

"Ah, there she is," he said waspishly. "The crusader who believes she knows better how to solve a murder than a thousand-man police force. By all means, Mrs. Bascomb, tell me how you would have done things differently."

"For one thing, I'd have made sure to interview every person working at the establishment where Betsy Creamer was last seen on the night before her murder." Her cheekbones were flushed with annoyance and her gray eyes blazed. "Maybe if you'd bothered to do that, you might have been the one to solve the case instead of that arrogant showman Adolphus Wargrove."

"On the subject of Wargrove, madam, we are in perfect agreement." Eversham scowled. "As for the rest of it, I suppose we'll have to agree to disagree. I only hope you won't live to regret your decision to play at being a detective. The man Dolph Wargrove has locked up barely matched Lizzie's description. Not to mention that there's no evidence tying him to the other three murders. But he's close enough to make the Home Secretary happy. And I suppose that's all that matters."

He'd never been particularly savvy at the political part of his job. His innate sense of right and wrong meant that he was often in conflict with those in the upper echelons of government who preferred speedy justice and triumphant headlines. But he'd never had one of his own investigations manipulated in such a way as to ensure the wrong man was faced with hanging. Wargrove, with whom he'd had run-ins over ethics before, hadn't surprised him. But he'd thought Max was better than that. Or at least that he had a strong enough backbone to withstand pressure from the Home Office.

Eversham might not be able to change the minds of his superiors with appeals to decency, but he hoped that bringing the actual murderer to them would do the trick. It was no longer his case—or anyone's for that matter— but he could do his best to ensure John Clark escaped the hangman's noose.

His determination—or ire—must have shown in his expression because he saw a flash of surprise, then remorse, in Mrs. Bascomb's eyes before she hid the response behind a cool mask of civility.

"You've said your piece. Now will you please get me a hansom cab so that I may return home?" Her full mouth was tight, as if she was trying to stop herself from saying more.

Eversham swept into a mocking bow. "Gladly."

As it happened, Kate spotted Caro beneath the glow of a nearby gas streetlamp a couple of streets away from where Eversham had seen her off.

It was only the work of a moment to get the driver to stop so that they could pick up her friend, and soon they were on their way toward Belgrave Square.

"I was so afraid I'd lost you forever," Caro said dramatically as she hugged Kate tightly to her. "What a debacle that was. Who knew that a simple announcement about a police investigation would turn into such a nightmare?"

"The Commandments Killer has been the most talked about subject among Londoners for nearly half a year," Kate said wryly. "I suppose we were foolish to misjudge the degree of interest there would be."

She was careful to maintain a bright tone, but inside she couldn't help thinking about what Eversham had said about John Clark, the suspect in custody for the killings. If the detective had been telling the truth, her column hadn't, in fact, helped capture a murderer. Instead it had only made it possible for the police to arrest a possibly innocent man.

It was a travesty of justice. And one thing she'd hoped to achieve with the column—along with helping women protect themselves from harm—had been to assist in bringing criminals to justice.

Now she wondered if her column had done more harm than good.

"Was it too terrible getting to somewhere you'd be able to find a cab?" Caro asked sympathetically. She must have assumed her friend was merely tired from her ordeal, for which Kate was grateful.

"It took far too long," Kate said truthfully. "And my poor feet are aching like mad."

"Mine too." Caro reached down to rub her toes through her kid boots. "I wish I could remove these entirely, but even I'm not brave enough to risk my stockings on the floor of a public conveyance. Who knows what sort of muck is down there?"

For the first time in hours, Kate laughed. "I wouldn't try it."

"So, what shall the next column be about?" Caro asked, switching subjects in that quicksilver way of hers. "Now that our first has managed to help apprehend a killer, I'm not sure how we can possibly make the second any more successful."

At the mention of the column, Kate bit back a wince. "Maybe we should wait a bit before we write another one."

Caro frowned. "Is there something wrong? I thought you were merely tired, but now you seem as if you don't wish to write with me after all. Which is perfectly fine. You only need to tell me and I'll—"

"No!" For a second, Kate considered sparing her friend the knowledge that their interview had been used to imprison an innocent man. But that would be fair to neither of them. "It's not you, I promise."

Never one to shy away from a difficult subject, Caro pressed her. "Then what is it? Did something happen in the crowd?"

Quickly, Kate told her what Eversham had said about the suspect the police had arrested.

Caro's eyes widened and she paled. "And you believe him? It wasn't sour grapes because he'd been taken off the case?"

"What reason would he have to lie?" Kate asked. "He was angry with us, of course. But I have no reason to doubt he was telling the truth. John Clark bears little resemblance to Lizzie's description."

They were both silent for a moment, the air in the enclosed carriage thick with regret.

"It never occurred to me," Caro said finally, "that our column could be used by the authorities to bolster their own incompetent police work. We were supposed to be illuminating the truth. Not helping to cover it up."

"Nor I," Kate agreed. "Since I took over the newspaper, I've made it my mission for our writers to adhere to the truth. Sensationalist rags in Fleet Street might traffic in exaggeration and outright lies, but *The Gazette* does not. But I never thought that the truth might be manipulated in such a way. Which I now realize was naive of me."

"Naive of both of us," Caro said firmly. "Our intentions were good, but to quote Samuel Johnson, 'hell is paved with good intentions.'"

"When we first conceived of this column, we aspired to help women protect themselves from just the sort of crimes committed by the Commandments Killer." Kate shook her head. "But we lost sight of our goals because we were—or at least I was—too caught up in the thought of catching the killer and, honestly, the accolades that might bring."

"I was just as enthralled by the notion as you were," Caro argued, "especially given how many missteps the police have made."

"And this doesn't mean that I intend to let the Yard get away with their deceptions," Kate assured her. "*The Gazette* has a very talented reporter who covers corruption and the like. I'll pass along what I learned from Detective Inspector Eversham to him. In the meantime, I think we should put off continuing with the column until we've come to a better understanding of just who it is we intend to help and how we can best do that while remaining true to ourselves."

"Agreed." Caro's expression was resolute, but her eyes were still troubled. "What can we do in the meantime about poor John Clark? What did Eversham say?"

"He didn't," Kate said. "And from the spectacle the police put on today, I doubt they're prepared to listen to the exhortations of the two ladies whose interview provided the very ammunition to arrest Clark."

"Just another thing to consider going forward." Caro scowled. "Why must men be such scoundrels?"

"Eversham seemed honest enough." Kate thought back to how angry he'd been—at them, but also at his comrades who'd manipulated the facts to suit their own ends. "Though he was hardly what I'd call a pleasant man."

"Honest or not, I'm sorry you had to endure his censure alone." Caro patted her hand. "But I do think there must be something we can do to ensure that Mr. Clark is released from custody sooner rather than later. Perhaps we could contact the Home Secretary?"

Her words gave Kate an idea. "I received an invitation to a house party at a friend's country estate in the Lake District. I was going to send my regrets, but now I think I'll let him know I'll be going after all."

At Caro's blank look, she added, "His father is a duke. I'd ask him myself, but I feel sure the request would bear more weight coming from, alas, a man."

"Oh, a duke will surely carry some weight with the Home Secretary." Caro's eyes lit with excitement. "It's frustrating, but until we're given the power and influence that we deserve, we must work with the tools at hand. In this case, our abilities to persuade others to do our bidding."

Continuing, Caro asked, "Is this friend anyone I know?"

"Lord Valentine Thorn." Kate was startled to see Caro's brown eyes narrow. "Oh, do you know him? We've been friends since childhood. And he writes sporting articles for *The Gazette,* so you'll likely see him from time to time at the offices."

"Yes, we've met," Caro said. And while Kate would have expected her to elaborate, she left off there.

Interesting. If she wasn't very much mistaken, her two best friends knew one another far better than Caro was willing to let on.

"So, you'll be gone for a week or two?" Caro asked before the cab stopped in front of the Hardcastles' townhouse in Mayfair.

"Yes, I'll need to make travel arrangements, but I'm sure I'll see you before I go," Kate said as Caro descended from the carriage. "I'll likely take the train up on Friday."

"If you'd like, I can sort through the rest of the letters," Caro said. "I hadn't considered how difficult it would be for you to read them all, then send them on to me. I'm willing to work, Kate, but you have to tell me what to do. In the beginning at least."

Her words brought Kate up short. Perhaps she had been taking care of herself for too long. "I would be grateful for the help," she said. "Thank you."

But she would still take some of the letters with her to the country. And perhaps she'd speak to some of the women in the nearby village as well. If they were going to truly aid women with their column, then they needed to ensure that they took the opinions of all women into consideration.

Before Caro walked away, Kate tried to reassure her friend. "We'll set things right for Mr. Clark. Even if we must apply to the queen herself for help."

Chapter Four

Thornfield Hall
Lewiston, the Lake District

The weak morning sun was no match against the crisp lake air as Kate trudged along the tree-lined path. She and the rest of the party from Thornfield Hall had started out early on their explorations of their host's property.

Lord Valentine Thorn, their host, was one of her oldest friends, and that was the only reason Kate had managed to keep from using her walking stick as a cudgel against the American industrialist who was a member of the excursion.

"You've never seen anything like it, Lady Katherine," he said, having moved on from boasting about the private train he'd hired for the duration of his stay in England, to extolling the grandeur of the estate he'd leased on the south coast. "It's larger than Devonshire's house. Bigger than the palace even. I daresay poor Thorn could fit three or four of his little lake houses inside of it."

In Kate's experience, men who felt the need to boast

about the size of their...estates...rarely came up to snuff when it came time for the big reveal.

And Mr. John Barton certainly did a great deal of boasting. About everything.

Ever since the guests had gathered on the first night of the house party, Kate had felt like a fox on the run from a particularly slobbery hound. She'd hoped this week away from the chaos of town would give her a chance to reflect on how else she might work to see that the wrongfully arrested Mr. Clark was freed, but though she had requested Lord Valentine contact his father to request his assistance, any further contemplation had been stifled by the unwanted attentions of John Barton.

"I think it's a lovely house, Papa," said his daughter, Tabitha, with a not-so-veiled glance of longing at Lord Valentine, who was walking just ahead of them. Perhaps looking for an ally, she added, "Don't you agree, Lady Katherine?"

"It's charming." Kate nodded. "I've thought so ever since Lord Valentine took possession of it. It's perfectly situated on the lake, and the surrounding country is perfect for those times when one needs a bit of invigorating country air."

Barton harrumphed but didn't object, though his expression was not unlike that of a cross child who'd been contradicted.

"I suppose someone like Lord Valentine has reason to retreat to the country now and then," Tabitha continued, ignoring her father's mood. "He must live such an exciting life."

"You can just stop with that nonsense this minute, my girl," Barton said baldly. "We came here to land a lord for you, but not a younger son. I've indulged you enough to come up here away from London, where most of my business is, but if this is how you mean to go on, we will make our excuses and go back to town."

On the one hand, Kate supposed she appreciated the way the American just came right out and admitted that their purpose for being in England was to, essentially, purchase a titled husband for Tabitha. Certainly any number of matchmaking mamas made their way to town each season with a similar aim—though they generally were looking for wealth to go along with the title.

On the other hand, she was, after all, a lady and had been raised from practically the cradle to find any sort of plain speaking distasteful. If one was chilled, one didn't say so; one just rubbed her arms. If one was angry, one sniffed.

Caro had made her more comfortable about saying out loud the things that were normally whispered, if mentioned at all. But it was still rather a novelty for Kate.

And even so, there was plain speaking of the sort she and Caro employed and then there was rudeness.

Barton's way was decidedly the latter.

"No, Papa! I didn't mean anything by it. Truly, I didn't." Miss Barton's embarrassment at her father's words was evident in her expression.

"I'm sure what Miss Barton means is that she's heard the stories of Lord Valentine's exploits as a journalist," she interjected, unable to keep from coming to the girl's defense.

Kate turned to Tabitha and gave her a reassuring glance

before continuing. "I'm afraid Lord Valentine spends a great deal of time in rather unsavory company for the sake of his work with *The Gazette*. But he comes to Thornfield Hall as often as he can, I believe."

Not quite mollified by Kate's attempt to smooth the waters, Barton took his daughter's arm in his and continued to scold, though with less vehemence than before.

Seeing her chance, Kate bent down to tie her bootlace and allowed some distance to grow between herself, the pair, and in front of them, the rest of the party.

Alone at last.

She really had wanted to take the opportunity this week afforded to think about both her goals for the column, and how best to help Mr. Clark. But the guests her host had assembled hadn't been chosen with her preferences in mind.

Lord Valentine Thorn was like a mischievous little boy; he delighted in bringing disparate people together under one roof in order to generate as much drama and interesting conversation as possible. Sometimes it worked and sometimes it most assuredly did not.

The current house party included among the guests ex-prize-fighter-turned-farmer "Gentleman" Jim Hyde; the Earl and Countess Eggleston, whose marriage had been a sensation in society since they'd met while she was betrothed to his brother; and lastly, Mr. Reeve Thompson, who seemed like a gentleman, but who Kate was coming to believe was a handsome n'er-do-well. And that didn't count Mr. and Miss Barton.

She really must think better of it the next time Val attempted to convince her *this* house party would be different from the last. At least he'd written his father, the Duke of Thornfield, on her behalf. As much as she'd like to resolve Clark's incarceration on her own, she knew that a request from a member of the nobility, and one as powerful as Thornfield at that, would do more good than all her efforts, no matter how sincere.

Still, she had made a list and written letters to other acquaintances and family members she thought might have some influence with the Home Office. And though she hadn't broached the subject with the other guests, she had spoken with Valentine, whose opinion she trusted, and made note of his suggestions. She might not have freed Mr. Clark just yet, but she had made headway in her attempt to do so.

Spying a trail that forked away from the one they'd been following around the lake, she used her walking stick to climb the uphill path into the cool shadows of the wood.

It really was lovely countryside. She'd been to the Lakes only once before, when she was a child, and that had been as a guest of a school friend, but she'd loved it. And though she hadn't visited the neighboring village thus far since her arrival, she would do so soon enough. Without the other guests, if she could help it.

She could only imagine the sort of comments Lady Eggleston and Mr. Barton would inject into her conversations with the villagers about their daily lives and the women's concerns about safety when visiting larger cities. The very idea sent a shudder through her.

What a strange few years it had been, she thought as she trudged up the path. Two years ago, her husband, George, had been alive and making her life unbearable. Now, she'd taken his newspaper—which he'd nearly let collapse through mismanagement—and turned it into one of the most profitable in the nation. Fortunately, it hadn't been entailed with the rest of his estate, and she'd managed to convince his heir, a distant cousin, to sell it to her at a shockingly low sum since he didn't wish to be seen dabbling in trade.

She was pleased with the success she'd made of *The Gazette* as a whole, but she'd had even higher hopes for the column with Caro. *A Lady's Guide to Mischief and Mayhem* had the potential to become a means of serving the female half of the city's population in a way the other papers did not.

Hopefully, her stay at Thornfield would give Kate the time she needed to consider a way forward for the column. Perhaps that would mean not focusing on specific cases. Or maybe they would take questions from the public about how women might better protect themselves from the myriad of dangers that made them feel unsafe. Clearly she would need to discuss with Caro, but she wanted more time to think before she broached the subject.

The breeze had begun to pick up a bit, and as she followed the winding trail, she saw that just ahead was a flatter bit of ground—almost like a staircase landing. The trail was actually called The Staircase, she remembered belatedly. Val had told them about it last night at dinner when he described the local landmarks.

Grateful for a place where she could sit for a moment and catch her breath, she finally reached the top of the ridge and was startled to see someone there before her.

"I hadn't realized..." she began, then stopped short when she realized what she was seeing.

Propped against a large rock sat a man. Or rather, a man's body, for a second glance revealed to Kate the blood seeping from the corner of his mouth. And his head was tilted at an improbable angle.

It was the estate manager of Thornfield Hall, Mr. Fenwick Jones. Kate had only spoken with him briefly during her stay, but he'd seemed to be a decent sort.

And now he was dead. Her mind wanted to find some other, less horrific explanation for the sight before her. But she knew the body before her was no life-sized wax figure like the ones at Madame Tussaud's Chamber of Horrors. This was a man she'd spoken with. A man who was no longer alive.

As she stepped closer, she saw the message. *I bore false witness*, the note proclaimed, the words scrawled across a large piece of pasteboard in what could only be blood.

Dear God. Either someone in the Lake District was using his methods or the Commandments Killer himself was here. And she was very much afraid the latter was the truth.

And when she realized that, self-possessed, even stoic Lady Katherine Bascomb began to scream.

Scotland Yard, London

If he had to file one more bloody document, he was going to do someone—preferably Inspector Adolphus Wargrove—an injury.

Eversham had never counted Wargrove as a friend, but he couldn't have guessed the other detective would be willing to put an innocent man in jail merely to further his career.

He'd lost respect not only for his colleague, but also for his commanding officer, Superintendent Darrow, who had bowed to pressure from the Home Office and Parliament to approve the arrest. He'd always heard complaints from outsiders that the police were corrupt, but he had prided himself on working with men who weren't of that ilk. There were those in the institution who behaved badly—what large group was perfect?—but his own colleagues and immediate superiors were decent. He'd been sure of it.

The Commandments Killer case—and Wargrove and Darrow's handling of it—had changed the way he viewed his profession, and that shook him to the core.

Against the advice of his family—who had wanted him to enter a more respectable profession like the law, or the church like his father—he'd gone into policing to make a difference. And he was good at it, damn it.

However, if he was going to remain with the Met, at the very least he should be doing the work that relied on his strengths. Not trapped here in the basement filing documents and evidence cards. He might have borne the demotion with more grace if he was convinced the man Wargrove had locked up was, in fact, the actual Commandments Killer. But there were too many reasons to doubt that John Clark had been the one to perpetrate the crimes.

Though Clark bore a faint resemblance to the description Lizzie Grainger had given of the man she'd seen the final victim with, he was the wrong height. He also walked with a limp, thanks to an accident at the factory where he worked, and which Lizzie had said in a later interview was not present in the man she saw. And, as a factory worker, it was highly unlikely that John Clark owned the sort of expensive clothes Lizzie had seen the killer wearing.

If that weren't enough, there was no evidence whatsoever linking Clark to the other three murders. If Eversham had still been in charge, he'd have spent the following week searching for Clark's connection to the rest of the crimes or trying to eliminate him as a suspect. Instead, Wargrove, in concert with Darrow, had rushed to arrest Clark just so they could claim the case had been solved.

Eversham prized the truth above all else. And scapegoating a man for the simple reason that the government wanted the case solved went against everything he stood for.

Thinking back to that farce of a day when Wargrove had announced Clark's arrest, Eversham was livid all over again. It had been nothing more than a performance put on for the benefit of the Home Office.

The only good thing to come about as a result was that Eversham had the opportunity to give a piece of his mind to one of the authors of the interview that had brought all of this about. Perhaps Katherine Bascomb hadn't known what would happen as a result of her interference, but that didn't excuse her.

Yes, it was his fault that Lizzie hadn't been interviewed in the first place. He took full responsibility for not making sure Wargrove had done his job. However, Mrs. Bascomb and her cohort should have come to the police as soon as they discovered Lizzie had seen something.

Lizzie's account of what she'd witnessed, and her description of the man who must have been the actual killer, was just the sort of detail he'd needed while the case was still his to investigate. As it was, he'd been kept so busy with mundane work, he'd not been able to go out and pursue new leads.

He was so lost in his own thoughts that he almost didn't hear the young constable call to him from the doorway to the file room.

"Super wants to see you, Eversham. He said don't dawdle."

Andrew straightened. For a split second, he considered that Darrow had come to his senses and had decided to reinstate him as a detective and allow him to finish his investigation. But his more realistic side suspected he was only in for an interrogation as to whether he was ready to acknowledge Wargrove had apprehended the right man.

As he neared the level where the upper echelons of the department kept offices, the floors were cleaner, the air was sweeter, the light was somehow brighter. The leadership at the Met were the *haute ton* of the police force and they lived like it.

When he reached the polished mahogany door with

a shiny brass nameplate reading *Chief Superintendent Max Darrow*, Eversham knocked briskly, and at the muffled sound of a voice on the other side, he opened the door and strode in.

The office was nearly as large as some houses Eversham had visited in the course of his work. The walls were papered in a finely drawn pattern of fruit trees intertwined with vines. Like his door, the super's desk was polished to a high sheen, and every fixture in the room was clean enough to show a reflection.

The man himself was much less polished. Eversham knew from gossip that Darrow had married into a prominent London family, and that had been his entree into his current position. But the fellow had spent years in the army in India, and his sun-weathered complexion bore witness to that. He was a strategic thinker, and far better at the politics of this job than Eversham could ever be. He'd thought they were friends of a kind, but that illusion had dissolved when his boss had knowingly allowed the arrest of the wrong man for the sake of those politics.

If turning one's back on one's principles was what it took to be effective, then Eversham was glad he'd never aspired to gain a higher rank.

"Ah, Eversham." Darrow removed the spectacles from his hawk-like nose and gestured for his guest to step in. "Have a seat. Have a seat."

The super had a habit of saying things twice in a row.

Inclining his head in acknowledgment, Eversham lowered himself into the leather-covered armchair across the desk from his superior.

Darrow leaned back in his chair and scanned him for a moment. "Well, I won't beat about the bush, man." He slapped the desk top with his open palm. "There's been a murder up in the Lake District that bears all the hallmarks of the Commandments Killer."

Eversham sat up straighter. "What does this mean, sir?"

Darrow steepled his fingers. "I know you'd like to think it means Wargrove was wrong, but it's too soon to determine such a thing. For all we know, it's someone up there who decided to put paid to his brother-in-law and cover it up by copying Clark's crimes."

"So, why tell me?" Eversham wasn't a fool. Darrow wouldn't have called him here only to inform him there'd been a similar killing.

The older man raised a bushy brow. "You argued very strenuously to me that Wargrove had arrested the wrong man. I told you that you were mistaken then, and I don't think anything has changed."

Eversham said nothing. He could sense something else was coming.

And he was right.

"However," Darrow continued, "this murder up at Lewiston does bear some striking similarities to Clark's crimes here in London. I won't jump to any conclusions just yet, but I am willing to send you up there to investigate."

Quickly, the superintendent outlined the details of the case. At the mention that Lady Katherine Bascomb had been the one to find the body, Eversham frowned. He didn't, as a general rule, believe in coincidences where crime was concerned. He wasn't sure how she might be involved in this new killing, but it was damned odd that the woman whose interview with a witness had led to an arrest was now a witness in another, similar murder investigation.

Then there was the fact that she had neglected to tell him her title. That she'd allowed him to call her Mrs. Bascomb for the entirety of their conversation was minor in the grand scheme of things. But it still annoyed him. Not that he'd have treated her any differently if he'd known she was a member of the nobility. But it would have been courteous to let him know.

He took notes as Darrow told him about the rest of the houseguests, and gave a brief outline of what to expect and a general sketch of the locale.

"I don't have to remind you, I hope, that you're not to make any public statements about whether or not this crime is linked to the London murders," Darrow warned him. "I've had enough trouble from the Home Office without your muddying the waters with baseless speculation."

Darrow's superiors would find out about the similarities between this murder and the Commandments Killer cases as soon as the London papers found out, Eversham knew, but he didn't point that out.

This was his chance to redeem himself and he wouldn't risk it by pointing out the obvious.

"Thank you, sir," he said, and meant it. "I won't let you down."

Darrow handed over a page that was the formal request from the local authorities in the village of Lewiston. "They're expecting you on the evening train. From there you'll need to take a cart to Thornfield Hall, the estate where the body was found."

"Very good, sir."

He was almost out the door when Darrow called out. "For the love of all that is holy, man, tread carefully around Lady Katherine Bascomb. She ruined your career once. Don't let her do it again!"

Chapter Five

Thornfield Hall

A full day had passed since she'd found the body of poor Mr. Jones, and Kate was still unable to get the sight of his body out of her mind.

She had followed crime in the press for years, but seeing a corpse in person was very different from reading about the details of a murder in the abstract. Aside from the gruesome nature of the sight, there was also the emotional toll of finding someone she'd interacted with in such a state.

Pulling her shawl closer around her, Kate looked up to see Lord Valentine, or Val as she had called him since they were children, watching her from the other side of the room, where he was in conversation with Gentleman Jim Hyde.

The members of the house party had been loath to go out of doors since the discovery of Jones's body the day before, and they were currently in the drawing room, scattered across the various clusters of chairs and sofas that could afford a degree of privacy even in a room filled with other people. Moonlight streamed through the long windows, as the sequestered house guests awaited after-dinner drinks with the enthusiasm of a nursery full of children who had been kept indoors for too long.

As Kate watched, Val excused himself from the boxer and moved to take a seat next to her on a long settee.

"You know you needn't remain down here with the rest of us if you don't wish to," he said quietly. "No one would blame you for taking to your bed with a headache."

"It wouldn't do any good." She sighed. "At least here I'm surrounded by people—even if they are talking nonsense for the most part."

Val laughed. "I only promised you that the guests at this party would be interesting. Not sensible."

"At least Mr. Barton has decided that he doesn't hold with females who discover bodies." She glanced over to where the American was no doubt regaling Lord Eggleston, another of the guests, about the size of his personal train car. Or perhaps it was his estate back in New York. Really it could be any of his possessions if she were honest.

Her host had the good grace to wince. "Now *that* I will agree was a misstep on my part. He did seem amusing when I met him, but I was quite drunk at the time, so perhaps my judgment wasn't at its best." They both laughed and then fell silent in that way two people who have known one another for decades could be.

"It's the same killer," she finally said in a low voice. Not wanting the rest of the party to hear her. "I know they've made an arrest in London, but I've followed this case from the beginning. The Commandments Killer is still uncaught and he's killed here, Val. He's *here*."

Val's expression turned serious. "I know. And I'm going to make sure that you—that all my guests—remain safe. That's why I sent for someone from Scotland Yard."

"But Scotland Yard bungled the case in London," Kate protested. With the exception of Eversham—who was no longer even involved in the investigation—the police believed John Clark was the Commandments Killer. "Worse, they arrested the wrong man. I told you that when I asked you to write your father. Whoever they send here is going to be investigating with an eye toward proving Jones's death was merely the work of an imitator. But that's not what this is. I'm sure of it."

Val's expression softened. "I believe you. But the village constable hasn't had to deal with this sort of thing before. The worst crime he's faced here has been the odd cow theft or a bout of fisticuffs between local lads. Like it or not, Scotland Yard is the only authority equipped to investigate this sort of thing."

"Besides," he added, "some of them must be honest. What about that fellow who told you what they were up to in arresting Clark in the first place?"

"Eversham," Kate said grudgingly. "But they're hardly going to send him. And even if they do. he was decidedly unpleasant, no matter how good the reasons for his anger may have been."

"Well, whoever they send," Val said, "perhaps you can have a word with him about your suspicions. My experience with detectives has been that they're more interested in discovering the truth of things than in fitting the facts of the case to their own theories."

After what she'd seen in London, Kate wasn't so sure, but she didn't tell that to Val. He was trying to make her feel better, which she appreciated for the moment.

Really, it was a shame that she felt not a scintilla of interest in him as a lover. He was handsome and funny and charming. And if she were to think of marrying again—and she most certainly wasn't—he would be an excellent choice. But having married once at the behest of her parents, she'd decided that she would never again put herself in a position where she ceded authority over herself to someone else. Even someone she trusted as much as Val.

"What?" he asked, his eyes narrowed with suspicion. "You look as if you're plotting."

"Only thinking." She wryly smiled. "He doesn't know it yet, but the killer has made a mistake by striking again so soon. Now I can prove that John Clark is innocent."

"I hope you don't mean that you intend to put yourself in danger by chasing after a murderer." Val's frown was severe. "I know better than to tell you what to do, but let me instead strongly suggest that you leave this sort of thing to the professionals."

"And so I shall," Kate said. So long as the professionals did their jobs.

No sooner were the words out of her mouth than the butler, Austen, entered the room. He spoke in a low voice to Val, who rose. "It would appear that the detective is here. And interestingly, it's someone you'll be familiar with."

Kate braced herself. If Adolphus Wargrove had been sent

here, then there was little chance the actual Commandments Killer would ever be apprehended.

"Detective Inspector Andrew Eversham." Val handed her the man's card.

To Austen, he said, "Show him in. I'm sure he'll wish to speak to all of us. He can arrange separate meetings after that."

Kate glanced down at the cream-colored card with Eversham's name embossed in black script across it. She wasn't sure whether to feel optimistic that Scotland Yard had sent someone to investigate who didn't believe John Clark was guilty, or concerned. For herself, she wondered what his reaction would be when he learned she'd been the one to find the body.

At their chance encounter, he'd shown in no uncertain terms that he held her to blame for the wrongful arrest of Clark. She hadn't considered how their interview with Lizzie might be manipulated to suit the police's needs, and that was something she regretted. But there was no denying that he'd neglected to interview Lizzie himself while he was in charge of the case. Which was what she'd tell him if he tried blaming her again.

A few minutes later, Eversham strode into the room after Austen. He was taller than she remembered. And unlike that day in London, the suit he wore was well tailored and neat. His light brown hair was neatly trimmed and his clean-shaven face was serious but not unpleasant. His nose was slightly crooked, but instead of marring his looks, it made his visage, which might have been too symmetrical without it, more interesting.

Though he had an air of authority, he managed somehow to blend into his surroundings. It was as if observing were his preferred mode of interacting with the world. Kate would wager that made him a better investigator.

She watched as Val greeted the newcomer and they spoke quietly for a moment. While they talked, Eversham scanned the room and Kate saw him notice her. His expression was inscrutable, but whatever he was feeling, she knew, given their last exchange, it wouldn't be pleasant.

"May I have your attention, everyone," Val said. "I'd like to introduce Mr. Eversham, an inspector from the Scotland Yard. He's come to look into the matter of Mr. Jones's death. And I'd ask that you answer whatever questions he might have for you so that we can get to the bottom of this business as quickly as possible."

Val introduced the assembled guests, and it appeared that Eversham made an effort to greet each of them by name, as if trying to commit them to memory.

"How soon can we leave?" John Barton asked when the introductions were complete. "I don't like my daughter here when there's a murderer on the loose. And I've business to attend to in London."

If he was flustered by the American's blunt questions, Eversham didn't show it. "I understand your concerns for your daughter's safety, Mr. Barton. However, I would ask that you remain here until I've had a chance to make a preliminary investigation into the matter. I want to clear each of you before you leave."

A few of the ladies gasped. "You don't think that we could have done this, surely?" Lady Genevieve Thorn asked. Val's sister was serving as his hostess for the party, and she was also an author of sensation novels, which Kate found intriguing.

Eversham seemed eager to assuage Genevieve's worries. "I don't suspect anyone at the moment, my lady. But you were all residing in the same house as Mr. Jones, so it would be remiss of me if I didn't question all of you if only to eliminate you from suspicion."

He hadn't actually said they were all in the clear, Kate noted. But his words seemed to have a calming effect, as he'd no doubt intended.

When she felt his gaze on her again, Kate felt a fluttering in her belly.

"Lady Katherine." His voice betrayed none of his thoughts. "Since you found the poor dead man, I'd like to speak with you first."

She rose and made her way to the door, where the inspector and Val waited for her.

"I've put the library at your disposal, Inspector," Val said as they walked together down the hall toward the book room.

When they arrived at the door, Val turned to Katherine. "If you'd like me to sit in for your interview..."

But Kate knew the discussion would be fraught enough without having Val along to witness it. "That won't be necessary," she told him before he could finish.

And before she could change her mind, she moved past where Eversham held the door open for her and stepped inside.

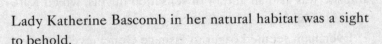

Lady Katherine Bascomb in her natural habitat was a sight to behold.

It was difficult to believe the woman he'd seen at the police assembly in London was the same polished sophisticate who stood before him now. It was even more of a stretch to believe that this was the same woman who had interviewed a Spitalfields barmaid about what she'd witnessed the evening before a murder.

Eversham watched her, as if for the first time, while she crossed the lushly carpeted floor and couldn't help noticing the sway of her hips as she walked. Her gown—a bright blue silk that complemented her dark hair—was expertly made and accentuated her figure in a subtle, but nonetheless enticing manner. Her nose was a bit too long and her lips too thin for her to be called beautiful, but there was a liveliness in her eyes that belied the placidity of her face as a whole. This woman would not be a good liar. Her eyes would always give away the game.

She was also rather tall, which he'd noticed in London. It would have been impossible not to when all those curves had been pressed tightly against him the day they'd met. He'd forgotten in the time since then, but he certainly remembered it now.

Realizing the direction of his thoughts, Eversham shook his head a little and moved to take the chair opposite hers. This was the woman whose writing had seriously endangered his career and made it possible for a murderer—

perhaps the one who'd killed the man she found dead—to go free. He could not afford to forget it.

His wandering thoughts firmly back under control, he was about to begin the interview when he was forestalled.

"I don't believe I ever thanked you," she said, "for rescuing me that day. You certainly didn't have to. And if you hadn't, well, I'm not sure what would have happened." She perched on the edge of her chair, very obviously not relaxed, but to her credit, didn't avoid his gaze as she spoke.

He hadn't expected it, and for a moment he was taken off guard: both by the apology, and by the fact that she, too, was thinking about the circumstances under which they'd met.

Still, he was here to do a job. A job he wanted very much to hold on to. So it would be best if he stuck to the matter at hand.

"It was no more than I'd have done for any other lady who found herself in need of assistance that day," he said curtly. "Though you might have told me about your title. You didn't correct me when I called you 'Mrs.'"

"Would it have made a difference in the way you treated me?" she asked. He felt as if he were being subjected to some sort of test. But he wasn't here to play games.

"Yes," Eversham said baldly. "But not the way you think, I imagine. If possible, I'd have been cooler. I have no great fondness for the aristocracy."

The way Eversham's father's family had treated him after his marriage to someone they considered beneath them had long colored the way Eversham felt about the upper classes. Not only because of his affection for his mother, but also because he'd seen the toll his family's rejection had had upon his father. He was a man who cared deeply about people. It's what made the elder Eversham such a good clergyman. But that was neither here nor there.

Lady Bascomb winced at his words. But she didn't look away. "You have every right to be angry, Mr. Eversham. But you must understand that we had no inkling that our column would be used by Wargrove to arrest the wrong man. You must believe me when I say that."

"Ignorance of the possible consequences of your actions is no excuse, my lady," Eversham said sharply. "You could have come to me when you realized I'd missed interviewing Lizzie Grainger. Instead you published her words for all the world to see. Not only did you give my colleagues a means of bolstering their arrest of the wrong man, you let the actual killer know that he was seen that night, possibly putting Lizzie Grainger's life in danger."

All the color drained from Lady Katherine's face and Eversham cursed himself for a fool. "Is that true? I should go back to London at once. Or at the very least send word to have her checked on. It never even occurred to me— though it should have—that by giving us that interview, she was risking her own life."

Striving to reassure her, where just a moment before he'd been intending to frighten some sense into her, Eversham said quickly, "There's no need for that. I have a man I trust keeping a close watch on her while I'm here. There hasn't been any sign that the killer has designs upon her."

"That is something, I suppose." She shook her head. "And I'm grateful to you for looking after Lizzie's safety."

"It wouldn't have been necessary if you'd only told me about her in the first place," he couldn't help saying. "There is something to be said for allowing the police to take care of things like this. Not only did you endanger Lizzie, but you endangered yourself as well. A lady should be mindful to know her place in matters such as these."

If he thought Lady Katherine would sit idly by at that bit of criticism, however, he soon learned his mistake. "First of all"—her eyes flashed with pique—"I've apologized. And I'm still considering how to make amends for the consequences of my actions. Whether you forgive me or not is your own business. But I will not listen to you speak about what a lady should and should not do. There was a time when I would have heard your words and bit my tongue and let them pass. Because that's what ladies are supposed to do. Well, for me, the time of holding my tongue has passed."

Eversham was surprised by her vehemence. He was about to make some remark intended to calm her when he realized she wasn't finished. She'd only been drawing breath so that she could continue her speech.

"Who do you think must deal with the aftermath of these murders you investigate, Mr. Eversham? Is it the men of the house who must wash and prepare the body for burial? No, it's the women. Who comforts the poor children of the dead when they wake up crying in the night? It's not the men of the house. It's the nursemaid, or the governess, or the mother. And then, other times, they can't be there to perform these duties, because they themselves are the victims. In fact, I'd wager you've deduced on your own that when women are the victims, the culprit is most likely to be the husband or lover. I'd wager that in your position as a detective, you don't even get called out to investigate most murders of the lower classes, because their killings don't merit the kind of resources reserved for the all too rare murders of the middle and upper classes. After all, the women of the lower classes are interchangeable and one is just as good as another."

Eversham blinked. Clearly she'd spent a great deal of time thinking about this. And perhaps she had a point.

"Lady Katherine, it wasn't my intention to suggest that—"

But, her spleen vented, she seemed to deflate a little. "There's no need to paper it over with niceties, Mr. Eversham. We each know where the other stands now. You believe my interview of Lizzie Grainger was careless and improper. I think you are a gifted detective but have little understanding of what life is like for the female population. You aren't the first man to suffer from this failing and you won't be the last. I simply ask that you consider my words the next time you think to dismiss some act by a lady as improper. Consider how much of what we've designated as proper and improper is less about manners and more about keeping ladies in their place. Where they won't get in the way of the men."

She sat back in her chair and waved a hand in his direction, as if instructing him to get on with it.

Lady Katherine Bascomb was certainly not dull, Eversham thought. He could admit to himself, even if he would be flogged before admitting it aloud in her presence, that she wasn't wrong in her assessment of how society treated women. And he couldn't help thinking of how difficult life must have been for someone like her—outspoken, clever, ready to stand for her principles when threatened. She was unlike any woman he'd ever known. In his experience, women—especially ladies—were coy and at times manipulative. He didn't blame them. It was, in some instances, their only means of wielding any control over their lives. But there was nothing of those traits about Lady Katherine.

She said what she meant. And she spoke with conviction, her eyes lighting up with a fire that made him think of how she might respond in other passionate situations.

Which was an entirely inappropriate line of thought, he reminded himself ruthlessly. Even if he could recall with an embarrassing degree of detail just how magnificent she'd been with her eyes flashing and bosom heaving.

Needing to wrest control of the conversation, he said, "Now that we've settled our previous disagreement, let me ask you some questions about what happened when you found Mr. Jones. Why don't you tell me, in your own words, exactly what happened?"

Her expression turned somber. "Should I begin from the moment I spied him or before that?"

"Wherever you wish."

Slowly, carefully, she told the tale of how she'd become stuck with the Bartons and had effected her escape by wandering up the secondary path.

"Had you known about this other path before you came upon it?" Eversham asked.

"No, Mr. Thompson had a guidebook to Lewiston, but it contained descriptions of walks closer to the village itself.

Val did tell us that there were any number of trails leading from his property around the lake and up into the hills, but he was never specific. This has been a rather relaxed house party, aside from the murder obviously."

She spoke with a straight face, but it took only a moment for the absurdity of her words to sink in, and Lady Bascomb gave a little gasp of laughter. "I do beg your pardon. I know it's not funny, but my goodness, what an odd few days this has been."

It was not uncommon in Eversham's experience for those affected by sudden death or bereavement to respond with unexpected mirth. Death was an odd business, and everyone dealt with it differently.

He rose, came around the desk, and lowered to his haunches in front of her. "You have nothing to be ashamed of, my lady. Now, why don't you tell me about finding the body."

She seemed comforted by his nearness—or at least that was what he hoped—and in a remarkably steady voice told him about hiking up the hill and seeing the horror there. When it came to details about Mr. Jones's body, she was remarkably thorough, even going so far as to note that he was slumped to the left. And that the note pinned to his shirt was secured with a ladies' hat pin.

"It's him, isn't it?" she asked when he didn't speak up right away after she'd finished. "It's the Commandments Killer."

But while he might have somewhat forgiven her, Eversham wasn't about to trade details of this investigation with her. If Jones's death was the work of the Commandments

Killer, then it wouldn't do to go spreading details of it in public. This was his chance to regain his position, and he wasn't going to jeopardize that. Even if it meant he'd have to work his hardest to ensure the only other person in Cumbria who knew as much as he did about the Commandments Killer was kept in the dark.

"I don't know yet," he said truthfully. "But I must request that you let me do my job."

Then, unbidden, a quote from Machiavelli flitted into his brain about keeping your friends close and your enemies closer. "If you'd be interested, I might request your assistance in some parts of the investigation."

She pursed her lips and looked as if she were about to give him a ringing scold. But after a moment's silence, she offered her hand. "I'll consider it. But I have a condition."

He'd already taken her delicate hand in his when she added that last bit. His curiosity overcoming his good sense, Eversham mentally shrugged. "What's the condition?"

"Why, that you let me do *my* job."

"And what's that? You know I can't allow you to write about this while the investigation is still ongoing. I can't have you jeopardizing it."

"Nothing like that," she said firmly. "I'd like to learn as much about your methods as I can while you're investigating this case so that I can ensure that I don't endanger innocent lives with my ignorance again."

Before he could respond, she continued, "I'd also like, for *A Lady's Guide to Mischief and Mayhem*, to interview you for suggestions as to how the fairer sex might keep themselves safe from harm in their daily lives."

"Is that all?" he asked with a scowl. However, he grudgingly admitted to himself that she was more willing to take responsibility for her mistakes than most men he knew.

"That's all," she responded primly.

He didn't normally give interviews. And the profiles that had been written about him thus far were either overly glowing or utterly dismissive.

But if she was working on a profile of him, then she wouldn't be writing newspaper articles about the latest victim of the Commandments Killer.

"You have a deal."

"Excellent." She smiled, and for a brief moment, he was dazzled by the full power of her smile.

And with that, Lady Katherine left the room without looking back—her head held high, her dark hair shining in the lamplight.

Eversham stood staring at the door long after she was gone, the faint whisper of her scent—something clean and floral—lingering behind her.

Chapter Six

Kate didn't see Mr. Eversham again until the next evening when everyone was gathered for drinks before dinner.

"I've asked Inspector Eversham to join us at Thornhill," Val was saying as she accepted a glass of sherry from a footman. "Since Jones was a member of this household, the investigation must start here, obviously, and I would request that all of you make yourselves available for any questions the inspector might have for you as he looks into the matter."

Beside him, Eversham, who was looking annoyingly handsome in evening clothes, wore a somber expression. "I have thanked his lordship for his hospitality, but I will not forget the reason why I'm here. A man has had his life taken from him, and though there are some who like to view such matters as fodder for entertainment—"

Kate narrowed her eyes.

"—I can assure you that I take murder very seriously. If you have any information that you believe can shed light on what happened to Mr. Jones, I most earnestly request that you tell it to me sooner rather than later. The smallest detail might be the clue that leads my investigation to the culprit."

A low hum of murmurs went through the assembled guests at his words.

"Do you really think I might help you solve your murder, Mr. Eversham?" The Countess of Eggleston had turned all of her focus on the detective, and Kate didn't miss the way her husband scowled. She was enough years younger than him that Kate wondered whether Eggleston was jealous-natured or if the countess had given him reason to doubt her.

Either way, Kate wasn't overly fond of the way the countess looked at Eversham either.

"Any of you might find us the culprit, Lady Eggleston," Eversham said neutrally. "I encourage all of you to answer my questions openly and honestly so that we might apprehend the murderer of Mr. Jones as quickly as possible."

For all that man had pooh-poohed the idea of treating murder as a parlor game, Kate couldn't help noting that his request for information had set her fellow houseguests to doing exactly that.

"Poor Jones," Val said from where he'd come to stand beside her. "If finding his killer is left down to a clue from Lady Eggleston, then I fear his murder will go forever unsolved."

"Eversham's only just arrived. Give him more benefit of the doubt than that, Valentine."

Val tilted his head and took a hard look at her. "I thought you were convinced that Eversham couldn't find his way out of a square with a map."

She felt her face heat. "I never said any such thing."

"Your opinions about the way he handled the Commandments Killer cases were hardly flattering, my dear." He took a sip of sherry. "He seems rather more serious than your usual type."

"I don't have a type," she hissed. "And I would request that you not say such things in a room full of people."

"Since old Bascomb's death, you've been escorted to various society functions by what I've come to think of as the upper-class featherbrain brigade, Kate."

"That's not fair." She frowned. Though there was some truth that the gentlemen she'd allowed to accompany her about town were not particularly well known for their intellect, there were hardly enough of them for a brigade.

Besides, she'd once thought that by avoiding clever lovers, she would be safeguarding herself against the sorts of manipulations and tricks her husband had practiced on her. But it hadn't taken long to figure out that it wasn't her husband's intellect that made him terrible. It was simply that he was a bad person.

"Lord Chelmsley is a nice enough fellow, Kate, but if he didn't have a valet, I don't think he could lace his own boots."

Though she'd never admit it to Val, while she'd been

genuinely fond of her lovers, he wasn't entirely wrong. There had been times when she wondered if Chelmsley knew any adjective other than "capital" because he used it to describe everything.

Still, she couldn't let Val get away with deriding her taste in beaux.

"If we are to go down this road, then pray let us talk about the string of opera dancers you've been linked with over the past few years, shall we?" Two could play at this game.

"You won't put me to the blush," Val said, spiking her guns rather effectively. "I'm quite aware of the talents of my paramours, and what's more, I have no compunction about admitting to it. But I don't think you're availing yourself of the same kinds of skills from your gentlemen friends, no matter what the gossips say."

And that was the way she wished to keep it, Kate thought. No matter how many times it was said that widows were allowed to take lovers without fear of social stigma, she knew all too well there was a double standard applied to women. Valentine might be lauded for his choice of mistress, but Kate, if her exploits were known, would be shunned.

"Is there a point to this inquisition?" She managed to keep a cool expression, but inwardly Kate was cringing at how much she'd had to keep from her friend.

"The point is that you're looking at the inspector as if you'd like him to investigate you, and I'm surprised. That's all. I hadn't thought you'd be interested in a policeman, no matter how much you might seem to find murder itself a fascination."

If they weren't such old friends, she'd have boxed

his ears for asking such impertinent questions. But he had known her since they were children and had been a good friend after Bascomb's death. Only, suddenly she wondered if there was an underlying hint behind his teasing.

"You aren't jealous, surely?"

His eyes widened and then he laughed heartily.

"It's not that funny," she said crossly.

"You find me as attractive as a head cold in the middle of summer." He shook his head. "And with all due respect to you and your admittedly lovely exterior, I feel the same about you."

There was also the small detail that she suspected there was something between him and Caro, though she had nothing more upon which to base her suspicion than Caro's reaction to Kate attending the house party. She would need to see them together to determine if her suspicions were well founded.

"I suppose we are doomed to friendship, then," she said. "Unless, of course, you continue to suggest that I have anything but the utmost platonic respect for Inspector Eversham."

"You did spend quite a while alone together during your interview yesterday." Val shrugged. "And you keep stealing looks at him beneath your lashes, as if you're afraid he'll catch you out."

"I found poor Mr. Jones. So of course he would spend a great deal of time questioning me about what I saw."

At the mention of Jones, Val's expression sobered. "Poor old Jones. I didn't know the man all that well, but he was a good steward. And he cared about the estate. He didn't deserve that sort of end."

"If it's any consolation, I do think Mr. Eversham will do his best to find the killer." She glanced over to where the inspector was deep in conversation with Gentleman Jim. Perhaps she was a little intrigued by Eversham, but only because she'd spent so much time attempting to understand his actions and decisions in the Commandments Killer case. He was so different than what she'd imagined.

That day in London she hadn't really seen him. She'd been too overcome with guilt over Clark and the urge to defend herself against his accusations. But when he'd walked into the drawing room yesterday, she'd been assailed by memories of his strong arm around her waist and his hard chest against her back as he ushered her safely from the unruly crowds.

It wasn't so much that she was fascinated by him because she'd followed him in the papers. That man had seemed dense and plodding and she'd never in a million years expected him to solve the case.

The actual Eversham was rational, quick thinking, and to her surprise, possessed a voice that seemed to act on her like a tuning fork.

"Oh, I don't fear he won't work hard at it." Val shook his head. "I just can't think of why anyone would wish Jones dead. And since this has all the hallmarks of the Commandments Killer, then I'm doubly baffled. Why the devil would someone like that come to our little corner of Cumbria and do such a thing?"

"Why does any killer decide to do it?" Kate had only just started writing about murder in her column with Caro, but she'd followed any number of cases in the papers over the years. And though many did seem to stem from concrete reasons like jealousy or avarice, there were some that didn't seem to have any sort of rational explanation behind them. "It's possible that Jones got in the way of things, but it's just as likely that he was in the wrong place at the wrong time."

Val nodded but didn't say anything.

"It just so happens that Mr. Eversham and I have come to an agreement of sorts."

Her companion snorted. "I knew it!"

"You know nothing, Valentine." She frowned. "As I was saying, Mr. Eversham has agreed to let me observe his methods. Of course, he is a professional investigator, but there are certain avenues that are easier to navigate for a lady than they are for a policeman. And I expect when those kinds of skills are necessary, I shall be the one employing them."

"How the devil did you manage that?" Val looked over at the inspector with something akin to disappointment.

"It was a mutually agreed-upon decision." Kate lifted her chin. "Just because you think my journalistic skills are wanting doesn't mean everyone does."

"You know I hold your journalistic skills in the highest regard, my dear. But that man entered this house earlier today with nothing but disdain for you and your column."

"Did he tell you that?" Kate couldn't help feeling a little

hurt that Eversham would have said such a thing aloud to his host.

"He didn't have to, Kate. I saw him when he caught sight of you in the drawing room. You weren't close enough to hear, but he uttered a curse under his breath."

"Well, I hope I was able to convince him that he was wrong." She had, hadn't she? She thought back to her conversation with Eversham and wondered if her assessment of the way they'd left things had been entirely wrong. Kate wasn't used to feeling unsure about matters. She ran a household, managed her own fortune, and oversaw the running of a newspaper, for heaven's sake. She was a mature lady of means.

"If he agreed to let you observe him," Val said with a huff of laughter, "then I'd imagine you were. Of course, the way you look probably didn't hurt."

"I thought you didn't think about me that way," she said with alarm.

"I don't, but I've got eyes in my head. You're not a hardship to look at, and you're a decent conversationalist. Otherwise I'd have quit your beastly newspaper years ago."

He didn't quit her beastly newspaper, as he called it, because he enjoyed writing about sporting events. The fact that his position with the paper made his family cringe with shame that one of their own had not only a profession, but also one that required him to spend his days with characters like Gentleman Jim, a man born in the Bowery and who had earned his fortune with his fists, was just a bonus in Val's eyes. So long as he had something to prove to his father, the Duke of Thornfield, he'd keep his position with the paper, family reputation be damned.

At that moment the butler came to announce that dinner was served, and Val moved off to escort the countess into the dining room.

Allowing Mr. Barton to take her arm, Kate couldn't help feeling Eversham's blue eyes on her as he led in Miss Barton behind them.

The detective might have ulterior motives for agreeing to let her work with him, but that didn't nullify the fact that she *would* be working with him. His prejudices against her were immaterial. She would be able to see that justice was done in this case, both for Mr. Jones and Mr. Clark.

And justice was all that mattered.

Eversham was both relieved and disappointed to see that he'd been seated between Lady Eggleston and his host's sister, Lady Genevieve Thorn. But, he reminded himself, he was there to conduct an investigation, not to trade verbal barbs with Lady Katherine.

"Were you well acquainted with Mr. Jones, Lady Genevieve?" he asked the bespectacled redhead when Miss Barton paused to draw breath.

"I'm not sure anyone was well acquainted with the fellow, if I'm honest." She took a spoonful of the excellent first course, a flavorful leek soup. "He was a rather enigmatic fellow and didn't spend a great deal of time in conversation with the other members of the household."

She paused to wipe her mouth, and Eversham had the sense that she was judging her words carefully.

"Steward is one of those uncomfortable positions in a household that is neither fish nor fowl. Rather like being a governess for a lady. A steward is most often gently born and may even be a member of the family that employs him. Jones was no relation to us, of course, but he was rather come down in the world. He told me once that his father is a wealthy landowner in Wales. But he didn't elaborate."

Eversham couldn't help thinking of his own position in the house. Though his father was the son of a baronet, he'd hardly been raised as a member of that class. Yet here he was breaking bread with a table of guests whose upbringings far eclipsed his own as the son of a vicar in rural Sussex. With, perhaps, the exception of the Bartons, who were doubtless wealthy, but hardly seemed to be of the same social refinement as the others. And Jim Hyde, the pugilist, of course. But both Barton and Hyde had wealth and fame to distinguish them.

Seeing Lady Katherine in animated conversation with Lord Eggleston, he corrected himself. He had a certain level of fame, thanks to his occupation. But like a governess, or the departed Mr. Jones, he had clearly been invited to partake in this meal with his betters at his host's invitation, not because he belonged here.

He would be sure to keep that in mind as he mixed with these high society folk and to not forget where he came from. And, in turn, where he belonged.

Loudly, he said, "Did Jones seem to chafe at his position in the house? I should imagine it would be difficult for a man raised in luxury to be relegated to the role of upper servant."

Lady Genevieve seemed to think his words over. "I don't know that he was resentful, exactly. He wasn't a particularly gregarious man, nor was he angry. He did his job looking after the estate and kept mostly to himself."

It would have made his job easier if Jones had boasted a village full of enemies who might be suspected of doing him in, which would have made it more plausible that the murder had been staged to resemble the Commandments killings. Though he still believed that the wrong man had been arrested for the crimes, having the actual killer move from London to the Lake District was not something he wished for. It might go a ways toward convincing Darrow that Clark was the wrong man, but it would mean that the culprit had a new hunting ground.

Whatever he might have said in response to Lady Genevieve's assessment of Jones was forestalled by one of the gentleman guests, a Mr. Thompson. "We are unable to speak of anything besides the obvious parallels to the Commandments case, Mr. Eversham. Surely you have some thoughts on the matter. It's rare that one has the opportunity to carry on a conversation with the lead investigator of one of such a sequence of killings."

Eversham turned his attention to the young man, who even to his own eye was angelically handsome. He noted that the man's suit likely cost more than Eversham earned in a year with the Metropolitan Police. Which, for some reason, made him distrust the fellow. Unfair, but there it was.

"I'm sure Mr. Eversham isn't able to discuss the details

of his investigation into the Commandments killings, Mr. Thompson." Lady Katherine had turned a narrow gaze on the man. The detective would have been grateful for her championship, but her next line put paid to that notion. "The culprit hasn't been convicted yet, has he?"

Butter wouldn't melt in her mouth, he thought wryly.

"Yes, Lady Katherine, as you so kindly point out, the man arrested for the Commandments killings has not yet been convicted. Though I can assure you"—he addressed the table at large—"that I will do my utmost to ensure that Mr. Jones's killer is apprehended."

"But doesn't Mr. Jones's murder bear a striking resemblance to the crimes of the Commandments Killer?" Thompson pressed. "There was the note, after all. And Jones was stabbed. It seems very similar to me."

"Thompson, watch yourself," Lord Eggleston snapped. "There are ladies present."

The younger man looked defiant for a moment, then, with a shrug, apologized. "I'd forgotten where I was. I'm so sorry to have offended. But perhaps I can ask a less upsetting question of Mr. Eversham. Why would you say some murderers are easily caught while others go free?"

Eversham considered the question. He'd had to adjust his opinion after the arrest of John Clark, but he was hardly going to share his newfound doubts in the Yard's leadership with the assembled company.

"The truth of the matter," he began, "is that there are those whose refusal to be honest with us make it nigh impossible for murderers to be caught."

"This is fascinating, Inspector." Thompson shook his

head. "You're saying that someone knows the truth of the killer's identity but chooses not to tell? Who would do such a thing?"

"There needn't be a desire on the part of the witness to let a killer go free," Lady Katherine said before Eversham could respond. "I should imagine there are all sorts of reasons a witness might not tell the full truth. A parent might wish to shield their child from suspicion—not knowing that the child is guilty, mind you, but wishing to remove them from the picture altogether. Or perhaps the person was engaged in some embarrassing situation at the time of the murder that makes them reluctant to discuss what they saw. I know some of the people interviewed in the Commandments killings were—ahem—of less than pristine reputations, shall we say."

"They were prostitutes and pimps, you mean?" Thompson challenged, which brought a frown to Lady Katherine's lips.

"I won't warn you again, Thompson." Lord Valentine was not known for his sense of propriety, but he apparently was not going to let such disrespect pass without comment.

"I beg your pardon, Lord Valentine," the younger man said with a show of remorse. "I forgot myself for a moment."

"As it happens," Eversham said, "I find that when one of their own has been taken from them, members of the aforementioned professions can be quite forthcoming. It's those who fear damage to their reputations that make the least honest witnesses, in my experience. Those with little to lose have little to keep secret."

"Are you saying that you suspect we will be poor witnesses,

Mr. Eversham?" Lady Eggleston clutched a hand to her bosom. "What an absurd notion. Everyone knows that the lower classes have a natural inclination to commit crime. One has only to look at the backgrounds of those sitting in this nation's jails to prove my point."

"My dear Lady Eggleston." Lady Katherine's voice was deceptively soft. "I will ask you to have a care when making such nonsensical pronouncements. Especially given that not everyone at this table had the good fortune to be born into the upper echelons of society. And yet, I feel I can safely say that none of them are known to have been culpable in any crimes."

Lady Eggleston had the grace to color at her rudeness. But Eversham heard her mutter about what happened when upper and lower classes mixed.

What had prompted Lord Valentine to invite people with such views to a house party that included guests from such a variety of backgrounds? Eversham wondered.

"I beg your pardon," said the countess, her lips pinched. "It was not my intention to insult my fellow guests."

"Very prettily said, Lady Eggleston," said the American, Mr. Barton. "Of course, in the States we enjoy a freer mixing of the classes than you do here. Why, it's not unheard of to see a coal miner seated at the table with the owner of the mines where he's employed."

"I don't recall ever having any of your miners seated at our table in New York, Papa," said Miss Barton with a guileless expression that surely covered a mind bent on mischief. "In fact, I believe you said once that—"

"Never mind what I said, daughter." The industrialist

scowled. "I was merely indicating that things are very different back home."

Eversham took the opportunity to ask, "You are a very long way from home, Mr. Barton. What brings you to our fair shores?"

"He means to find me a noble husband," Miss Barton said baldly.

At the same moment, her father said, "Business, Mr. Eversham."

"Of course," Eversham continued without letting on that he'd heard Miss Barton. "Business. And is there much business to be had in the Lake District?"

Perhaps taking pity on the father and daughter, Lady Katherine spoke up. "A trip to the Lakes is *de rigueur* for any visitor to England, Mr. Eversham. You must, if you haven't been here before, take a few days for yourself to explore the countryside."

"I will be sure to do so, my lady." He inclined his head. "I understand you all were exploring one of the local walks when Mr. Jones was found."

And the conversation moved on to the reason for his presence here at Thornfield in the first place.

But he couldn't help reflecting on Lady Eggleston's pronouncement about the propensities of the lower classes. He knew such notions were wrongheaded, but there was no mistaking that class differences could cause conflict. Especially when one found they had fallen several rungs on the social ladder, serving those they once rubbed shoulders with.

The note on the man's body had said he "bore false

witness." Could Jones have angered someone by lying about the circumstances that had led to his change in fortune? Or perhaps he'd been putting on airs he no longer had the right to?

He would need to speak with the servants first thing tomorrow to find out.

Chapter Seven

To Kate's relief, the inspector didn't insist upon questioning the assembled guests about the murder right there at the dinner table. Despite that small mercy, however, she was relieved when it was finally time for the ladies to withdraw to the parlor for tea, leaving the gentlemen to their port and cigars.

Under normal circumstances, she would have chafed at the ridiculous social convention that held ladies up as too fragile to drink strong spirits or hear ribald jests. But after the fractious conversation at dinner and the frisson of awareness she felt every time she glanced in Eversham's direction, she was grateful for the respite.

Not for the first time, she wished that Caro had accompanied her on this trip. If only so she'd have someone to discuss the fact that the detective they'd only a couple of weeks ago been criticizing for his handling of the

Commandments killings was here investigating a murder that was eerily similar to the earlier ones.

Her reverie was interrupted by the appearance of Lady Genevieve Thorn at her side. "I hope you're not suffering any ill effects of your encounter on the trail."

Kate had always found Val's sister to be a pleasant, if somewhat distant, sort of person. Try though she might to become closer to her, Kate's overtures of friendship had always met with friendly, but firm, rebuffs. Perhaps it arose from Genevieve's writing, which must keep her in the role of observer rather than participant. Or maybe she just didn't feel any kind of kinship with Kate. Despite the fact that both ladies were wordsmiths, there was a rather wide gulf between the sort of essays and articles Kate wrote and the high melodrama that Lady Genevieve penned. Just because Kate counted her brother as a close friend didn't mean that Genevieve would get on as easily with her.

Still, she was grateful for the concern she saw in the other woman's expression. "I am well, thank you." Genevieve offered her a cup of tea, which she accepted with a nod. "I won't pretend that the entire incident wasn't upsetting, but my concern is for poor Mr. Jones rather than myself. Did you know him well?"

Lady Genevieve lowered herself to the settee beside her. A childhood accident had left her with a rather severe limp, but as far as Kate could tell, she didn't let it keep her from doing as she pleased. "He was already employed as the estate manager here when Val took over the estate. I met him a few times prior to this visit, but we were hardly close. He seemed pleasant enough, poor fellow."

There was a pause and Kate noted the way that she plucked at the folds of her gown, her hands restless. As if sensing Kate's gaze on her, Genevieve colored.

"I know I should probably tell Mr. Eversham," she said with a slight frown, "but you know as much as anyone about the Commandments Killer, and I rather think you're in a better position to know whether what I saw could be related to Mr. Jones's murder before I bring it to the inspector."

Kate's brows lowered. "What did you see?"

Genevieve glanced at the other side of the room, where the rest of the ladies chatted over the tea tray, oblivious to the seriousness of the conversation taking place here. "It's just that when I was in the village a few days ago, I stopped in at the stationer's for ink and I overheard an argument between Mr. Green, the proprietor, and Mr. Jones. I don't think they'd heard me come in, you see, and well"—she leaned in closer—"it got rather heated."

Her mind racing, Kate said in a low voice, "What were they saying?"

"I didn't hear the beginning of the discussion, so I don't know what precisely they were arguing over," Genevieve said slowly, "but Mr. Jones said very clearly, 'I'll see you in hell first,' then strode out of the office with his face as dark as a thundercloud. I don't even think he saw me there. And when Mr. Green came out a moment or two later, he was scowling until he saw me and he seemed to get hold of himself. Of course, I couldn't ask what had happened without revealing what I'd heard. So I pretended as if nothing was amiss and requested my ink."

Kate had been prepared for the tale to be a little overblown, if she was honest. She was rather fond of Genevieve's novels, but they were nothing if not sensational. But Jones's words spoke for themselves. He must have been angry indeed to have threatened Mr. Green like that. Could the stationer have been responsible for the steward's death?

Aloud she replied, "You handled the matter exactly the right way. You had no way of knowing what would happen to Mr. Jones. Not to mention that it's doubtful either man would have appreciated your intrusion into what was doubtless a private matter."

"I certainly couldn't have brought it up to Mr. Jones even if I'd wanted to." Genevieve shook her head ruefully. "He stormed off before I'd even had a moment to draw breath."

Her eyes, so like her brother's, were troubled. "Do you think this might have had something to do with the reason Mr. Jones was murdered? I know there was a note on the body, like in the other Commandments killings, but it's possible the killer wanted to draw attention away from himself by implicating someone else."

It was a theory Kate had contemplated from the moment she saw the note pinned to the dead man's chest. She wanted to discuss the matter with Eversham, but given he thought she was responsible for the near demise of his career with the Metropolitan Police, she didn't think he'd be willing to share with her what he knew.

"It's possible," she told Genevieve. "You needn't worry about telling Mr. Eversham about this. I'll tell him for you."

The relief on the other woman's face was palpable. "Thank you. I know I should have the courage to tell him myself, but I dislike too much attention. I am supposed to be using this visit to work on my next book, but Val will insist that because I'm acting as hostess, I need to be sociable."

Kate laughed. "You are acting as his hostess, my dear. It seems as if being sociable is part of the bargain."

"You needn't remind me. I'm only grateful he doesn't parade eligible men before me like our mother does in the hopes that I'll marry one of them."

"It is the way of things." Kate smiled. "Even when the daughter in question is wealthy in her own right and has no need of a husband to keep her in pin money."

"I don't suppose you're willing to marry Val so that I might have some peace?" Genevieve's normally serious face broke into an impish smile.

"Not a chance." Kate shook her head. "I've had quite enough of marriage to last a lifetime. Besides, your brother is far too stubborn to suit me. If I marry again, and that's a rather emphatic *if*, it will be to someone who is willing to make a partnership of it instead of ruling the roost."

At that moment, the gentlemen began to drift into the room. Kate couldn't help noting that Eversham, in his borrowed finery, was every bit as handsome as Valentine. His light brown hair, a little shorter than was the fashion, shone gold in the lamplight, and the planes of his face were as finely drawn as a Greek statue's.

"He's not what I'd have expected of a policeman."

Genevieve smiled wryly. "In that suit he could almost pass for a gentleman."

Despite her antagonism for Eversham, Kate felt herself bristle at the implication he was somehow inferior to the other men here. "He is the grandson of a baronet, I believe. So I hardly think the claim is as outlandish as that."

Perhaps recognizing her snobbery, Lady Genevieve colored. "Pay no attention to me. Sometimes, despite my determination to be nothing like her, my mother's views on the world slip out of my mouth. Of course he's a gentleman. And even if he weren't gently born, it should hardly matter. Next I'll be spouting off the same sort of nonsense as Lady Eggleston about the lower classes being born to commit crimes."

Kate acknowledged the apology with an inclination of her head.

They were forestalled from further conversation by the arrival at their side of Mr. Barton. But across the room, Kate saw Eversham glance their way, her eyes meeting his for the barest moment before Kate looked away.

Not daring to look again, she plied her fan to cool the flush she felt in her face and turned her attention to the blustering industrialist.

Later, when the assembled guests were making their way up the grand staircase toward bed, Eversham found Lady Katherine at his elbow.

"I wonder if I might have a word, Inspector."

Though he'd begun to reconcile himself to the agreement he'd made with her about allowing her to assist him with the case, his conversation with Lady Genevieve about Jones's position in the household had reminded him just what sort of world Lady Katherine hailed from.

While she seemed to hold more egalitarian views on the British class system than most aristocrats, she had still been born the daughter of an earl. And in Eversham's experience, the upper classes weren't entirely to be trusted.

He was honest enough to admit he found her desirable. But he'd do his best to keep from succumbing to his attraction for her.

"How can I help you, my lady?"

Eversham noted that they were now several feet behind the others and it was with a sense of inevitability that he watched her pause, ostensibly to look closer at a particularly ugly painting of a sheep.

"It rather looks like my great-aunt Ermentrude." He nodded toward the pastoral scene.

"She had curly white hair, then?" Lady Katherine asked in a deceptively serious tone. "Or perhaps you mean she had hooves?"

"None of that. It's just that she was a bit of an embarrassment to the family."

Lady Katherine frowned. "How so?"

"Well, for starters," Eversham said gravely, "she was a very baa-d card player."

There was a long moment of silence before she let out a low laugh that resonated along his spine. And lower parts.

"You're awful."

He shrugged slightly. "You chose this bit of distraction. I would have gone with the battlefield scene over there."

Shaking her head, she pushed past him into a doorway to the right of the sheep. Curious despite his earlier warning to himself, Eversham followed.

It was a small sitting room with a fire burning genially and a pair of deep armchairs arranged invitingly near the hearth.

But Lady Katherine was not interested in the comfort of the scene.

She strode dramatically forward and turned, the skirts of her deep crimson gown whispering over the thick carpets.

"Lady Genevieve overheard Mr. Jones in a heated conversation with the local stationer a few days before his murder," she said. "It must mean something, don't you think?"

He could see that she was intrigued, but he'd followed too many false clues over his career to allow such a circumstance to raise his hopes.

Still, it was promising. "Tell me everything."

Quickly, Lady Katherine outlined what she'd been told by the other woman.

When she got to the threat Jones had made against Mr. Green, he stopped her. "Those were the man's exact words?"

She nodded. "It's obvious Green was going to do something that Mr. Jones didn't agree with."

"Or Green was making some sort of demand of Jones. Blackmail? Extortion?"

"Whatever it was, it was enough to make the—by all

accounts—straightlaced Mr. Jones raise his voice and make a public threat against a local tradesman." Lady Katherine's eyes were lit with interest, and Eversham bit back the inclination to warn her against optimism about this development. She may know a great deal about writing for the papers, but reporting about things after the fact often ignored the daily drudgery of following up on details and taking statements from people whose accounts added nothing to the eventual resolution of a case.

Good police work was made up of patience and what was frequently hours of poring over documents, tracking down alibi witnesses, and assembling enough pieces of a mosaic to get a general impression of what happened rather than a full picture.

"You don't think it's important?" she asked, obviously sensing the direction of his thoughts.

Eversham found himself wanting to soften the blow, so instead of speaking his thoughts aloud, he said, "It's important, but far too soon to know if it has any bearing on Jones's murder. Thank you for telling me, though. I'll be making a visit to the village tomorrow to get the full story from Green."

"Excellent." She looked as if she would say something else, but she must have decided against it.

There was a sudden silence between them, and Eversham cleared his throat. "Thank you for giving me this information, Lady Katherine."

"We did promise to work together, after all," she said with a nod.

Eversham got the sense that she was waiting for

something. An invitation for her to accompany him to-morrow perhaps? Well, if that was what she wanted, she'd be waiting for a long while. He might have agreed to co-operate with her, but that hadn't changed his opinion on the advisability of her getting involved in police work. A man had been murdered here. He'd be damned if he let Lady Katherine anywhere near this killer—whether the criminal was the Commandments Killer or just some opportunist looking to cover up his crimes by using the signature of another, more notorious, murderer.

"Would you like to go up first?" he asked after the silence had lasted long enough to make even him uncomfortable.

She sighed, as if she'd heard his mental rationale for keeping her at arm's length. "There's no need for subter-fuge. This is hardly the sort of house party with the kind of goings-on that inspire gossip."

He felt his cheeks heat. "I didn't mean..."

The amusement in her voice was evident. "I know you didn't, Inspector," she said. "But your gallantry is appreci-ated. You go on up. I'm going to stay down here for a bit."

Her eyes, which had been intrigued earlier, were shad-owed with fatigue now.

Eversham recalled that it had been less than twenty-four hours since she'd come upon the dead body of a man with whom she'd been acquainted.

He'd often felt that one of the aspects of his job at which he was the most skilled was his ability to put people at ease during what was often the most traumatic experience of their lives. But with Lady Katherine he'd been too distracted by the knowledge of her writings about him to see her for what she was—the witness to a horrific scene of the worst kind of violence a person could visit upon another human being.

"All right?" he asked, gentling his voice in a way he'd not bothered to do with her earlier.

But if he thought she'd allow any kind of softness from him, he was very much mistaken.

He watched as she steeled her spine and lifted her chin. "I'm fine." Then, as if wishing to forestall any further show of sympathy, she said, "Good night, Inspector."

Recognizing that he'd been told in not so many words to take himself off, Eversham did just that.

Chapter Eight

After a restless night, filled with flashbacks of the moment she'd stumbled upon Jones's body, Kate stepped into the breakfast room the next morning to find that Eversham was conspicuously absent. No doubt he was already on his way into the village to question the stationer, Mr. Green.

She'd been disappointed, he'd been right about that, that he hadn't seen as much promise in the news about the argument between the dead man and Green as she had. Or perhaps his experience with the Commandments Killer in London had made him cautious about anyone jumping to conclusions.

Still, this might be the best opportunity to catch the killer who had been responsible for so much death and terror. And she would do whatever she could to make sure the opportunity wasn't squandered.

She still had difficulty reconciling the Eversham she'd

read about in the papers with the man himself. What she'd dismissed as a reticence to act, she now saw for what it was: caution and deference. He listened more than he spoke, and over dinner she'd felt those watchful eyes on her more than once.

Perhaps he was as curious about her as she was about him?

Or, she reminded herself with a jolt, it was more likely he was trying to figure out how he could retaliate against her for nearly ruining his career.

She shook her head at her tendency to romanticize the man. He was just that, a man. And however handsome he may be, he had rather effectively managed to cozen her into giving him her information about the argument without giving her a promise in return that she could accompany him to the interview with Green. Which, she would remind him in no uncertain terms, went against their deal. He'd promised to let her follow him through the investigation, and a witness interview was a vital part of such, as they both well knew.

"Lady Katherine, good morning."

Kate had helped herself to tea and toast, and as she found a place at the table, she noted that she was among the last to be seated.

"I trust you were able to sleep after that horrible policeman's intrusive questions?" continued Lady Eggleston, her mouth pursed with distaste. "If I'd known we'd be treated like criminals, I never would have accepted this invitation."

"Come now, Countess," said Val from where he sat at the head of the table, "I hardly consider Mr. Eversham's questions as bad as that. He merely asked you to recount what happened on the walk."

"Much too polite, if you ask me." Barton forked eggs into his face with the gusto of a blacksmith shoveling coal. "In New York, our police aren't afraid to ruffle a few feathers. They don't hold with tiptoeing around society folk."

This was met with a gasp from Lady Eggleston, and even her husband, the earl, who was taciturn at his most talkative, uttered a heartfelt "I say."

"I, for one," Kate said mildly, "think it's clever of Mr. Eversham to gather the facts before he begins making accusations. After all, we want the actual culprit apprehended, do we not?"

"Indeed, we do, Lady Katherine." Miss Barton, who had remained quiet throughout the conversation, blushed, as if she disliked calling attention to herself. To Kate's surprise, she then addressed her father. "Papa, you must admit that the police in New York are quite deferential to our class of people—as you well know from the beating they gave our groom when they mistook him for that escaped convict. It's those without influence or wealth upon whom they visit their most violent tactics."

Kate's estimation of the young lady rose several degrees.

"I know enough, daughter," Barton said gruffly. "But like everyone else I want this fiend captured before he kills us all in our beds."

"Mr. Eversham is an experienced detective." Kate was not unaware of the irony that she was the one defending Eversham against criticism. And yet, she did trust him to do a better job here than Adolphus Wargrove, for example. Eversham had the good sense to recognize when important steps in the investigation process were being skipped in order to rush to a hasty result. "He is renowned throughout the nation for his solutions to some very complicated crimes."

"You haven't been his greatest supporter, though, have you, Lady Katherine?" Mr. Thompson, who had watched the ongoing conversation in silence, narrowed his eyes as he posed his question, as if trying to gauge whether his barb landed. "Didn't you insinuate in your interview with the witness in the Betsy Creamer murder that Eversham had failed to interview her first?"

Hearing a reader throw her own criticism of Eversham— which at the time she'd thought was just—back at her made Kate cringe inwardly. "You're not wrong about my criticism, Mr. Thompson. However, my issues with certain actions on Mr. Eversham's part don't mean that I think him incompetent. Indeed, quite the opposite. I would not expect so much of him if I didn't think he was more than capable of greatness."

"I'm not sure what to think, Lady Katherine. After all, Scotland Yard was able to find the killer thanks to your interview with the witness. He's locked up in jail awaiting trial right now, isn't he?" Thompson shook his head. "And yet, poor Mr. Jones was killed here in a manner eerily similar to that of the other Commandments killings."

"It is troubling, Mr. Thompson, make no mistake." Kate wasn't sure how to reconcile the man's questions.

Everything he'd said was true. All they could do was let Eversham do his work and hopefully find the real killer.

"I suppose I shall have to mark your change of heart about Eversham down to the mysteries of the female mind." Thompson smiled. Kate thought she heard a note of mockery in his tone, but his expression was guileless.

"There's no mystery there, Thompson." Barton guffawed. "The mind of a lady isn't complicated at all. It just needs a bit of praise every now and then. Indeed, I suspect that dwelling on such dark topics has overset Lady Katherine's nerves a bit, eh?"

"Must I remind you, Mr. Barton, that I am seated at this table?" Kate counted to three in her mind to prevent herself from speaking any more harshly to the man. It would do her case no good to become visibly incensed by his nonsense. He would merely state that she'd proved his point.

"Oh, I do know it, Lady Katherine." Barton had the temerity to wink at her, and Kate felt her jaw clench.

"I think the sooner this business is concluded, the better." Miss Barton, who seemed to wish the floor would open and swallow her up, nonetheless tried to get the conversation back on topic. "We had intended to travel to London tomorrow, but I don't think Mr. Eversham will agree to that yet."

"He can't keep us here." Lady Eggleston frowned. "Especially if the Commandments Killer was responsible."

"Unless he suspects one of us of being the Commandments Killer." Thompson took a sip of tea, and Kate got the distinct impression the man enjoyed stirring up mischief.

Well, she'd had enough of his provocations.

"I think we need some diversion," Kate said firmly. "I was planning a trip into Lewiston this morning to buy some stationery. Would anyone like to join me?"

She knew she'd likely regret making the invitation, but Kate didn't wish to draw attention to herself by going into the village on her own. And since she was still not sure whether she trusted Eversham to share what he learned with her, she wanted to question Green herself.

When the group set off on the footpath leading into the village, they numbered six. Kate and Val, who had agreed to join them once he'd returned from his morning ride, brought up the rear, while Miss Barton, her father, Mr. Thompson, and Genevieve walked ahead of them.

"I don't suppose this trip into the village has anything to do with what my sister told you about Jones's conversation with Green?" Val asked as they neared the outskirts of the little village that was closest to his estate.

Kate felt her cheeks heat. "I don't know what you mean."

"You know precisely what I mean." He rolled his eyes. "You cannot just trust the fellow to do his job, can you?"

"I trust him to do his job," she said tartly, "but I don't trust him to keep me apprised of what he finds."

"Why hasn't he already asked you to write about it for *The Gazette*?" Val asked thoughtfully. "I'd have supposed he'd be shouting it from the rooftops that he was right all along. I mean, clearly he was if poor Jones is another Commandments Killer victim."

"I believe he wants to make sure first that this is indeed by the same killer." Kate shrugged. "Besides, I have no wish to write anything having to do with the Commandments Killer without knowing how it will affect poor Mr. Clark."

"That makes sense." Val heaved a sigh. "I just feel terrible about poor Jones. I had to write to his family in Wales yesterday. I hardly knew what to say."

And of course, he'd known Jones better than anyone else in the household, Kate realized with a beat of remorse for not offering more sympathy to her friend. "I'm sorry, Val. That's awful. But I'm sure they will appreciate your letting them know."

"Thank you." Val ran a hand through his artfully arranged curls, a sign of just how overset he was. "It's a sorry business all around. And I suppose I've been trying to come up with a reason to explain why it happened. And there is none. Not really."

"Eversham will find out who's responsible." Kate was surprised to realize she meant the words.

"Even though you're conducting your own investigation alongside his?" There was a teasing note in Valentine's voice.

"That's not what I'm doing."

That was precisely what she was doing. But how else could she ensure that the real killer was apprehended so that John Clark could be set free?

"Very well," she said after a pause. Val knew her far too well to be put off with an outright lie, so she settled for a half-truth. "Perhaps that's what I'm doing. But it's only because I want to verify all the facts for myself first."

Val laughed softly. "You always did want to see something with your own eyes before you would believe it."

Instead she shrugged. "Call me a doubting Thomas all you like. But I won't apologize for it."

"Nor should you, my dear. I only hope you don't run afoul of Eversham again. He already has reason to distrust you."

"I can handle Mr. Eversham, never you fear," she said with more confidence than she felt.

While it might be true that she and the enigmatic detective had come to an understanding of sorts, there was something unsettling about the way he made her feel.

As if there was unfinished business between them that had nothing to do with murder.

Eversham had spent the better part of the morning questioning the servants about their whereabouts the morning of the murder and gathering information about Fenwick Jones.

No one stood out as a possible suspect, but he had learned more about the man himself.

Jones had been hired on at Thornfield by the previous owner of the estate, a minor poet who had rather famously lost the house and grounds in a card game, which was how Lord Valentine came into possession of it.

Like Eversham himself, Jones was the younger son of a gentleman—in the dead man's case, his father was a classics scholar who had been cut off for making a love match of which his family hadn't approved.

Jones had been close to a local squire's family, where he had learned the rudiments of running an estate, and with a letter of character from the man in hand, had come to Cumbria from his native Norfolk to take the position at Thornfield.

Though the servants in the house hadn't known the man well, they seemed to like him, and he'd endeared himself to the housekeeper to such a degree that she'd shed tears while speaking of him. Of course, Eversham didn't know the woman well enough to tell whether this was a common occurrence for her, but her emotion seemed genuine enough to him.

After an initial survey of the household, mindful of what Lady Katherine had told him about the argument with the stationer, Green, he'd set out on foot for Lewiston.

Like all of the country hereabouts, the path leading into the village was tree lined and picturesque, with the rolling hills punctuated with neatly bordered pastures dotted with sheep. The path itself was flanked on either side by a rustic stone wall that looked as if it might have emerged from the very ground.

Eversham had lived in London for so long, he'd forgotten how to enjoy the pleasures of the countryside. He found the hum of street vendors, the clatter of hooves, and the roar of the underground comforting in a way that the eerie quiet of the green fields and dramatic hills was not.

Even so, he had to admit that the air here was cleaner, and without the soot of London factories, he could see the sky above and the world around him in a way that was impossible in town.

His position with the Metropolitan Police had made it possible for him to see more of England than he'd have dreamt of as a boy, and while he could appreciate the variety of landscapes and vistas, he was never happier than when he got back to the city—dirt and all.

Once he made it into the village itself, he noted with interest just how many tourists—identified by their guidebooks and maps in hand—crowded into the narrow streets. He wouldn't have thought it possible for a stranger to go unnoticed in such a small village, but he hadn't accounted for the fact that this area, because of its geography and having been made famous by the Lake Poets, was a destination for travelers from all over the world.

Was it possible that the killer had hidden among these visitors? The locals, so used to having their environs invaded by unfamiliar faces, would hardly have noticed one more among them.

It was a possibility that would make his job more difficult, but Eversham was determined not to let this killer slip past him again.

With that in mind, he made his way toward the stationer's, which was easy to find, given the size of the town, situated as it was between the bustling inn and a leather merchant's shop.

As he neared the shop, he saw a group from Thornfield approaching, with Barton, the American, leading the way, followed by Lord Valentine, Lady Katherine, Mr. Thompson, and Miss Barton.

He'd disliked the industrialist on sight, not only because of his general air of superiority but also because the fellow's greedy eyes were frequently pointed in the direction of Lady Katherine's generous bosom. The man was a boor and

a buffoon. Eversham did try not to let his personal prejudices get in the way of an investigation, but he would have
dearly loved to be a civilian for ten minutes so he could give
Barton the tongue-lashing he deserved.

Unfortunately, he was still an officer of the law and had
been unable to find a flaw in the man's account of his
whereabouts the day of the murder. Thus he would have to
shield Lady Katherine from the man with means other than
a verbal warning.

Even now he could see that the American had taken her
by the arm. Eversham hurried forward, thinking to catch up
with them.

As he neared the group, however, he realized the lady
was not in need of rescue.

"I have already declined your kind offer, Mr. Barton."
Her smile was fixed in a rictus of politeness, though her
eyes flashed with annoyance. "Now, please do not ask me
again for my answer will be the same."

Wrenching her arm away from the American's grasp, she
turned her attention to Eversham, and he couldn't help
noting the relief in her eyes. "Mr. Eversham, there you are.
We did wonder if perhaps you would come into the village
this morning."

"I had a few errands to take care of here, Lady Katherine,
as you may have guessed."

"Indeed." She managed to convey a wealth of meaning
into that single word. Doubtless she was annoyed with him
for not asking her to come along, but he could hardly invite
a member of the press, however comely, to follow him
as he made his inquiries. A man's life was at stake. And

though he might once have balked at her presence here for fear of endangering his career, his entire focus now was on ensuring that the right man was apprehended so that Clark might be freed.

"Were you able to speak to the staff, Eversham?" Lord Valentine stepped up beside Lady Katherine, and Eversham couldn't help noting the ease between them. Valentine was a handsome devil, and not for the first time, he wondered just what the nature of their relationship was. If they were lovers, they were discreet about it. But then one could never tell with the upper classes. Some of them might flaunt their affairs in public, but in Eversham's experience, which was, of course, limited, they were just as likely to keep any obvious signs of affection behind closed doors. He much preferred the honesty of the common folk. At least one knew where one stood with them.

"I did, thank you, Lord Valentine."

"We've come to visit the shops," offered Miss Barton from where she'd stepped into the circle of conversation. "Lady Katherine was coming to the stationer's and invited us to join her."

"Did she indeed?" Eversham turned his eyes to Lady Katherine, who gave a slight shrug.

"I am a writer, you know." As if he could forget it.

They stood just before the green-trimmed window of the mercantile shop, where a display of ladies' hats held a place of pride.

"We are indeed blessed, are we not?" Thompson, who had been lingering just off to the side, made his presence known. Eversham wasn't sure what had brought the man to

Lord Valentine's house party. The Bartons', the Egglestons', and even Lady Katherine's invitations could be explained away, but so far as he could tell, Thompson wasn't close friends with Lord Valentine and he didn't seem to have a previous acquaintance with any of the other guests. "When Val invited me, I had no notion that the newspaper writer Lady Katherine Bascomb would be here. You may not know it, Miss Barton, but this fine lady is very much in demand in town. I've heard that she is even the object of pursuit to such a degree that she's had to hire extra servants to protect her at times."

Eversham hadn't heard that. Though, of course, he'd been busy over the last year with his pursuit of a killer.

Miss Barton gasped at Thompson's revelation, but Lady Katherine waved it off. "It's hardly worth mentioning, Mr. Thompson. I beg you will not make more of it than it is. A man who had read my columns wished to meet me, that's all." This had happened before her work with Caro.

"You were afraid for your life at one point, Kate." Valentine frowned. "Do not make light of it."

"How awful for you, Lady Katherine." The magnate's daughter's eyes had widened, and she clasped a hand dramatically to her bosom. "I am so glad you weren't harmed."

Eversham didn't like the idea of her having to fend for herself. There were a great many men who would have no qualms about harming a woman as lovely as she was.

Clearly discomfited by the talk of her ordeal, Lady Katherine held up a staying hand. "Let us speak no more of it. It's a hazard of being in the public spotlight even in such a limited way as I am. Now, I should like to go into the stationer's and purchase my ink." She nodded to them and made her way to the door of the shop, and Lord Valentine hurried to open it for her.

Not wishing her to speak to Green before he did, Eversham moved to follow them.

Perhaps realizing his pursuit of Lady Katherine was fruitless, Barton had gone in some moments earlier, and when he stepped into the brightly lit establishment, the detective saw the American was engaged in conversation with a balding man with a naturally hangdog expression. Even so, whatever Barton was saying must have been pleasing to the shopkeeper because his eyes were wide with excitement.

Lord Valentine turned to Eversham, cutting off his view of the conversation near the sales counter. In a low voice, he said, "She won't thank me for it, but I would ask that you keep an eye on Kate while she's here. I don't trust Barton as far as I could throw him, and I've business on the other side of the village."

"I will see to it that she's returned to you safely, Lord Valentine," Eversham said stiffly.

He must have revealed more in his words than he'd meant to because the nobleman gave a bark of laughter. "I think you misunderstand things, old man."

"And what precisely is it that I misunderstand?"

Eversham knew he was being purposely obtuse, but some small part of him wished to hear Valentine say it out loud.

"We are friends." The other man rolled his eyes. "I have

known Kate since I was in short trousers, and she is as close to me as my sisters. But nothing more."

Something loosened in Eversham's chest, but he wasn't ready to examine it more closely.

"I'm sure it's none of my affair," he said. Before Valentine could retort, he added, "I will do as you ask."

His eyes alit with something that seemed suspiciously like amusement, Lord Valentine nodded. "Then I'll wish you good day."

Turning his attention to the front of the shop, Eversham saw that Lady Katherine had moved to stand behind where Barton continued to harangue Mr. Green. Striding forward, he was just in time to hear her say into the silence of a pause in the conversation, "I believe I saw your daughter and Mr. Thompson headed for the mercantile, Mr. Barton. If you wish to join them."

Eversham couldn't help appreciating Kate's calculation. A man like Barton, who was on the hunt for a title for his daughter, would not countenance the girl spending time alone with a nobody like Thompson.

And sure enough, no sooner had Lady Katherine spoken than Barton made a hasty excuse and hurried toward the door.

Though Green was no doubt frustrated by the American's having left without making a purchase, he turned his attention to Lady Katherine and Eversham with the ease of a man who knew how to make a sale.

"Lady Katherine." The shopkeeper bowed. "It's a pleasure to welcome you. *The London Gazette* is quite popular even this far from the city. Though I am sorry for the terrible occurrence up at the Hall. Mr. Jones was a favorite around these parts."

Turning to Eversham, Green continued, "And you must be Mr. Eversham from Scotland Yard."

The two men shook hands, and Eversham searched the man's round face for signs of nerves at having an officer of the law in his shop, but could find none.

Green's round face, framed by bushy side-whiskers that gave him a leonine appearance, seemed innocent enough.

Of course, there were hardened criminals who relied on such traits to exploit others. Eversham much preferred hard evidence.

"It's a bad business, what happened to Jones," the stationer continued. "Things like this don't happen in Lewiston."

Then, showing the first sign of nerves, Green took out a handkerchief to mop his brow.

Interesting, Eversham thought. Perhaps Green wasn't feeling as innocent as he looked.

Chapter Nine

"Of course, it's what happened to poor Mr. Jones that brings us here this morning," Kate said to the shop-keeper, not bothering to keep up the pretense that she'd come here for paper and ink.

"I wonder if there's somewhere we might speak privately?" Eversham asked, moving closer to her and sheltering their conversation from the villagers behind them in the shop.

Green ran a finger beneath his collar, then asked his wife to watch the store. Stopping to mop his brow again, Green led Eversham and Kate to an office at the back of the shop. The room itself was dominated by a large desk, and once Kate was seated, he sank into the chair behind it. Eversham remained standing.

"Why don't you tell us about your interactions with Mr. Jones." Kate strove for a nonthreatening tone.

"He was a nice enough fellow, my lady. Always paid his bills on time, and I never heard anyone in the village speak ill of him."

"It's interesting you should say so, Green." Eversham had taken up a position with his back to the small fireplace, his height doing more to emphasize his authority than his voice did. "We've heard that you and Jones had a rather heated argument before he was murdered. Can you please tell us about that?"

Green's eyes widened, and for a moment Kate thought he might actually run from the room.

"You can't mean you think I had something to do with the man's death." Green laughed nervously. "Of course I didn't, Mr. Eversham. It was just a disagreement. Nothing to kill a man over."

"Perhaps if we knew what the argument was about, Mr. Green, we could better determine—" Kate broke off at a speaking glance from Eversham, who clearly was not happy with her asking the questions.

She might have known his tolerance of her questioning Mr. Green was only temporary. Even though she was getting results from Green without making the man shake like a frightened rabbit.

Seemingly oblivious to the interplay between his questioners, Green kept his attention focused on Kate. "It was just that Jones wished to buy some letters I had. But when I said I wasn't interested in selling, he made some threats."

At the last word, Eversham straightened. "But you said Jones was 'a nice enough fellow.' I don't think making threats are the actions of a nice fellow. Do you, Mr. Green?"

The stationer looked toward the detective and had the grace to appear sheepish. "Well, that was before I knew you'd heard about the argument, sir."

She bet it was, Kate thought with amusement. Really, if the people the police normally questioned were this transparent, she wondered that they didn't catch the criminal at the outset of every investigation.

"Now that you know we know, I'll thank you to tell us everything, Green. This is a murder investigation. And right now you're the only person I know who had a disagreement with the dead man."

At Eversham's words, the shopkeeper paled. "No, sir. It wasn't me. I was angry with him, it's true, but not enough to kill him."

"Why don't you start at the beginning?" Kate said in a soothing tone. "Do you have a bit of spirits to help calm your nerves?"

When he indicated a decanter on the sideboard, she poured him a glass and carried it to him, for all the world like they were in a drawing room instead of a mean little office in the back of a village shop.

Eversham remained silent the whole time while she saw to Green's comfort, but once she'd resumed her seat, he spoke up. "Now, tell us what happened."

Between sips of brandy, Green told them what had led to his argument with Jones.

Green's late father, it seemed, had been valet to the man from whom Lord Valentine had won Thornfield Hall, which at the time had been called Philbrick Close, and its surrounding farms. Sebastian Philbrick, in addition to being a prominent landowner in these parts, had been a protégé of Wordsworth, Coleridge, and the other Lake Poets. While never quite as famous as the others, he'd been popular enough to earn a tidy living, and he'd reveled in the success until his excesses had led him to gamble away his estate and he'd died in obscurity not long afterward.

Upon his father's death, Green had received a bequest of a cache of letters between Philbrick and various people of his acquaintance. Green had sold one between the poet and Wordsworth several years ago and used the proceeds to purchase this very shop.

"Somehow, Jones learned that I had more letters." Green shook his head a little, as if he still couldn't believe it. "And he wanted to buy them from me, which I declined. I've held on to them this long, and I want to save them so I'll have something to pass on to my children one day."

Like everyone else in England, Kate was familiar with the works of Wordsworth and his circle. She'd even read a bit of Philbrick's verse when Val had first invited her to visit his estate. There was something tragic about the man reaching such celebrity only to fall from such heights into the proverbial gutter.

"From whom are these other letters?" If they were as valuable as the one Green had sold to finance his shop, they might offer a strong motive for murder. Though if that were the case, then it would have been Green rather than Jones who was killed. Unless Green had killed the other man to protect his treasure trove?

"I don't like to say, my lady." Clearly the stationer had been spooked by Jones's interest. "My father was loyal to

Mr. Philbrick for many years. I'll save these until enough time has passed that they won't bring shame on Mr. Philbrick's good name."

Of course, that made Kate want to know more than ever whom the letters were from. But, she reminded herself, they were here to discover who'd killed Jones. Not to satisfy her curiosity about a long-dead poet.

"What was the nature of Jones's threat?" Eversham moved from his position before the fire to stand next to Kate. So close she could smell the sandalwood scent of his shaving lotion.

It was not, she admitted before suppressing the thought, unpleasant.

Green's expression turned mulish. Before he could demur, however, Eversham barked out, "You'd better tell us unless you wish to find yourself before the magistrate. A man is dead, Green."

"I'll need your word, Lady Katherine, that this won't end up in the papers," Green persisted.

"You have it." Kate had no qualms about giving the promise.

He must have believed her, because Green gave a nod. "Jones claimed to know to whom the letters should have gone after Philbrick's death. He offered me a chance to sell them to him for less than they were worth. If I didn't, he said he'd tell the rightful owner so that they could sue me for them."

"But if Philbrick gave those letters to your father, then they belong to you." Kate frowned.

A flush crawled up Green's face.

Eversham gave a low whistle. "Your father stole them, didn't he?"

"I don't rightly know, sir," said Green hastily. "But I know he worked for months for the man without any wages. And when Philbrick lost the estate, my father might have helped himself to a few things to cover expenses."

"Lord Valentine won both the contents and the house from the previous owner, yes?" Kate asked. "That's hardly a secret."

The word of Philbrick's former home going to the disgraced son of the Duke of Thornfield had spread like wildfire through London society. Once word had reached Lewiston, Kate had little doubt every inhabitant of the county had known within hours. The gossip networks of town were fast, but that was nothing compared with country word of mouth.

"Jones claimed it wasn't Lord Valentine." Green shrugged.

"Philbrick died without issue, didn't he?" Eversham asked, his brows furrowed. "Could there be some heir we don't know about?"

"He was lying to get the letters for himself." Green seemed to believe what he said. "A man like that, come down in the world, he wanted a way to get himself out of service. I know what that's like, thanks to my father. So he hit on a scheme to trick me out of my inheritance."

Someone's inheritance anyway, Kate thought.

"He was overheard saying he'd, ah"—Eversham glanced at Kate with apology—"'see you in hell first.' What did he mean?"

"I told him that if he didn't take himself off, I'd have a

word with Lord Valentine about what he was trying to do." He rubbed his shining pate in discomfort. "I wouldn't have done it, of course."

"Because you couldn't risk Lord Valentine learning about the letters, you mean?" Kate asked sweetly. "The letters that might rightly belong to him?"

"All I can go by is what my father told me," Green said defensively. "And he did say that Mr. Philbrick gave them to him for safekeeping so—"

Perhaps not wishing to spook the man any further, Eversham spoke before he could finish. "Was that the last time you saw Jones?"

"Yes, sir, Mr. Eversham." Green had perhaps recognized that he couldn't afford to get on the bad side of the law now that he'd revealed his secret about the letters. "The next I'd heard was that he'd been found murdered. And I swear to you I had nothing to do with it. I was in Bristol picking up supplies in any event."

Recognizing that they'd learned all they could from the shopkeeper, Kate rose. She and Eversham were nearly out of the office when Green called after her. "You won't tell Lord Valentine, will you, my lady? About the letters?"

Kate turned back to look at him.

Though her father was the Marquess of Edgemont, they'd hardly been wealthy—which had been the primary reason her parents had been so keen to secure her marriage to George Bascomb, a wealthy businessman. Before the influx of cash from her marriage settlement, they'd only been able to employ a few loyal servants who were willing to work for low wages. A man like Philbrick, whose fortunes had risen and fallen based on the success of his writing, couldn't have been the steadiest of employers. Even loyal servants needed to be paid.

Perhaps the elder Mr. Green had been given the letters; perhaps he'd taken them in lieu of payment for his services. Either way, she didn't see that they would be of interest to Valentine, who was wealthy in his own right, thanks to a legacy from his grandmother and some shrewd investing.

"I won't tell him." She tried to imbue her tone with all the reassurance she could muster.

Once they'd stepped back onto the street outside the shop, Eversham said wryly, "You were quick enough to give away Lord Valentine's property. Remind me never to let you act as my broker."

"Val has more money than the queen." Kate dismissed him with a wave of her hand. "Besides, I promised Green I wouldn't tell Val. I didn't say about what."

Eversham's laugh was long enough to frighten a nearby horse.

Eversham accompanied the rest of the party from Thornfield back to the house. He'd hoped to use the opportunity on the way to speak to Val about his relationship with Jones, but that had proved impossible. While he and Kate were speaking to Green, the master of Thornfield had returned to the household ahead of them.

Not long after they set out, Eversham noticed that Barton

seemed intent on monopolizing Lady Katherine for the duration of the journey. He could hardly tell the American to desist when the man's only other choices for conversation were his daughter and the feckless Mr. Thompson. Given the same choice, he'd have chosen Lady Katherine, too. Still, he noted the strained nature of her expression when Barton began to describe, yet again, just how large his house on Fifth Avenue in Manhattan was.

So, he set himself to draw the other man's attention away from her by peppering him with questions about the nature of American policing, and though Barton seemed frustrated at the diversion at first, his desire to extol the virtues of his own nation in opposition to England was too strong to ignore.

They'd reached the main entrance to Thornfield by the time Barton grew weary of the topic and made his escape, and Eversham watched him go with some degree of satisfaction.

"That was a very nice gesture, Inspector." Lady Katherine spoke in a low voice that could be heard only by him as they stepped into the marble entryway of the house. "Though I don't need rescuing. I could have put him in his place easily enough."

Watching as she handed her pelisse to the waiting servants, Eversham noted the wisps of dark hair along the nape of her neck and, in his mind's eye, saw himself lowering his lips to them.

What the devil? He shook his head a little, and by the time she'd turned to face him, he'd got himself back under control.

"So, I take it from your silence that you agree with me?" Her eyes were lit with amusement.

Belatedly he realized he'd missed her words entirely.

Get it together, man.

Before he could form a response, however, he heard a high-pitched noise coming from the direction of the staircase followed by a cry of "Katie!"

A petite brunette in a deep purple silk gown and carrying a disgruntled-looking Siamese cat approached them as quickly as her narrow skirts would allow.

"My dear! I came as soon as I read about the murder in *The Times*!"

It was the lady who had been with Lady Katherine the day they'd met in London. Her writing partner, Miss Caroline Hardcastle.

If she'd seen news of the murder in London, that meant that Darrow would be busy answering questions from the public, who'd been assured the Commandments Killer had been caught. It was perhaps unbecoming of him, but he couldn't help feeling the man—and Wargrove, too—was reaping what he'd sown.

"Caro, why on earth are you carrying Ludwig around with you like the villainess in a penny dreadful?"

Lady Katherine's voice, tinged with amusement, brought him back to the scene before him.

Her next words, however, gave him a start.

"Where is Ludwig's leash?"

As if he'd heard his name and knew he must respond, the cat gave an aggrieved yowl that sounded remarkably like a human baby.

"Hush, dearest," Caro soothed, and Eversham was unsure of whether she meant the lady or the cat. "I would have put him on the leash, but the stationmaster forbid it. Can you imagine? Now the poor mite is put out with me because he had to remain in the basket for the duration of the train ride."

"Poor Ludwig." Kate smoothed a hand over the cat's head, and while she did so, Miss Caroline Hardcastle's gaze turned to the man standing behind her friend.

As Eversham watched, her mouth formed an "O" of surprise and her eyes widened to a comical degree.

Perhaps noticing her friend's lack of speech, Kate glanced behind her and saw just whom her friend was reacting to.

"Oh yes," she said, as if she'd only now recalled that Eversham, whom she'd spent that morning questioning a murder suspect with, was there.

"Caro, this is Mr. Eversham of the Metropolitan Police," Kate said in a remarkably calm voice. "He's been called here to investigate poor Mr. Jones's murder."

To Eversham, she said with a speaking look—though he wasn't sure what the look was saying precisely, "Inspector, this is my writing partner, Miss Caroline Hardcastle, and this unhappy fellow is Ludwig, her…well…her cat, I suppose."

Caroline Hardcastle unceremoniously passed Ludwig to Kate and offered Eversham her hand.

Feeling as if he were performing in a Drury Lane farce, he took her proffered hand and bowed over it. "Miss Hardcastle, it's a pleasure to meet you."

"I have so many questions" were her first words after a perfunctory response to his greeting.

"Later," said Lady Katherine in a quelling voice. "Can we please remove ourselves from the entryway before you begin peppering him with questions he'll no doubt be unable to answer?"

As if she'd only just realized where they stood, Caro gave a nod, then took her very large cat from her friend and extended a hand, as if asking Kate to lead the way.

"I'll leave you two ladies to your reunion," Eversham said before they had a chance to walk away. "I promise you may ask me anything you like later, Miss Hardcastle."

Lady Katherine glanced in the direction of Lord Valentine's study and gave Eversham a brief nod.

"Thank you for this morning," she said before turning to a once-more wide-eyed Caro and ushering her up the stairs.

For a moment, Eversham stared after them, feeling more confused than ever.

Putting the oddity of the encounter from his mind, he asked the butler about his master's whereabouts and soon found himself in Lord Valentine's blissfully calm study.

"I apologize for returning to the house before the rest of you." Lord Valentine was seated behind his desk with an inkpot at his elbow and a stack of newly sanded sheets of paper beside him. "A servant came to inform me of the new arrival and then I decided to bury myself in my work." He said this as if the two occurrences were connected, but Eversham didn't comment.

"It's no matter," Eversham said. "While we were in

Lewiston, however, Lady Katherine and I had an opportunity to speak with Mr. Green and I have a few questions for you."

"Before we begin," the other man said, "I wonder if you will call me Val? I do appreciate the benefits that come from having a courtesy title, but it can be quite stuffy in an informal setting. And I like to think that we are on the way to being friendly if not friends."

"Perhaps you'd better wait until I finish my questions before you ask that," Eversham said wryly.

The lord's eyes widened a little. "Green must have had something interesting to tell, then."

Not wanting to prolong the situation with small talk, Eversham outlined what Green had told them about his argument with Fenwick Jones and the steward's attempt to blackmail him into giving up the letters with threats of a "rightful owner" of the missives.

"You won this estate in a card game, did you not?" he asked, watching Lord Valentine's expression for any hints of deception or discomfort.

But if he felt any sort of guilt or worry over the detective's question, Valentine didn't show it.

"It's common knowledge." He shrugged.

"What about the contents of the house?" Eversham asked. "Were those included with the house, or were they auctioned to settle more of the debt?"

"I honestly don't know." Valentine shook his head. "There were things here in this house when I bought it that seemed to date back to Philbrick's time, but I wasn't particularly interested in maintaining it as a museum to the fellow. I know it's probably sacrilege to say so around these parts, but I never was one for poetry. Much less his."

"So you don't know who Jones could have been speaking of when he mentioned the rightful owner of the letters, then?" Eversham asked.

"I wish I did. Jones was a competent steward, but we weren't particularly close." Valentine stared off for a moment, as if trying to remember something. Turning back to Eversham, he said, "I did get the feeling that he may have been hiding something. There wasn't any particular thing he did or said. Just a sort of discretion about his movements, I suppose. I gave him free rein over the running of the estate, and I must say, he was quite good at bringing it back into productivity after lying fallow for many years. But we didn't speak of personal matters. And whenever he left for a few days, I got the sense he was seeing someone, but I didn't ask and he didn't volunteer."

Leaning back in his chair, Eversham sighed. He'd hoped finding out what the argument between Green and Jones had been about would clarify things, but that was not the case.

"It can't be that bad," Val said, a note of commiseration in his tone. "It sounds as if this lead about the letters gives you more than you had before at least."

"The trouble is I don't know if Jones was being truthful or not." Something about what Green had said concerning the threat from Jones was bothering him, but he wasn't sure what. "And I've searched the man's rooms and there was no trace of correspondence or anything that might have let us know whom he's been in contact with."

Valentine frowned. "I know the man received a great deal of mail. But that's to be expected when his family didn't live nearby. I saw a few of his letters myself a time or two before they were brought to him." He rubbed his chin thoughtfully. "In fact, I distinctly remember one letter in particular because my butler brought it to my attention a few weeks ago."

"What stood out about it?" Eversham asked, curious.

Val huffed out a laugh. "I always forget how starchy servants can be. Austen complained to me because it was very obviously from a woman. I believe it was heavily scented, and Austen thought it set a poor example for the impressionable young male servants. They looked up to Jones, I think. And Austen felt that letters from 'a paramour,' as he called them, were improper."

Eversham wasn't the least bit surprised. The rules that governed the behavior of servants were often more rigid than those that regulated the strictest members of the middle class. It was easy enough for people like Val and Lady Katherine, who were the offspring of peers, to ignore niceties. They would carry their courtesy titles for the rest of their lives. Which, in turn, bestowed upon them the automatic respect of most of the people they met.

Lady Katherine might own a newspaper, and Val might write for it, but those endeavors could never entirely erase the privilege that came of being born to a noble family.

For someone like Jones, whose position of steward was far above every servant in the house he served, to behave without a care for propriety was an affront to every servant who had to follow every rule of the household to the letter or risk being sacked. Jones might have been born into a higher station than they were, but he was a servant now, and if he didn't behave as one, then it endangered the structure by which Austen and the rest of the servants ordered their lives.

Could one of the servants, angry about his cavalier attitude toward their way of life, have killed Jones, then tried to cover up the motive with that note?

"What was the outcome of Austen's complaint?"

"I told him I'd see to it." Val shrugged. "And I told Jones to be more discreet. I didn't give a hang about the fellow's affairs. But Austen is worth his weight in gold and I won't have him disrespected. No matter how much of a prig he might be at times. I suppose he has his reasons."

For someone who was writing a biography of a prize-fighter who grew up in the London Rookeries, Eversham thought wryly, Val was blithely unaware of the degree of his own ignorance. He rather wondered that Lady Katherine hadn't made him see his own folly, but then again, perhaps it wasn't her responsibility to school her friends on their blind spots.

Thinking of Katherine reminded him of his earlier encounter with Miss Hardcastle, and deciding he'd learned as much as he could from Val, he said, "I left Lady Katherine heading upstairs with Miss Caroline Hardcastle just now. She's an unusual young lady."

At the mention of Miss Hardcastle, the other man's expression turned grim. "If I didn't know her presence would ease Kate's mind—and no matter how she will insist that finding Jones's body was of no consequence, I know it alarmed her—I would have locked the gates to the estate and turned her away."

Eversham felt his eyes widen. "She wasn't that bad. A little eccentric perhaps, but—"

Interrupting him, Val said tartly, "The queen is a little eccentric. Miss Hardcastle is a bloody *Punch* illustration come to life. She is perhaps the most irritating person it has ever been my misfortune to cross paths with. Even her damned cat, who loathes me, by the way, is a better judge of character than Miss Hardcastle."

"Were we talking about her ability to judge char—?"

But Val hadn't even heard him. "I tried to do her the courtesy of warning her off a chap who I know for a fact frequents one of the ugliest sorts of brothels in London— you'll know about those dark corners, Eversham, you're a policeman after all—and of course I couldn't tell her why because she's a damned lady. And do you know what she said to me? Have you any notion what she said?"

Since he didn't think his response was necessary, Eversham let him continue.

"She told me to mind my own affairs." Valentine looked as if he wanted to tear his hair out by the roots but settled on running a hand through it instead. "As if I were just interfering with her for my own amusement."

"That is frustrating," Eversham said carefully, not sure whether he was expected to comment further. When Val didn't continue, he offered, "If Miss Hardcastle is anything like Lady Katherine, then I would guess she is rather headstrong."

"But Kate is a widow and runs her own household." Val shook his head. "Caro—that is, Miss Hardcastle—might consider herself to be past the age where it matters, but she is still an unmarried young lady, and as such, she should guard her reputation."

"She cannot be above one and twenty, surely?"

"Seven and twenty," Val said, to Eversham's surprise. "Though she behaves as if she's barely out of the school-room sometimes."

"If she's still unmarried, should not her family be en-suring she avoids characters like the one you warned her about?" Eversham asked.

"They can't control her," said Val dismissively. "Her father works in the city and is rich as Croesus. He'd give her the moon if she asked for it, I daresay. Her mother has tried, but I think she's given up. So Caro—that is, Miss Hardcastle—does as she pleases. Which makes her vulnerable to the sort of men who only want her for her fortune."

"You're a good friend to try to protect her," Eversham said.

"We've run in the same social circles for years. I'd do the same for any acquaintance."

Eversham could tell plainly it was a lie. He wasn't sure, however, if Val was lying to himself, or only to Eversham. Either way, it was clear he didn't dislike the unusual Miss Hardcastle as much as he pretended.

"Of course." He nodded. "She's lucky to have you."

Thinking back to Katherine's words after they left Green's office, he noted to himself that he hadn't clarified which "she" he referred to.

"I suppose I should go make sure she hasn't caught the

eye of Barton," Valentine said, his jaw set. This time, it was clear enough to Eversham which "she" *he* was referring to.

As the two men neared the door, Val stopped as if just remembering something. "I wonder if there might be some of Philbrick's things stored out in the folly."

Eversham frowned. "Folly?"

"It can't be seen from the house," Val explained, "but I know when I first came here, Austen had some of the items that remained in the house stored there temporarily. But it's entirely possible temporarily turned into permanent." He shrugged. "It's not as if it's actually in use."

Which meant if there were items belonging to Philbrick there, they'd be undisturbed, Eversham thought with a spark of interest.

"Excellent," Eversham said. If there was a clue as to the identity to Philbrick's mystery heir, he'd lay odds it would be in the man's abandoned belongings.

Chapter Ten

Kate could practically feel the vibrations of curiosity emanating from Caro as the two ladies made their way upstairs to the bedchamber the latter had been assigned.

It was only the fact that her friend had to use every ounce of her physical strength to keep Ludwig from leaping down and running amok through Thornfield like a whirling dervish that saved Kate from discussing her odd partnership with Eversham on the stairs, where anyone could overhear.

"Perhaps you have some task that might be more easily completed below stairs, Harrison." Caro's words to her maid after they'd closed the door to the chamber behind them were less a question than a request.

Used to her mistress's need for confidentiality in her discussions with Kate, Harrison gave a brief curtsy and took herself off.

Once the servant was gone, Caro, who had settled Ludwig into his cushioned basket with a bit of catnip, turned to her friend and gave her a hard hug.

"My poor dear," she said, then pulling away, she looked Kate over as if searching for visible signs of trauma. "Was it very dreadful? I know we've talked enough about the horrible things that can be done by one person to another, but we've never seen an actual murder for ourselves. You must have been overcome with nerves."

Allowing her friend to lead her to the corner of the room with a pair of comfortable chintz armchairs and an overstuffed footstool, Kate took a seat and let Caro fuss over her a little. She, herself, wasn't a particularly demonstrative person. But Caro, despite her rejection of many of the social expectations put on women, was a caretaker, and seeing to Kate's comfort was her way of showing she cared.

Harrison must have known they'd be needing refreshment, because a tea tray was arranged on the table tucked between the chairs.

"It was upsetting, I will admit," Kate said once they were both seated and each had cups of tea in hand. "I don't even think I realized at first that he was dead. There's an impulse, I suppose, for the mind to offer some other, less awful, explanation for what you're seeing."

"Had you spoken with him very much?" Caro asked, her dark eyes shadowed with concern.

But Kate was quick to reassure her. "No, we hadn't spoken more than a few words to one another. I gather he wasn't particularly close to anyone in the household, though he did spend some time with Valentine discussing estate matters."

At the mention of Val, the sympathy in Caro's eyes was replaced with a glint of cynicism. "Why am I not surprised that Lord Valentine was the one most familiar with the man found murdered on his property?"

This startled a laugh from Kate. "I hope you don't mean to suggest Val is a killer, Caro, because though I understand you might not be overly fond of him, I don't quite think his interference in your affairs warrants wishing him to hang for murder."

Caro sighed. "Of course I don't want him to hang," she said with a grudging degree of remorse. "But you cannot deny me my right to loathe him. More than once, he's seen fit to put his aristocratic nose in my business."

"I can see now why neither of you has mentioned knowing the other to me," Kate said with amusement. "Your antipathy knows no bounds."

Then her expression turned serious. "I think he's been more upset about what happened than he lets on. You know how men are. Always intent on keeping their emotions in check."

The noise Caro made might have been sympathetic, but it also might have been critical. When it came to Lord Valentine, Kate wasn't quite sure where her friend's feelings might go.

"Enough about our infuriating host." Caro leaned back in her chair. "I want to know how it is that you and Andrew Eversham appeared to be so cozy when you came in just now. Who knew the famous Eversham was so attractive?

You certainly made no mention of it after you met him in London."

Leave it to Caro to see romance where none existed.

"We weren't cozy," Kate protested. "It was just that we'd been discussing the murder and what we'd learned in the village."

"You'd better tell me everything." Having removed her shoes earlier, Caro tucked her feet beneath her and settled in. Kate knew from experience that she would receive her friend's undivided attention for as long as she needed it. "So, has it been determined if the murder here was definitely committed by the same person as in London?"

It was a good question, and Kate gave it some thought before she answered. "There is nothing to suggest that the murder was committed by someone other than the Commandments Killer. But we haven't been able to rule out some local motive to kill Mr. Jones either."

"What of the rest of the houseguests?" Caro asked. "Might one of them have had a quarrel with Jones?"

"Nothing's been discovered so far," Kate said. Then she went on to describe in detail each of the houseguests Val had invited to Thornfield for the week. When she got to the Bartons, her friend made a face.

"I don't particularly mind the Americans coming here to buy titled husbands for their daughters—most of the noblemen I've met are weak-chinned old roués without two thoughts in their heads to rub together—but I do wish they'd send better examples of their own stock. This Barton fellow sounds positively dreadful."

"I didn't have a very good impression of his daughter at

first," Kate said thoughtfully. "She seemed an insipid creature, if I'm honest. But I think perhaps she's not so bad as I'd thought. Genevieve seems to have made a friend of her anyway, and I think she's not a bad judge of character."

"What of the pugilist? I suppose that's Valentine trying to thrust another of his protégés upon society." Caro wrinkled her nose as if she'd smelled something bad. "Lord knows we need some new blood in the mix. But I'm not sure it's always the best thing for them. It can't be easy to be gawped at like a zoo animal every time one attends a social function. That's what debutantes are for."

Caro had never quite recovered from having been forced into a season by her mother.

Kate gave a soft laugh. "I think Jim Hyde will fare well enough if he decides to allow Val to introduce him in society. Though I'm not sure that's a given just yet. This was just an opportunity for him to get more comfortable in polite company. And since Val is writing the man's biography, I suspect he's preparing the poor fellow in case he's asked to lecture. It will be much better for him if he's got a bit of experience with the odd rituals of the middle and upper classes before he's thrust into the thick of it."

"I suppose that makes some sense." Caro's response seemed subdued, but Kate was sure that had more to do with Val's involvement in the scheme than with Jim Hyde.

"The rest of the guests are of a certain type," Kate continued. "Of course, you'll recall the scandal surrounding the Egglestons' marriage. She might behave as if she's above reproach, but transferring one's affections from one's fiancé to his brother is enough to mark one's reputation for life.

And Mr. Reeve Thompson, while innocuous enough, isn't precisely the highest of society. I very much suspect Val chose this combination of guests from those who wouldn't cut up rough about being in the same house as someone like Mr. Hyde."

"I'm not sure whether that's a slight against yourself or not." Caro raised a brow. "Though I suppose you are good enough friends with Lord Valentine that he knew you were unlikely to decline his invitation for snobbish reasons."

"Just so." Kate could be accused of many things, but snobbery wasn't one of them.

The conversation lulled and Caro stretched. "I must say, you've had quite a busy several days since you left London. I knew you'd be thinking over the future of the column, but I supposed you'd have some time to observe the beauty of nature and perhaps enjoy some stimulating conversation."

She pursed her lips. "Instead you've discovered a dead body, dodged the advances of a boorish American, and been forced to endure the company of a man who blames you for the downfall of his career. Whoever said the country was more restful than town has never been to Lewiston."

"There certainly hasn't been much time for reflection." Kate smiled ruefully. "And now that you're here, there should be even less."

"I do have that effect on a party." Caro grinned impishly.

Then her gaze turned speculative and Kate braced herself for an inquisition.

"I thought you said Eversham was angry with you in London. He didn't seem angry today." It wasn't a question, merely a statement of what Caro saw as fact.

"Do not imagine there is more between us than is there, I beg of you." Kate might find the detective handsome, but that didn't mean anything. "I am conducting my own investigation in an effort to find the real killer. That means I must, at times, be in the company of Mr. Eversham."

"If you say so." Caro didn't believe her; that much was obvious from her tone. Kate knew from experience that she could no more control her friend's expectations than she could knit a sweater from Ludwig's fur—or wool, for that matter, since she had no skill at the craft.

Caro and Kate might share similar perspectives on the role of women in society, but Kate was well aware that she was the more pragmatic and cynical of the two. Caro, on the other hand, was sentimental and saw love around every corner. Even where there was no hope of it ever coming into being.

Perhaps sensing that Kate was having none of her flights of fancy, Caro said, "Tell me more about the investigation."

Once Kate told her about Green and the letters, Caro asked, "But what does a secret heir to Philbrick have to do with the Commandments Killer? The note on Jones's body called him a liar. Did it mean he was lying about the existence of an heir, or was it something entirely unrelated?"

"We can't know that until we know more about Philbrick," Kate said. "If there is some connection between Philbrick and the killer, then perhaps this is what will finally make it possible to catch him."

Caro tilted her head in thought. "Didn't you say this house belonged to Philbrick before Valentine came into possession of it?"

Startled that her friend had voluntarily mentioned Val, Kate blinked. "Yes, this was his house. Why?"

"Well, if Philbrick lived here, it's possible some of his things are still here. Maybe we can find something that will give us a clue as to who this rightful owner is that Jones was going on about."

"That's a brilliant idea." Kate grinned. "What are we waiting for?"

As it happened, Kate had to endure a tedious hour at the luncheon table with her fellow guests before she could make her way to the attics to search for Philbrick's left-behind belongings.

Though she now had Caro there to divert the attention of Mr. Barton, who seemed somehow to have learned about her friend's family wealth—doubtless from Lady Eggleston, who kept sneaking amused glances Caro's way, as if she were enjoying the fruits of her devious labor—and had directed all of his attention her way through the meal.

Caro seemed to find her own sort of pleasure in insulting the American to his face, but so subtly he thought the taunts were jokes and showed no sign of taking offense. Of course, given the man's obliviousness to his off-putting effect on others, he likely couldn't conceive of a woman who wouldn't find him utterly irresistible.

By the time the meal was over and the other guests were headed off to find some diversion for themselves, Kate felt the familiar pinch of a headache beginning behind her eyes. But headache or not, she was determined to make some sort of progress in the investigation.

She met Caro on the stairs on her way up to check on Ludwig.

"You weren't exaggerating about Mr. Barton," her friend said with wide eyes. "He's even more impervious to my insults than Lord Gordon, who thought it was a compliment when I informed him his views on suffrage were Byzantine. I'm not entirely sure he knows what Byzantine means, of course, but still."

Kate winced. Lord Gordon, a friend of Caro's father, was notoriously thickheaded, but Barton did threaten to outdo him in ignorance. "I am sorry he seems to have turned his attentions to you. Though I can't say I didn't appreciate the respite. I haven't actually been able to enjoy a meal since my arrival."

Caro shook her head. "I didn't mind it a bit. Puncturing male self-importance is one of my favorite activities, as you well know. And though I suspect it may be an impossible task in this case, since the male in question doesn't seem capable of understanding when he's been rebuffed, I look forward to making it my mission to do so before I return to London."

Changing the subject, she glanced upward toward the stairs leading to the third floor. "I take it you are on your way to the attics to investigate?"

"Yes. I was on my way to invite you now."

Her friend glanced down at her gown, an exquisitely tailored blue silk from Worth. "Of course I'll come. Someone must protect you from the skeletons in Lord Valentine's closets."

"I have nothing to hide, Miss Hardcastle," said the man in question from where he'd just emerged from his study down the hall. "Perhaps you are simply deflecting your own guilt."

To Kate's amusement, Caro, who never blushed, turned pink. Clearly there was far more history between these two than she'd realized.

Turning to face her nemesis, the younger lady looked at him from head to toe. "If we are to speak of guilt, Lord Valentine, then I am quite certain you bear far more of that than I."

"Perhaps we'd better make our way to the attics now," Kate said before the conversation devolved further. She sensed there was some long-standing hurt between them that was far too deep to be resolved here in the hallway.

"If you're intent on searching through Philbrick's things," Valentine said, "then I'm afraid the attic isn't where you'll need to be. I double-checked with Austen, and he said that the bulk of the items left behind in the house when I took possession were moved out to the folly."

The ornamental gardens at Thornfield had been laid out in the first part of the century by a previous owner, before even Philbrick, who had done what he could to restore the acres closest to the house to their natural state, albeit with help from some of the best landscape gardeners in the country. Beyond that, however, was the folly and a shrubbery maze, which was so overgrown as to be nearly impassable.

"It's quite secure," Val said, perhaps reading the fears of weather damage and vermin in Kate's expression. "I believe the interior was intended to be finished at some point, but the fellow from whom Philbrick purchased the estate ran out of funds before he could set anyone up there.

"Lest you think I, too, have run out of funds," Val continued, "I've been waiting for the fellow I want to restore the grounds to finish a job elsewhere. So, I'm afraid you'll need me to escort you through the wood to the folly."

Kate looked down at her morning gown, then glanced out a window at the overcast skies. "I'll need to change first. I don't suppose there's a working fireplace in the folly?" The spring had been a chilly one and rain would only make it more so.

"Afraid not," Val said with an apologetic look. "I can have one of the servants bring a brazier if you like."

"Oh," he continued. "I should mention that Eversham was headed to the folly when last I spoke to him. So you may have company for your search."

Kate stifled a sigh. Of course Eversham had thought of searching Philbrick's belongings before she had.

"Mr. Eversham seems to have forgotten he was supposed to be letting you observe him at work." Caro raised a brow.

Not bothering to rise to her friend's bait, Kate said briskly, "We'd better get changed so that we can be off."

"At least he'll be an extra pair of hands," Caro said as they climbed the stairs.

If he hadn't already found what they were looking for, Kate thought with a pang of disappointment. She knew a man had been murdered, but she'd been looking forward to doing something that would help solve this mystery.

Ah well. It wasn't about who it was that found the information that would help, so long as they found it and it led to the arrest of the right man.

Kate donned her warmest wool gown, kid boots, and wrapped herself in a woolen shawl as well. For her part, Caro, who apparently packed for travel with more clothes than she could possibly wear, had donned an ermine coat with a jaunty fur-trimmed hat and matching muff.

"One would have thought you were expecting to stay away through the decade, rather than a mere week," Kate said wryly as they followed Val along the path leading from the neatly tended grounds nearest the house toward what looked like an expanse of thick woods. Only as they neared where the grass gave way to trees did she see that they hid a wall of tall shrubs, which must be one side of the maze Valentine had talked about. She'd never have known it was there if he hadn't pointed it out.

"You never know when the weather will turn, Kate." Caro didn't look the least bit abashed. "Besides, I did offer you my coat before we left the house."

"Caro, I'm six inches taller than you," Kate replied. "At best it would work as a shawl."

She and Caro chatted, with occasional input from Val, as they climbed. When they'd finally reached the edge of the clearing that surrounded the white marble edifice, which had been crafted to resemble a smaller version of the Parthenon, Kate noticed that the door beyond the columns was ajar and she saw a flash of light in the darkness.

Caro clasped both Kate and Val by the arms and said in a stage whisper, "There's someone in there."

"Not to worry, Miss Hardcastle," said their host. "It's Eversham, remember?"

The trio made their way up the marble stairs and walked between the enormous columns of the folly. Despite the likelihood that it was Eversham inside, Val insisted on entering first. There was still a murderer on the loose, after all.

But the sound of Eversham greeting Val was enough to let the ladies know it was safe, and careful to ensure the way was clear, Kate and Caro stepped inside.

If she'd been expecting an interior that matched the grandeur of the folly's exterior, Kate would have been sorely disappointed. Though unlike some follies, which were nothing more than a facade with no interior, this one did boast a rather large inner chamber. It was, however, as plain as the outside was fancy, which made sense if it had been built with the idea of turning it into a hermitage.

There were no windows, and without the lantern hung on a hook on the wall behind him, Eversham would have been impossible to make out.

"I see you were able to find the place," Val said as he hung his own lantern on a hook a couple of feet down from Eversham's.

"Yes," the detective replied. "Though I hadn't expected you to give a guided tour while I worked."

His tone was sardonic, but Kate could hear a bite of annoyance in his words as well.

Which was really just too bad.

He might have forgotten his promise to work together, but she hadn't. Before she could speak, however, Caro sneezed. The sound of it echoed through the mostly empty chamber.

Then, before anyone could speak, she sneezed again. And again and again.

"Goodness, Caro, are you well?"

Her friend wiped her streaming eyes with a handkerchief she'd pulled from some inner pocket in her coat. "I'm afraid I forgot just how much my nose doesn't care for dust," her friend said, her voice muffled. "I'm sorry, Kate. I had meant to help you search Mr. Philbrick's things."

Kate glanced at Eversham, who had gone back to shuffling through a sheaf of pages in the lantern light. "Of course you mustn't apologize. You can't help how dust affects you."

She turned to Valentine, who was in the process of prying open a trunk alongside the wall. "Val, would you mind terribly walking Caro back to the house? She's feeling unwell."

Her friend stood and moved closer to where the ladies stood. As if to punctuate her plight, Caro sneezed again loudly.

"It's the dust," Caro said, though it sounded more like "duth" instead of "dust."

Though he might have reacted with annoyance, Valentine was a gentleman and merely gave Kate a look that seemed to say she owed him, before offering Caro his arm. "Let's get you back to the house, Miss Hardcastle." Over his shoulder, he said to Kate, "I'll send a servant up in a short while to carry back anything you wish to look over in the house."

Once they were gone, Kate turned to Eversham, who hadn't looked up from the documents he was examining.

"Don't just stand there," she said in an exasperated tone. "What have you found?"

Chapter Eleven

E versham had known as soon as Lord Valentine had arrived with the ladies in tow that his concentration over the job at hand would be broken. "I only arrived here a quarter of an hour before you did. I haven't found anything yet."

"Oh."

Her tone was so flat, he almost wished he'd invented a discovery to blunt her disappointment.

Realizing what he'd just considered, Eversham nearly groaned aloud. That would never do. He needed to make sure he kept her at a distance from now on or he'd find himself doing all sorts of things simply to improve her moods.

"Here." He gestured to the trunk Valentine had just pried open. "These need going through." To her credit, Kate lowered herself to her haunches—possible thanks to the old-fashioned gown, sans hoops, she'd donned before coming out here—and in the dimness of the lantern light began sorting through the papers inside the walnut trunk. The wider skirts and higher waist suited her, he thought before purposefully turning back to his own search.

They worked silently together for some time before Katherine, as he'd begun to think of her, said, "I shouldn't have thought a policeman would be afraid of the dark."

Eversham had been scanning a bill from Philbrick's bootmaker when her words penetrated his consciousness. "I'm not afraid of the dark," he said pettishly.

"I'm quite sure that's what you said earlier." Kate raised her brows. "When a gentleman says he wishes to be indoors once night has fallen, one can only assume it's a deathly fear of darkness that precipitates that wish. I believe it's been proven by science."

He huffed out a laugh. "You're teasing me." It had been a long time since anyone had bothered to be playful with him.

Most of his friends from university had been appalled at his decision to join the police. And his colleagues on the force looked down on him because his grandfather had been a baronet.

He'd almost forgotten what it felt like to laugh over something foolish with a friend.

It was unfamiliar, but not unpleasant.

"I'm trying." Katherine shrugged. "But you don't seem to know how it's done. You're supposed to play along. As if you truly are afraid of the dark. But I suspect you're too much of a policeman for such a thing. It's a shame really."

This made him frown. "Why?"

She rose to her feet and brushed off her gown where

it had been in contact with the floor. "Because the papers I've been looking at have been as dull as dishwater and I was looking for some sort of diversion. Sebastian Philbrick might have been a passable poet, but so far his correspondence has been as entertaining as a prayer meeting."

Eversham coughed.

"I forgot." Katherine gasped, her cheeks coloring. "Your father was a minister, wasn't he? I do apologize. I never intended...that is to say, I didn't mean..."

He stepped closer and touched her on the arm. "I take no offense, Lady Katherine, I assure you. Prayer meetings can be deadly dull. There's a reason why I'm with the Met and not a clergyman."

She looked up at him and smiled, a pair of dimples bracketing her mouth, like an emphasis on where precisely he should put his own. "You're being kind. I'm always saying the wrong thing at just the wrong moment. For the most part, I'm cool and calm, but every once in a while, I manage to truly say something that puts me to the blush."

Was it his imagination or were her eyes darting to his mouth?

Breaking their gaze, he thrust a hand into his hair. "Well, no harm done. Though we should make sure there aren't any other trunks that we should ask the servants to bring up to the house."

"Of course," she said, her tone falsely bright to his ear.

Her tone didn't matter, he reminded himself. He had a job to do.

"I'll take these." He gestured to a stack of crates.

"Just so," she said. "I'll make sure these two are what we're looking for."

They turned away from each other and set about opening crates and trunks and riffling through them to scan the contents.

They worked in silence for some minutes until he heard a cry of pain from Katherine.

Eversham let the lid of the trunk he was holding up slam shut and hurried to her side.

"What happened?" he asked as he arrived at where she knelt before an open trunk. She was shaking out her hand and her face was creased with pain.

"I pinched my finger in the hinge," she said through clenched teeth. "Stupid, stupid, stupid."

From experience he knew he had to let her get all her shaking out. There was something about pain that made one unable to remain still.

It was as if concentrating on some other action took away some of the sting.

Once the worst of it had passed, she peeled off her glove so that she could look at the injury more closely.

"Look how red it is." She extended her finger to him so that he could see it better.

The light was dim, but he could see that the pad of flesh was an angry red where the metal hinges had pinched the skin.

He would wonder later what impulse had prompted him, but in that moment, he acted on pure instinct.

Gently he brought her hand to his mouth and pressed his lips to the wound.

Her fingers were cool in his, and this close he could see her gray eyes widen in surprise. But she didn't pull away.

"Thank you," she said softly, her dark lashes fanning over her cheeks as she glanced at his mouth.

Andrew was no green boy. He knew what a woman who wanted to be kissed looked like. And yet, even as he leaned close enough to smell her jasmine scent, he whispered, "May I kiss you, Katherine?"

"Oh yes." Her assent came just as his mouth captured hers in a kiss that felt at once like nothing he'd ever known before and like coming home.

He was, he knew, in a great deal of trouble. But he'd think about that later.

Kate had never been kissed quite like this. She would have expected a man like Andrew Eversham, a policeman who had spent most of his adult years among the hardest characters England had to offer, would be rough and without finesse.

But she realized as soon as his soft lips touched hers that she'd utterly misjudged him.

Of course a man who had the ability to adjust his approach from tact to bluntness as the situation required would kiss with every bit of finesse at his disposal.

Her injured finger forgotten, she clutched the front of his shirt as he took her face in surprisingly gentle hands and stroked the skin of her cheek with his thumb.

She'd begun to think herself immune to passion. The

first affair not long after her husband's death, when she'd thought herself ready to partake of all the freedoms of widowhood, had proven unsatisfying. And the next lover she'd chosen, despite his good looks, had been selfish—perhaps *because* of his good looks—and she'd ended the affair after a few months. But though she hadn't enjoyed the act itself, the closeness and the long, drugging kisses that preceded it had been heavenly.

Eversham, however, was entirely different.

Pulling back a little, she looked up at him, seeing the dark glint of desire in his eyes. "You're exceptionally good at this." She could hear the husky tone in her own voice.

"I'm glad you think so." He kissed her again, this time pulling her lower lip between his teeth, in a move that made her lose her breath. "I aim to please."

With deliberate slowness, he licked into her mouth and she pressed closer to him, tilting her head to get better access to that delicious warmth. She was assailed by all her senses at once, feeling the rough wool of his coat against the skin of her fingers and inhaling the clean sandalwood scent of him. All the while, pulses of sensation coursed through her, fanning out from where their mouths joined, from the peaks of her breasts pressed against his chest, then lower still where she most wanted him.

"What were we talking about?" He pulled away a little. "I wouldn't want you to think I was ignoring y—"

He broke off as she pulled him closer, kissing him back until they were both breathless. "Who cares?" he muttered, and took her mouth again. When she heard a noise of hunger, she wasn't sure if it had come from him or her.

She only knew that when she felt his hands thread into her carefully arranged hair, she slid her arms over his shoulders and did the same, liking the feel of his cool, unfashionably short locks against her fingers.

It took a moment for the sound of a throat clearing to penetrate the cocoon of their own making. But when it did, Kate gasped and pulled back from him with more speed than she'd have thought herself capable of in her languorous state. It took Eversham a beat longer, but once he'd realized they had company, he muttered a curse beneath his breath and called out to whoever it was, "A moment, please."

"Very good, Mr. Eversham." The voice came from one of Valentine's footmen.

Glancing at Eversham, who was straightening his cravat and pulling down the cuffs of his shirt and coats, Kate noted that his hair was sticking up at all angles and reached out to smooth it down.

"There's no help for your hair, I'm afraid." He nevertheless attempted to smooth it where Kate could feel some of the pins had come loose. She reached up to reaffix one and their hands met.

Unlike only seconds before, they pulled away as if they'd touched hot coals.

When they were satisfied they'd repaired their appearances to the best of their abilities, they turned as one to walk toward the open doorway to the folly.

Anyone might have found them, Kate thought with alarm at her own recklessness. She might be a widow with more liberty than an unmarried miss, but she wasn't so immune to social judgment that she could engage in licentious behavior without fear of consequences.

What had she been thinking?

"What is it, Jennings?" she asked the footman, whose ears were red, though from cold or embarrassment she couldn't say.

"Begging your pardon, Lady Katherine." He bowed. "But Lord Valentine asked me to fetch the inspector. There's been another murder."

"Good God, not at the house?" Kate put a hand to her throat and would have gone running from the folly if Eversham hadn't stopped her with a hand on her arm.

"Who and where, lad?"

"It was in the village, sir." Jennings swallowed. "Mr. Green was stabbed, and they said it was something terrible to behold. Please, sir, Lord Valentine says you must come at once."

Their search through Philbrick's belongings forgotten, Kate and Eversham took up the lanterns inside the folly and followed Jennings out from the marble building, to under the darkening afternoon skies.

Chapter Twelve

When they reached the house, it was to find a grim-faced Valentine, surrounded by the rest of the houseguests in the drawing room.

"I thought you were supposed to be keeping us safe," Barton said as soon as Eversham entered the room. He would have bypassed the group altogether, but he needed to speak to Lord Valentine and this was where the footman, Jennings, had brought him.

He'd very carefully stopped himself from looking at Katherine once they'd entered the house. He was frustrated at his own lack of self-control when it came to her, and as he had a job to do—as Barton had pointed out—he needed to remain focused no matter how delicious a distraction she was.

Yet she hadn't entered the drawing room with him and

that felt wrong, no matter how much he might tell himself it was as things should be.

"I've been conducting an investigation, Barton," he said to the American, who stood beside his daughter's chair, patting her hand in what Eversham supposed was meant to be a comforting gesture. However, it looked as if giving reassurances wasn't an activity with which the man had a great deal of practice.

"We were just at Mr. Green's shop this morning." Miss Barton's pallid complexion was turning even whiter with nerves. "Do you think the killer was there, too, Inspector?"

The room's inhabitants all began talking at once, and Eversham took the opportunity to speak with Lord Valentine. "What do you know?" he asked the nobleman in a low voice. "How did you learn of it?"

Gesturing for Eversham to follow him, Valentine led him out of the room and into a small antechamber, which appeared to be a parlor of some sort.

"The local constable came about an hour ago looking for you." He looked angry. "Green was a good man. I've known him since he moved to the village to set up his shop. That's two good men this monster has killed in this locale now. I want you to catch this villain, Eversham."

"That's what I intend to do." Eversham didn't remind Valentine that he'd already gone up against this killer before and failed to catch him. That knowledge hung between them like a dank fog of disappointment. "And with every move he makes, he's giving more clues to his identity."

"Did you find anything in the folly that might help?" Valentine asked.

Eversham felt his face heat but managed to maintain an even tone. "No. Nothing."

"I've had the carriage brought around for you." Valentine rubbed a finger between his brows in fatigue. "The constable is already waiting inside."

With a nod of thanks, Eversham made his way back downstairs.

Her face burning with embarrassment, Kate parted from Eversham and hurried upstairs. Valentine had instructed Jennings to bring them both, but she could hardly go into a roomful of people looking as if she'd had a man's fingers running through her hair. And she had little doubt that's exactly what it looked like.

The wind was up, but it wasn't quite that good at loosening a well-placed hairpin.

She'd thought to have a quick word with Eversham before she headed to her rooms, but as soon as they entered the house, it was as if the passionate, warm man who'd held her in the folly had been replaced with an ice sculpture.

Of course, she could hardly expect him to say tender things when someone had been murdered, but he might have said something.

Not for the first time, she castigated herself for giving in so easily to the temptation to see what his kiss would taste like. She knew better than most how complicated such activities could make things. Her previous liaisons had been with men she'd respected but hadn't been in love with or even infatuated with. Yet even though she had been the one to call things off between them, it had taken time for her to disengage her feelings. How much more difficult would it be when the man was Eversham, whom she felt pulled toward like metal to a magnet?

Just the fact that she was so hurt by his ignoring her to go chase a murderer now was proof enough she wasn't in control of her emotions where he was concerned. And she would do well to remember that the next time she saw him. It would be better for both of them if they forgot about what had happened in the folly altogether.

When she reached her bedchamber, however, she knew there would be no forgetting it, at least for now.

"Kate, your hair!" Caro gasped from where she was tucked up in the window seat next to Katherine's bed, Ludwig purring audibly from her lap. "I hoped my little ruse of a sneezing fit would lead to some kissing, but goodness, you look as if he positively ravished you!"

Shutting the door behind her, Kate hissed, "Lower your voice, you madwoman! Do you want the entire house to hear you?"

Not one bit chastened, Caro laughed. "My dear, no one is up here. They're all in the drawing room driving Valentine to distraction with questions about poor Mr. Green's murder. I remained for all of five minutes before I knew there was nowhere on earth I'd rather be less than in the same room with Lady Eggleston practicing a swoon until somebody noticed. Really, if she wants to do a credible one, she should take lessons from an actress. She's much too stiff. You have to let yourself go limp. Otherwise you give yourself away."

Though she was exasperated at Caro's unexpected presence in her bedchamber, Kate was glad for her stream of chatter while she pulled the bell for hot water and began searching through her wardrobe for a clean, and possibly warmer, gown.

"So, tell me everything," Caro continued. "Was it lovely? He looks as if he'd be very good at kissing. It's always the quiet ones, you know?"

"Of course, I won't tell you anything." Kate laughed. Stepping behind a screen, she sat down on a stool and began removing her boots. "That's private. And besides, nothing's going to come of it."

"Why not?" Caro sounded more than a little disappointed. "He's attractive, if a bit dour for my taste."

Standing to unbutton her gown, which fastened down the front, Kate peeked around the edge of the screen. "Did you forget that we nearly ruined his career? At the first sign of trouble, he'll bring it up to use against me. Mark my words."

"You don't know that."

Kate heard Ludwig give a yowl of annoyance as Caro no doubt pushed him out of her lap.

They paused their conversation at the sound of Kate's maid, Bess, who entered the room to fill the bowl with hot water and take away Kate's soiled clothes.

Wrapping herself in a dressing gown, Kate emerged and

sat down before her vanity mirror and began to unpin her hair. "Thank you, Bess," she told the maid with a smile. The girl had been with her for a few years now and they'd grown to be friends. "Will you please ready the blue wool so that I can change in, say, half an hour or so?"

"Of course, my lady." The girl nodded. "I'll get it now."

Before she could go, Kate turned to face her. "Oh, and I have a task for you that will require your acting skills."

The maid's eyes brightened. "What is it?"

"I need you to have one of Lord Valentine's carriages brought round, but whatever you do, make sure he's not informed of it."

"Is that all, my lady?" Bess asked with a grin. "I've already made friends with one of the grooms. He'll do that for me without even blinking."

"Where are you going?" Caro asked once the maid had departed. "And in one of Valentine's coaches without his knowledge?"

"Valentine knows everything that goes on in this house." Kate waved her hand. "I just don't want to make a circus of it."

"Of what?"

"We're going into the village." Pinning her hair into a simple but well-secured chignon, Kate turned around to look at Caro, who was, for once, speechless. "You'd better go change if you intend to go with me."

Caro looked down at the dressing gown she'd changed into after her sneezing fit. "All right."

Then, gathering a protesting Ludwig into her arms, she asked, "But what about Eversham?"

"I have little doubt he was in the coach I heard leaving a few minutes ago." Kate went over to the hot water and began scrubbing her hands. "He'll be going to the shop where poor Mr. Green was found. We will be going to the man's home. I intend to speak with his wife to find out whether she knows more about the letters than he told us. And tactful as Eversham is, I don't think he'll manage to get as much information from her as we will."

"I'll be back," she heard Caro say just before the bed-chamber door closed behind her.

Turning back to the mirror, Kate checked her hair once more and sent up a little prayer of hope that whatever they found at the Green house would help them find the man's killer.

Eversham found a hamper of sandwiches and a jar of tea in Valentine's carriage when he climbed in for the short ride into the village. Having missed luncheon, he was grateful for the sustenance.

The rain that had been threatening all day had finally come, and he tried to clear his mind of anything but the case as the well-sprung coach rumbled over the narrow lane toward Lewiston.

That Green had been killed so soon after speaking with him could be a sign that the murderer had been alarmed by whatever Green could reveal. But Eversham hadn't had the feeling that the man was holding back anything more about the altercation with Jones or the letters. It must be something that he hadn't even realized was connected to the killer's identity.

If there was an unknown heir to Philbrick's estate with whom Jones had been working, then there were only two options: one, that some distant relative who had been heretofore unknown had surfaced, or two, Philbrick had fathered a child. But in order to be legitimate, the child would have to have been born in wedlock and there was no record of the man ever having been married.

Still, a child of Philbrick's body—even an illegitimate one—seemed more likely than a distant relation. For one thing, an illegitimate child would have reason to be angry. And there was a great deal of anger in the way Jones, and even the London victims, had been killed. For another, a child would not have been able to come forward at the time of Philbrick's death.

He knew from his years with the police that most murders were due to either money or familial strife, and this case had the potential for both. Or at least the overarching motive seemed related to both. But unlike Jones and Green, he'd never been able to find a connection between the four London victims.

His gut said that these murders were also the work of the Commandments Killer, but if that were the case, then the motives had changed. Had the killer altered his reasons for killing, along with the location?

It was something to consider.

He closed his eyes, but as soon as he did, he was back in the folly with Katherine.

What a well-named site for his most impulsive mistake yet. Still, attraction had been brewing between them for weeks. And like a long-awaited storm, once the tension broke, there was nothing but relief. At least temporarily.

She'd been as sweet and passionate as he'd hoped. And if the footman hadn't interrupted them, who knows what they might have done?

Though he did not intend to repeat the action, he was grateful to have gotten the need for her out of his system.

They were adults. There was no reason they wouldn't be able to put the matter behind them. One good thing about Katherine was that she was just as invested in finding the culprit—whether he was the Commandments Killer or someone else who was copying his methods.

He felt a small pang of guilt at having left her behind to go to the village, but a murder scene was no place for a lady.

And if he knew her, she still hadn't dealt with the trauma of finding Jones's body.

The carriage drew to a halt, but before the coachman could let down the step, Eversham leapt down to the village street. He was only a few feet from Green's shop, which was lit from within, the interior hidden from view by the drawn curtains in the window.

Just outside the door he saw the local constable, a Mr. Miller, who even in the dim light was visibly pale.

Up and down the road running through the village, townspeople were milling around, talking in low voices to one another and darting glances toward the stationer's shop. The taking of one of their own by persons unknown made people question their own safety, as well as the motives and behaviors of their neighbors.

If the local stationer could be murdered in his own shop, what was to stop it happening to the butcher, the blacksmith, or the postmistress?

It would hardly make them feel safer to see their local lawman shaken to the core by what he'd seen.

"Let's go inside," Eversham whispered, opening the door to the shop and scanning the interior. The light he'd noticed before came from sconces lining the walls, and every last one of them had been lit, as if someone were trying to keep out more than just darkness. Fortunately, the shop itself seemed not to be where the murder had taken place, so he gestured for the constable to follow him and led the man to a chair near the counter, where Green had been talking with Barton just that afternoon.

Eversham knew that the men who kept the peace in rural villages were unaccustomed to the brutality that was all too common in the cities. There might be the occasional feud between neighbors or accidental deaths, but the sort of violence that the Commandments Killer wrought with the blade of a knife shocked the senses.

"It's worse than Jones, Mr. Eversham." Miller dropped into the chair, his round face lending him an air of youth despite his thirty-some-odd years. "Much worse. There's a lot of blood. I almost didn't see the note because it's"—he paused to swallow—"it's drenched, sir."

"Tell me exactly what happened." Eversham tried to get the man to focus on the job, to direct his mind away from the shock of what he'd seen and toward the retelling of how he'd got here and what he'd done.

"I was having a pint in the taproom at the inn." Miller looked wistful, as if he wished he were back there now. "Mr. Green's assistant, Jeffries, came in shouting that Green was dead in his office. I thought at first it was from something normal, like a fit or a fall or some such. But Jeffries kept saying 'the blood' and I got a bad feeling."

Eversham had questions but didn't interrupt, knowing that he needed to let the man finish the story in his own time.

"I didn't want to come," Miller admitted in a low voice. "But it's my job. And I'm no coward. But I'm not ashamed to admit I got Old Sullivan, who owns the taproom, to come with me."

The detective made a mental note to speak to Sullivan at some point.

"I could smell it before I saw anything." The constable spoke as if he were still surprised by the fact. "Like nothing I've ever known before, this killing, but it's got the smell of it. Once you get the scent in your nose, you don't soon forget it."

"What did you see?" Eversham prompted.

"There was just a lamp burning on the desk, but even in that dimness, I could see he was cut up awful. Lying on the floor beside the desk, like he'd fallen there, then the killer went to work."

He shook his head a little. "It wasn't until I was farther in the room that I saw the blood spattered on the wall. It's everywhere."

"Has anyone else been in the office since you and Sullivan left?" Eversham knew in the chaos of finding a dead body that people could do all sorts of things to disrupt the area where the murder had taken place. Some of it couldn't be helped, but he did prefer that the entire village didn't take a tour of the place before he had a chance to look it over.

"No, sir," Miller said. "Sullivan left almost immediately to be sick outside. And I wasn't long after." He gave a defiant look, as if expecting the London detective to chide him. But Eversham had no intention of doing so. "Then I sent for you. And waited here."

Something occurred to Eversham.

"You said you went outside to be sick, Miller. Was that out the front door or is there one leading out the back?"

"The back," Miller said. "And I made sure to lock it so no one could come in that way. I know those people out there want to see for themselves, but I'm not going to let them get that sight in their heads. No matter how much they think they want it."

"Good man." The constable might have been rattled by the sight of the murder, but he'd kept his head about him through the ordeal. Eversham had seen hardened police officers who'd had years of dealing with the worst London criminals who might not have acquitted themselves as well. "Now, I would like for you to keep watch at the front entrance to make sure that crowd out there doesn't try to venture inside. If there's a trustworthy lad, I'd like you to send him for the local physician."

"Very good, sir." Miller stood, seeming a bit sturdier on

his feet. He looked relieved to leave matters in Eversham's hands, and Eversham couldn't blame him.

Removing his notebook and pencil from his coat, he strode toward the door leading into the back offices and stepped inside.

Chapter Thirteen

Before they left Thornfield, Kate had Bess ask for the direction of Mr. Green's house. The gossip mill had been as busy downstairs as it had been upstairs, and Bess had learned not only that Mr. Green and his family lived in a tidy cottage on the other side of the village but that his death was said to have been even more gruesome than that of Jones.

Kate knew the public often exaggerated the details of killings. Perhaps for the same reason people enjoyed ghost stories—to frighten themselves in the comfort of their own homes. Or to distract themselves from the humdrum of their everyday lives. In this case, she suspected that the servants of Thornfield Hall were both shocked that another murder had occurred so soon after that of Mr. Jones and somewhat upset that they had a detective from Scotland

Yard staying in the house and yet he hadn't been able to prevent another murder.

The ride into town was in an aged carriage. The groom said it had belonged to Valentine, though Kate rather suspected it had belonged to Philbrick because the style was decades out of date.

As it happened, they had been found out by Valentine as they left. "I know better than to try to change either of your minds once you're set on a thing," he said as they climbed into the conveyance. Once they had been seated inside, he said through the open door, "Be careful." He directed his words to Kate, then, to her surprise, looked over at Caro as well. "Don't lead her into any more mischief and mayhem than necessary."

"I like that." Caro huffed after he'd closed the door and rapped on the side of the carriage to give the signal to the coachman. "I'm not the one who gets us into mischief."

"Of course you aren't," Kate said soothingly. "We are equally at fault for the amount of mischief we get ourselves into."

"Just because we are en route to conduct an unsanctioned investigation while Mr. Eversham is occupied at the scene of the crime doesn't mean we're causing mayhem." Caro's frown spoke for itself.

"Eversham may not like it," Kate said reasonably, "but we are far more suited to question Mrs. Green than he is. Who better than a woman to know what questions to ask about a husband's secrets?"

"No one," Caro said with conviction.

They didn't consider themselves the equals of the police

when it came to investigating murder, of course. Though they'd both been following crime stories in the papers for years—and Kate had actually written some as well—it was hardly equal to the training that Eversham and the rest of Scotland Yard went through.

What they did have was a reporter's ability to elicit information from people wary of the police. Like it or not, there was an inherent distrust of the law among many of the people who most often found themselves being questioned.

While there was also a distrust of the press, that was often dismissed when the interviewee learned their name would be printed in the newspaper. And Kate had learned how to make people feel so comfortable with her that they forgot they were speaking with a journalist. Something she hoped to employ tonight.

While Caro was still new to newspaper writing, Kate had been at it long enough to have figured out how to interview even the toughest subject.

Aloud, she mused, "There will likely be people at Green's house. Whenever something like this happens, there will always be those who come to offer comfort."

"And to stick their inquisitive noses into someone else's business," Caro said wryly. "I'll make sure to keep the worst of the busybodies at bay while you speak with Mrs. Green."

It didn't take long for them to reach the cottage. Every window seemed to glow with interior light, and in the dim twilight, it looked welcoming and like the very ideal of a cozy home.

Once she and Caro had been handed down from the carriage, Kate instructed the coachman to pull over to a stand of trees at the end of the lane and wait for them.

Their knock was answered by a maid who looked as if she'd been weeping. And when they asked if they could speak with her mistress, the girl shook her head. "She's been put to bed with a sleeping draught. But there's other ladies from the village here."

Caro handed her the pie the cook at Thornfield had insisted they bring the family, and the girl looked for a moment as if she didn't know what to do with it. Then coming to herself, she thanked the visitors and showed them to a parlor just off the main hallway before leaving, not bothering to make introductions.

The cottage itself was darker inside than Kate had expected. The interior walls were covered with intricately patterned paper and every surface was lined with ornaments, gewgaws, and trinkets, and though the lamps were lit, the dark furnishings and decor seemed to soak up the light.

There were only a few ladies in the parlor, and they all seemed to be gathered around a handsome older woman who bore such a resemblance to Green that Kate knew she must be either his mother or a close female relative.

The woman nearest them, whose gown, while not in the first stare of fashion, was well made, came forward to greet them. "You must be Lady Katherine and Miss Hardcastle, from up at the Hall." Her blue eyes were bright with curiosity. At their surprised faces, she clarified. "Word travels fast in a village. And you both look just as you were described." Then, as if recalling the reason why they were there, she colored. "Of course, it's a terrible tragedy about poor Mr. Green, of course it is. But I'm sure once she's awake, Marianne will be sorry she wasn't here to greet you herself."

"We came to offer our condolences to the family, Mrs. . . . ?" Kate let her words trail off as a reminder that they hadn't been introduced.

A pretty woman wearing a cap over her graying blond curls stepped forward to indicate that they should come forward. "This is Abigail Black, the doctor's wife, and I'm Mary Sullivan. My family owns the Rose and Crown."

She indicated the older woman who looked like Green. "This is poor Mr. Green's sister, Hettie."

Then gesturing to the last woman in the room, she said, "And on her other side is the butcher's wife, Constance Whitlow."

Kate and Caro greeted everyone and were soon seated on chairs that had been brought in from the dining room for the occasion. Mary, who seemed to be the one who had taken charge of things, pressed cups of tea into their hands and bustled between the parlor and the kitchen with efficiency that seemed to set everyone at ease.

While Caro answered questions about their newspaper column, Kate took the opportunity of the distraction of the rest of the group to speak with Hettie Green, who had the faraway look of someone who had received a great shock.

"Do you live in the village, Miss Green?" Kate asked the older woman, who was clutching her cup of tea as if it were the only thing keeping her from descending into the abyss.

She blinked at the question, as if coming back to herself. "I, yes, I live here with my brother and his family."

"Or I did," she added, realizing that her brother no longer lived anywhere.

"I'm so sorry for your loss," Kate said gently. "This must be awful for you."

"It was just so sudden." Hettie shook her head. She looked down at the cup of tea and frowned, then set it aside on a nearby table. "And in such a way. I don't even know what to think. I knew Josiah was involved in some untoward business, but he didn't deserve to be murdered for it."

Kate's heart quickened at Miss Green's words. "What sort of business?" she asked carefully, as if speaking too loudly would make the woman flee from her.

"Oh, he had some letters our father gave him that had belonged to his former employer, the poet Philbrick." Hettie frowned. "I warned him that he shouldn't let it get about that he had them in his possession. There are those who nearly worship the man, for all that he wasn't as popular as the other ones in his circle. When there's money or fame at stake, people are likely to lose their heads. He'd already fought with the man from the Hall about them."

As if the thought had suddenly occurred to her, the woman's eyes widened. "He was murdered, too, wasn't he?"

She stood up abruptly, and all the chatter in the room stopped.

"I have to find the letters before they get someone else killed," she said, hurrying toward the door to the parlor.

But the appearance of Eversham on the threshold halted her progress.

"I must ask you to remain here, ma'am," he said firmly. "In fact, I need all of you to stay here for the duration while I search the house."

If he was surprised to see Kate and Caro in the Green house, he didn't say. He gave the room at large a nod, pulled the door closed behind him, and was gone.

"Who was that?" Miss Green asked in a dazed voice.

"That was Inspector Eversham of Scotland Yard." Kate hurried toward the door.

And before anyone could utter a word of protest, she'd stepped out into the hall to follow him.

Eversham had never been particularly quick to anger.

Colleagues and criminals alike had often remarked upon his ability to look at most situations with a cool head. Even at the height of the Commandments Killer case, he'd managed to remain calm in the face of both personal and professional setbacks.

But when he walked in to see Katherine sitting in the Green parlor, after he'd spent the past hour grateful she was nowhere near the bloody crime scene, Eversham had to stop himself from shouting his outrage.

Even so, his teeth were clenched as he made his way upstairs to the study, where Green might have kept his important papers. He'd searched the office where he and Katherine had met with the stationer—was it only that morning?—for any sign of the Philbrick letters, but all he'd found was a year's worth of invoices for supplies, a business ledger that showed the shop, while not thriving, was breaking even.

The note pinned to Green's chest was, as Miller had said, soaked with the dead man's blood, and had read: *You were warned.*

That in itself had brought him up short. It was, as far as Eversham knew, the first time the killer had diverged from using sins from the Bible as a brand on his victims. But even with that divergence, it was obvious that this had been done by the same hand as the other notes.

It was the same man who'd killed Jones less than a week ago, leaving the dead man's body to be discovered by Katherine, who, instead of remaining at the Hall and keeping out of trouble, had come into the village, where the killer had struck again, to insert herself into his investigation.

He wasn't sure whether the fact that she'd brought Miss Hardcastle with her was a good sign or a bad one, considering that young lady seemed just as bent on mischief as Katherine and, to Eversham's mind, was even bolder about it.

Reaching the floor above, he saw that there were four rooms off the landing. The maid who'd answered the door had said the study was the one facing the back garden, which he calculated to be the one opposite the stairs. Hoping he wasn't intruding on the widow, whom the local doctor told him he'd sedated before coming to tend to the body at the shop, he turned the knob and saw that the room was dark except for a low-burning fire in the hearth.

Slipping inside, then closing the door quietly behind him, Eversham set about lighting the lamps so that he could conduct his search in some degree of visibility.

Unlike the rest of the house, which was cluttered with trinkets and ornaments, this room was plainer. The wallpaper was muted, and the rug on the floor was the only real bit of color with an Oriental pattern in reds and blues. The walls were lined with bookshelves that were filled to overflowing, and there were even stacks of books on the floor beside the large mahogany desk.

It was very obviously a man's room, and it would appear that Green had made it his inner sanctum. There was a humidor on the desk, and a faint whiff of cigar smoke hung in the air. The fact that he'd not been able to smell it in the rest of the house must mean that Green indulged in the habit infrequently, or more likely, he leaned out the window behind the desk.

He'd just stepped behind the desk to begin sorting through the papers there when the door opened and Lady Katherine stepped inside and shut the door behind her with a quiet click.

"You shouldn't be here," he said curtly, setting aside bills in one pile and other correspondence in another. "You shouldn't be in the village, period, but at the very least you should have remained in the parlor with the other ladies, as I asked."

He didn't bother to look up. He was still too angry.

"I came to help you search for the letters." Her tone matched his for shortness. "Miss Green, the stationer's sister whom you saw downstairs, said that he kept them in this study."

"I don't need help doing my job, Lady Katherine." Eversham began to open the drawers on one side of the desk, and to his frustration, she came around and began to open the drawers on the other side.

"It will be faster if we're both searching," she said when he stopped to look at her in disbelief. "I've been thinking about who this heir might be."

She'd continued speaking while she searched, as if they were simply carrying on a normal conversation in the course of their day.

Letting out a little growl of frustration, he decided to ignore her and went back to his task.

Katherine, of course, continued speaking.

"Since no one came forward at the time of Philbrick's death, at least that's according to the servants' gossip at the Hall, which my maid was able to glean for me, and he was last of his line, a distant relation seems unlikely. After all, he was famous, if impoverished. It's not as if they wouldn't have learned about his death."

Perfect, Eversham thought, shutting the bottom drawer of the desk with more force than he'd intended. He was now informing his investigation with servants' gossip and innuendo.

Standing from where he'd been crouched before the desk, he turned to her.

To his further annoyance, she was systematically riffling through each drawer with the skill of a seasoned policeman.

"It has to be a child." She rose from where she'd bent to look in the desk and placed a hand on her back. "It's the only thing that makes sense. If a man has no family, and no heirs have been named in his will, the only other option is a child of his blood."

Eversham had come to this conclusion himself earlier, but there was no way he was going to share that with Katherine. Somehow he had to dissuade her from her involvement in this case.

Deciding to try a different tack, he turned to her and said in an approving tone, "That's good, Lady Katherine. Perhaps you can go back to the Hall and see if you can learn more about this. Maybe the older servants have heard about a liaison he may have had. Or a marriage even."

But he must have put too much effort into sounding positive because her eyes narrowed.

"You are a terrible actor." She shook her head in exasperation. "And honestly, did you think to fob me off so easily? I intend to help you find these letters and the so-called 'heir' before someone else dies. We're close. I can feel it."

The way she chided him, as if he were a recalcitrant child, was the last straw for Eversham. Moving closer to her, he took her upper arms in his hands and said through his teeth, "You cannot help me with this case, Katherine. A man was murdered today, in one of the most gruesome displays of brutality I've seen in over a decade with the Yard. And I don't intend for you to expose yourself to the sort of danger that chasing someone like that entails."

"But you put yourself in danger like that every day," she argued.

"It's my job," he all but shouted. "I'm paid to look at the worst sort of things imaginable. I don't want you anywhere near that. I won't have it!"

"You won't—?" She stopped mid-question, as if she couldn't even repeat the words, so infuriating were they to her. "You have no right to make demands of me, Eversham. I'm neither your wife, your betrothed, your sister, your mother, nor anyone whom you have leave to order about. I can come and go as I please, and I won't have you dictating where I do and don't go."

She pulled away from him and walked out from behind the desk so that she could pace. "In case you've forgotten, I own a newspaper. I've been to crime scenes as a reporter. I've followed these cases in the press from the beginning. I might not have seen more than one body, but I know enough. And I'm not going back to that sheltered sphere where men insist that ladies belong. Where we don't know what really goes on in the world. Where we're kept ignorant of our own bodies, or what happens between men and women in the dark corners of the city. It's all pretense anyway. Well, I've had enough of pretense to last a lifetime and I won't go back. And you can't make me."

Eversham thrust a hand through his hair in frustration. "I want you safe, Katherine. I'm not trying to put you on a pedestal. I want to make sure you don't meet the same fate as Jones and Green. Is that so bloody wrong?"

Something in his expression must have revealed the depth of his genuine fear, because what began as surprise in her expression turned softer. "No, no, it's not wrong."

She stepped toward him, and before he even knew what she was about, she'd slipped her arms around him and tucked her head beneath his chin. On a sigh, he pulled her closer and kissed the top of her head. "Was it very awful?" she asked softly.

He didn't have to ask to what she was referring. He knew she meant Green.

He would never tell her exactly what had been done to the man. Some things she didn't need in her imagination no matter how she might insist she was strong enough to see the darker side of the world.

"It was bad," he said. "And I couldn't bear it if someone did that to you."

Speaking that thought aloud meant something, he knew. Some change in what they were to one another that neither was willing to talk about just now. But something about telling her he was afraid for her loosened a knot in his chest that he hadn't realized was there.

"Nor I you." She lifted her face to look him in the eye. "But I feel safe when I'm with you. When we're together."

"I'm only one man." He was flattered that she seemed to think he was strong enough to keep her safe from the sort of madman who would do what had been done to Green. But he could only protect against that which he could see coming. So far this killer had appeared and disappeared like a ghost in the night. "I can't be everywhere at once."

When she brought her lips to his, it was a kiss of comfort. There would be time enough for exploring what was between them. Now she only sought to reassure him.

"I know," she said once she'd pulled away to rest her head against his chest. "I don't expect you to be a magician. But I need to help you with this case."

He pulled back to look at her. "Why is it so important to you? As far as I can tell, you've never gotten involved in an investigation like this before."

With a sigh, she tugged away from him and turned to face the bookshelves. He watched her strong back as she seemed to struggle with some inner turmoil.

Finally, she said softly, "If Caro and I hadn't published the interview with Lizzie Grainger, then you wouldn't have been removed from the case and Mr. Jones and Mr. Green might still be alive."

Chapter Fourteen

K ate held her breath as she waited for a response. She'd admitted her fears about the repercussions of that Lizzie Grainger interview to Val and Caro, but she'd never fully admitted her guilt to Eversham. Not really.

Self-doubt was something she'd struggled with when she was younger, when her every move had been scrutinized by her parents, who were often critical of everything from her choice of attire to her taste in friends. She'd hoped that marriage would remove her from the worst of it, but George Bascomb had turned out to be more controlling than she could have imagined. Throughout the duration of her marriage, she'd come to question her every decision, lest her husband find fault with her and punish her for not meeting his exacting standards.

His death, however, had ushered in a kind of freedom that was almost too much. It had taken her some time to learn to trust herself again. To trust her own ability to make decisions for herself.

Slowly, she'd come to realize that widowhood offered liberties that life as an unmarried girl in her parents' house, and later a woman with a husband to answer to, had not.

But at times, those old self-doubts arose to make her question her decisions.

At the time, she'd been so certain that publishing Lizzie's interview, with her descriptions of the man she'd seen with Betsy, was the right thing to do. She was tired of reading day after day about Scotland Yard's failure to catch the man who was terrorizing London. And yes, she held Eversham responsible for that failure.

She'd thought that publishing the description would lead them to the culprit and the city would be safe again. The arrest of the wrong man, the demotion of a good detective and the elevation of a bad one, more murders hundreds of miles from the scenes of the first four crimes—none of those consequences had occurred to her.

And she had no one to blame but herself.

Caro was still too new at this to bear responsibility. Though Kate knew she would do so gladly.

The blame lay with her.

She wasn't sure what she wanted from Eversham. Absolution? Forgiveness?

Some betraying whisper deep in her soul hinted that she might want the kind of anger she'd grown so accustomed to during her marriage.

But Eversham wasn't that kind of man. And she was no longer that scared, dependent young wife who couldn't think for herself. "I won't pretend that I haven't been resentful," he said finally.

The relief she felt to finally hear his voice almost made her knees buckle.

"But no one was responsible for my removal from the case but me," he continued. "I was in charge of the investigation, and I should have made sure my men actually followed through on the interviews I'd delegated to them."

"As for John Clark," he continued, "there's no one to blame for his arrest but my superintendent and Adolphus Wargrove."

"But if we hadn't printed that description—" Kate began.

Eversham interrupted her. "If you hadn't printed that description, some other paper would have. Or maybe they'd have found some other way to frame someone for the murders."

Kate gasped. "You really believe they could be that unscrupulous?"

Eversham ran a hand through his hair and sighed. "I didn't want to believe it, but Darrow was under a great deal of pressure from the Home Office to arrest someone—anyone—for the Commandments killings. As you well know, the constant news about the murders in the papers had whipped the people into a frenzy of fear. And when people are afraid, they don't trust their government. It's not a reason to arrest someone when they've done nothing wrong, but it was the solution Darrow found."

Kate was shocked to her core. While she'd known they'd arrested the wrong man, she'd hoped—perhaps naively—that it had been less of a purposeful act than a mistake. The way Eversham described it, they'd done it deliberately and for political reasons.

Still, though they'd cleared the air about the grievance over their past, they still hadn't resolved the issue that had started their argument.

"So, you see now why I want—no, I *need*—to be part of this investigation." Kate wasn't going to back down from this. No matter how much Eversham might wish to protect her.

"I understand it."

She began to speak, but he held up a hand before she could do so. "I understand it, but I don't like it. As I said before, I'm trained to investigate crimes, and if necessary, to fight back when those criminals I'm chasing strike out. You are a writer. A good one, but still, that's no preparation for when a man without a conscience decides to turn his attention to you."

Kate sighed. "I suppose we're at an impasse then. Because I refuse to sit by and do nothing to help while you search for this person."

Badly needing to do something lest she give in to the tears of frustration she felt burning behind her eyes, she turned and began scanning the bookshelves. She wasn't sure what she was looking for, but the activity gave her something to concentrate on while she listened to Eversham blow out a long breath before turning his attention to searching the other side of the room.

They worked in silence for some minutes, the cloud of their disagreement still hanging over the room.

She was almost to the end of the third shelf on the last

row, nearest the window, when Kate noticed that the book on the end jutted out farther than the rest. Some impulse for symmetry and order made her push it so that it lined up with the rest of them, but it wouldn't budge. Frowning, she tried instead to pull it toward her. With a click, as if a latch had been undone, the entire row of shelving began to pull away from the wall.

"Eversham." Her heart raced. "Look."

In a trice, he was by her side, and together, they managed to move the shelf to reveal the hidden doorway behind it.

It was too dark to see inside without more light, so Eversham picked up the lamp from the desk and stepped inside, Kate pressed against his back as they moved forward.

The room was little more than an oversized closet. But it was clear at a glance that this was where Green had stored valuables.

Like the shelf that hid the compartment from anyone who didn't already know it was there, the far wall of the tiny room was lined with shelves. But while the ones on the other side held only books, these were stuffed full of papers, jewelry, objets d'art, and in one case a gold chest that, when Eversham attempted to lift it, weighed far more than it appeared to.

"What is all this?" Kate asked, reaching out to touch a jeweled snuff box that sat beside a stack of leather-bound books. "Was Green dealing in stolen goods to keep the stationer's shop afloat?"

But Eversham, who had managed to open the gold chest, pulled out a pocket watch and gave a low whistle.

Wordlessly, he showed her the lid of the watch, which was engraved with a monogram.

SLP

"It's Philbrick's." Kate looked at the shelves with new eyes, noting that many of the items seemed to be the sorts of things that a man with expensive tastes and newly acquired wealth from impressive book sales might purchase for himself. "Green's father stole more than just letters."

It was a statement, not a question. Now Jones's threats that there was an heir who might appear to claim what he was owed took on a more sinister meaning. The letters Green had would have been worth a couple thousand pounds, but this trove of items belonging to Philbrick—if auctioned as a whole lot—might bring a payday of ten to twenty thousand.

"It would seem that way," Eversham said. "Though there's no way to know until we find someone who can verify that these did indeed belong to Philbrick."

"But why would he keep them hidden? To be of any worth on the auction block, they'd need to have some sort of provenance tying them to the poet. The fact that Green kept them here seems to indicate he didn't have one. In which case, his best move would be to sell them off piecemeal."

"Perhaps that's what he was doing," Eversham said. "I'll need to make some inquiries in London to see if Green had offered anything for auction of late. Perhaps the man who sold the other letters for him will know."

"I suppose we'd better see if any more of Philbrick's papers are here." Kate had already begun pulling stacks of documents from the shelves and scanning through them.

Once she'd finished one set, which seemed to be correspondence between the poet and his publisher, she moved to the shelf above it, where a book was holding down another stack. Picking it up, a bit of gold on the cover glinted in the lamplight before she could move the tome to another location.

Bringing it closer so that she could read the embossing, she saw that a woman's name was there.

Miss Delia Hale

She wasn't sure why, but her heart began to beat faster.

Opening the cover, she flipped through the pages until it fell open to where an age-wrinkled rose had been pressed between two sheets.

Her eyes lit upon the words opposite and Kate gasped.

Today, I was married to my dearest Sebastian and we are to have a child.
  My cup runneth over.

Not only had Sebastian Philbrick been married. He'd fathered a child.

A legitimate heir.

Jones had been telling the truth.

"Eversham."

The thread of excitement in Katherine's voice made the detective turn from where he'd been examining a miniature of a pretty brunette. "What is it?"

But before she could show him the object in her hand, which appeared to be a book, the door to the study opened and Miss Hardcastle's voice called out to them. "Kate, the other ladies are beginning to ask questions, and Mr. Miller has come looking for Eversham. What shall I—?"

She broke off, no doubt noticing the door behind the bookshelf.

"What on earth is this?" she asked, stepping into the entryway leading to the secret room.

"Let's talk about this later." Katherine hurried her friend back into the study. The book she'd been holding, Eversham noticed, was no longer in her hand. And a quick glance at the shelves behind her revealed it wasn't there either. She must have pocketed it.

Before he could ask her about it, he heard someone else come into the room. He poked his head out the door to see Miller, looking much better than he had earlier that evening.

"Sir," the man said, his gaze taking in the presence of not one but two ladies in the private office of a recently murdered man. But some remnant of his upbringing must have asserted itself, for he bowed to each of them in turn. "I'm sorry to interrupt, Mr. Eversham, but the doctor is finished with, uh, his work."

"We'll get out of your way, then," Katherine said. "I know you've a great deal to do."

That she was leaving before she'd told him the contents of the book she'd pilfered was frustrating, but there was no help for it.

"Good evening, gentlemen," said Miss Hardcastle as she and Katherine slipped from the room and shut the door behind them.

Once they were gone, Eversham turned to Miller, who was gaping at the opening behind the bookcase. Quickly, the detective outlined the purpose of the room and gave a few examples of the contents.

"You think you know a person." Betrayal laced Miller's tone. "All this time, I thought Green was a good 'un. Many's the time I sat down with him and drank a pint and talked of this and that. And he was nothing but a thief."

"Technically," Eversham said dryly, "it was his father who was the thief, but I see your point."

"Should I stay here and keep watch over this?"

But Eversham, despite his instinctual liking for the man, wasn't quite sure he could be trusted. "I think you'd be of better use keeping watch over the shop to make sure that curiosity seekers don't make their way inside."

Miller didn't bother to hide his shudder of revulsion. "If they do manage it, they'll be sorry and that's a fact."

Eversham, who'd seen a leather satchel near the desk earlier, now brushed past Miller and carried the bag into the closet. Carefully, he began to fill it with the papers he and Katherine hadn't had a chance to examine. "I've never understood the impulse myself, but the crowds that gather to watch public hangings show us that some people have a high tolerance for the gruesome."

Finished with his task, he took the lamp they'd used to illuminate the secret room and carried it out.

"Help me with this, will you?" Together he and Miller shouldered the bookshelf back in place until a click sounded from the locking mechanism.

"It's quite clever, isn't it?" Miller tipped his head toward the shelf. "I suppose he had it put in when he and his family built this place."

That in and of itself was an indication that the stationer had a source of income besides his shop. While it was possible to earn a decent living as a merchant, it was a rare man who could afford to build his own house with his earnings in a town as small as Lewiston. No matter how much trade the tourists coming round to visit the natural wonders and follow in the footsteps of their favorite poets might bring in.

Something else occurred to Eversham as well. "Where are the children?"

Miller stepped toward the door leading into the hallway and opened it. He kept his voice down, presumably so as not to wake the sleeping Mrs. Green.

"There's just the two boys and they're both away at school."

If he hadn't already known about the extra money, that fact would have certainly raised his suspicions, Eversham thought.

Aloud he said, "Someone will need to send for them."

Before they reached the parlor where Miss Green and

the ladies from the village waited, he pulled Miller aside. "I'm relying on your discretion with regard to the existence of the secret room, as well as the fact that Lady Katherine was helping me search it. We don't want people coming to pry before we've had a chance to catalog the contents."

"Lady Katherine has a reputation for doing as she pleases, Mr. Eversham." Miller shrugged. "I figured you didn't have a way to send her away without stepping wrong. Quality ain't the easiest to deal with. Excepting Lord Valentine, of course. He's a good 'un and always makes sure to send a bottle at the holidays."

Thanking whatever bit of snobbery that assumed Katherine would have nothing romantic to do with a Scotland Yard detective, Eversham gave a quick nod.

Opening the door to the parlor, he saw that only Miss Green, the sister of the murdered man, remained.

"I told the others they could go." Her eyes were red from weeping. "They needed to be home for the evening meal."

Perhaps remembering he'd missed his own supper, Miller said to the woman, "I'll be going now, Miss Green. If you or the family need us, you know where to find us."

Once the constable was gone, Eversham said, "Tell me about your father, Miss Green."

At the mention of the man who'd served as Sebastian Philbrick's valet, the woman's eyes grew wary, and Eversham knew she was aware of the cache of items her father had stolen from his employer.

"What is it you wish to know?" she asked carefully.

"It's unusual for a manservant to marry and have children,

isn't it?" Though it wasn't unheard of for servants to marry, most households had restrictions that prohibited a person from remaining in service after marriage. Especially given that bed and board were included as part of their compensation, and marriage would mean either having the servant move out, which would inconvenience the master, who relied on round-the-clock service, or allowing the servant's spouse and later children live in as well.

"It is, sir," said Miss Green. "And my father didn't do so until after Mr. Philbrick was no longer able to afford his services. He was unable to find another position, so he returned to Lewiston—Mr. Philbrick was living in London at the time—to work in his father's shop."

"The stationer's?" Eversham asked. He'd thought her brother had used the funds from the first letter he'd sold to set up the shop. Could he have only taken over his grandfather's existing one?

"No, our grandfather was a butcher." Her nose wrinkled in distaste. "Papa loathed it. But he had little choice, given his lack of experience at anything else. And once he'd met our mother and they were set on marrying, he resigned himself to it."

"Why didn't he use the things he'd stolen from Philbrick to set himself up in some other business?" Eversham asked baldly. He had considered being more delicate about the way he worded the question, but he had little time for such niceties, given that there were now two murders in the space of a few days to solve.

She colored at his words. "I see you've found my brother's hidden room." She tilted her head defiantly.

"Did you always know about your father's collection of Philbrick's things?"

She shook her head and her tone turned bitter. "He pinned all his hopes for the future on his beloved son. A girl wasn't worth the time or trouble. Besides, I couldn't carry on the family name after all, so what good was I?"

"Why didn't he sell the items himself so that he could stop working in the butcher shop?" Eversham asked, genuinely curious.

"You'd have to understand my father, Mr. Eversham," she said. "Once he'd come back to Lewiston and taken that step back down the ladder, he put all his focus on making sure that my brother never had to work a day in the butcher's shop. I don't even think he cared about his own comfort once his son was born."

She gave a twisted smile. "From the time I was little, I heard my father talk about how much better things would be for his son. I think he said it to rile my grandfather at times. Because you can believe Grandfather made sure Papa was reminded at least once a day that he wasn't living like a gentleman anymore. But there was always a gleam in Papa's eyes when Grandfather said it, as if he knew something Grandfather didn't."

"When did you learn about the stolen items?"

"When Papa died and my brother's inheritance was the keys to a pair of sturdy trunks. I'd always seen them in the attics in our little cottage. They were engraved with Mr. Philbrick's initials, and I always thought they were a gift to Papa when he was forced to let him go. When I said as much, Josiah called me a fool and said that they were what

Papa took for his back wages that Philbrick hadn't paid him for months."

"Did he show them to you?"

"No," Miss Green said firmly. "He didn't trust anyone to see them. The only reason I knew about the little room was that the maid walked into the study thinking it was empty one day and saw the shelf pulled out. After that, he forbade anyone to go into his study without his express permission."

"Did your brother mention anything about letters from the collection in the past days?" Eversham asked.

She shook her head. "I didn't know there were more than the one he sold to set up the shop. Like I said, he was very closemouthed about the things Papa had from Philbrick. Why are you asking so many questions about them anyway? I thought my brother was killed by a burglar in the shop."

Not wanting to reveal too much, Eversham said, "We don't know just yet what the motive was for his murder. But I do want all of you in this house to be very careful about who you let into your home in the coming days."

She began to speak, but then must have thought better of it.

"I'd appreciate it if you'd stay out of the study for the time being, as well," he said firmly. "I'll send someone over to go through the closet, but in the meantime, I'd like it to remain undisturbed."

He didn't mention the papers he'd already secreted in his valise. The less Miss Green knew about the room's contents, the better.

"They said the killing of Mr. Jones up at the Hall was

like those Commandments killings in London," Miss Green said, her eyes wide. "Does my brother's murder have some connection?"

"It's too early to know if there is a connection," Eversham told her. "But as soon as I'm able to share more information with you and Mrs. Green, I'll do so."

At the mention of her sister-in-law, Miss Green pulled a face. "I suppose I'll need to find somewhere else to live now. She never did like me much."

It sounded as if her brother wasn't overly fond of Miss Green either, Eversham thought with a pang of sympathy for the woman. It wasn't an easy life for an unmarried woman of a certain age without an independent income.

Making his goodbye, he hurried from the house and back to the shop, where he could speak with the doctor about his examination of the body.

If there was any evidence to be found in the killer's handiwork to link this murder to the others, Eversham wanted it before the monster had a chance to kill again.

Chapter Fifteen

〜※〜

Once she had returned to the house from the village, Kate waited with barely concealed impatience. First for Eversham to return, and when that hadn't occurred by the time the household was ready to retire, for the hallway to quiet long enough for her to creep from her own bedchamber to his.

She'd already concocted a story, just in case she was seen, which featured a wrong turn and mistaking his door for her own. Not that she supposed anyone would believe it. But Thornfield was just labyrinthine enough to make it plausible. There were even similar-looking landscapes hanging in the hall outside each of their rooms.

Come to think of it, she should probably warn Valentine that his decor was just crying out for accidental compromises—something a bachelor with no wish to marry soon should really protect himself against if he wished to maintain his single state.

Finally, when there seemed to be no more chatter and she hadn't heard the close of a door in several minutes, she placed the diary she'd lifted from Green's hidden room back in her pocket and, as quietly as she could, opened her own door, stepped into the hall, then shut it noiselessly behind her.

Eversham's room was at the far end of the hall, and Kate sent up a silent prayer of thanks for whichever decorator had insisted upon especially thick carpeting along the passage. She'd already removed her shoes to ensure that the friction of her slippers on the floor would not be a factor. Unfortunately, short of sneaking about in her underclothes, she could do nothing about the shushing of her silk gown as she moved. She'd have to rely upon the thickness of the doors and walls to quiet that particular bit of noise.

After what seemed an age, she reached Eversham's door and tried the latch. It was unlocked and she slipped inside, silently closed the door, and leaned back against it with a gusty exhale.

To her relief, the room was empty. He was very likely still in Lewiston gathering information about Green's murder.

A helpful servant had lit the fire for when Eversham returned, and it cast a warm glow over the room, which Kate used to get her bearings.

The chamber was plainer than her own, but seemed comfortable enough. She averted her gaze from the bed, which seemed to demand her to imagine Eversham in it— something she was trying desperately to avoid. But the chair beside it, with a footstool tucked beneath, seemed perfect for reading.

The desk beneath the window was what piqued her curiosity the most, however, and once she'd lit the lamp there, she examined the items arranged neatly on the polished surface.

There was a ticket stub for the train journey from London, a few coins, and to her surprise, an old copy of *The Gazette* folded open to one of her articles. It had been a particularly difficult one to write, since it focused on the discovery of a drowned girl on the banks of the Thames. She'd been missing for some weeks, and it was rumored that she'd found herself with child with no hope of being offered marriage from the father, as he was already married. The death had been ruled a suicide by the coroner, but Kate had expressed her doubts in an opinion piece, casting suspicion on the lover, though his name hadn't been revealed publicly.

It was hardly a new story, that of a woman killed by a man who no longer found her useful, but the circumstances of this one had ignited a rage inside Kate that she'd rarely felt since before her husband's death.

Anger was not an emotion that women were allowed. In fact, if Kate hadn't been the owner of the newspaper, she was quite sure that column would have secured their termination from the roster of its writers. Even so, despite their usual reluctance to call attention to the fact that other publications even existed, *The Times* had published an opinion piece obliquely referring to her, and questioning the propriety of women writing at all. The author had likely wanted her to be cowed by it, but the criticism had only assured Kate she'd done something right.

Looking down at where the paper lay folded on Eversham's desk, Kate wondered what he'd thought of it. Had he recoiled from the righteous anger of it? It was hard to know, given how little emotion he showed on the surface. She supposed it was necessary for a man in his profession to maintain a certain calm, since he needed to be able to interact with all sorts of people without setting their backs up. But it made her own interactions with him frustrating. She liked to know where she stood with people.

She was still lost in thought over her discovery when she heard the latch on the door and the man himself stepped into the room.

For a moment, she took advantage of the fact that he didn't know he was being watched. Once he'd closed the door behind him, Eversham leaned against it just as she had done earlier. The fatigue fairly rolled off him in waves, and as she watched, he gave a languorous stretch that had her wanting to stroke her hands along the lines of muscle that he loosened with the motion.

She knew the moment he realized he wasn't alone because he stilled like a buck scenting danger in the forest. When his head turned in her direction, his eyes narrowed and all the relaxation of seconds before was replaced with taut alertness.

And, unsurprisingly, annoyance.

"I could have you brought up on charges for removing that diary from a crime scene." He stalked toward her with the renewed energy of one who had spotted an enemy.

"Were you aware of that? How would your readers react to having one of their heroes jailed for a crime?"

But far from being alarmed, Kate found his anger invigorating. A fight had been brewing between them for days and she was ready for it. "I don't think they'd mind," she said truthfully. The regular readers of her paper were tired of authorities hiding the truth from them. "They don't mind lawbreaking if it serves the greater good."

His mouth, which was really far too lush for a man who spent his days chasing criminals, tightened. "You don't get to decide that, Katherine. This is my investigation and I am responsible for every bit of evidence that it produces. I can't have you just taking what you want from a crime scene as if you're a child without any concept of right or wrong."

She stepped toward him, her own anger carrying her forward. "Do you think I don't know that?" she demanded, punctuating her words with a finger punch to his chest. "And here I was starting to change my mind about you. All that time I took you for a boring plodder, but after seeing Wargrove in action, I decided I'd misjudged you. Now I can see you care more about rules and regulations than you do about solving crimes."

His jaw tightened at the insult, but she was too angry to stop now. "And as for knowing right from wrong, I'm not the one whose superiors knowingly put an innocent man in jail. If you knew right from wrong, you'd have moved heaven and earth to free him."

"It's not just a matter of walking into the super's office and asking him nicely to let the man out, Katherine," he growled. "If that would have worked, I'd have tried it ages ago. There are forces beyond my control there. I'm doing what I know best to do, and that's trying to catch the man who actually committed the crimes!"

They were standing toe-to-toe now and Kate was as angry as she'd ever been. "I think you don't wish to blame yourself for your own failure to capture the Commandments Killer and you're taking out that anger on the nearest scapegoat, who unsurprisingly is a woman who you think has overstepped her place."

He leaned closer, so close she could feel his breath on her face. "You don't know anything about me, *Lady* Katherine, so I'll thank you not to put words in my mouth."

"I know that you're a bully," she spat out.

"And I know that you're a pain in my arse."

They stood glaring at one another for exactly two breaths before, like two magnets, they came together in a melding of furious passion.

Eversham wasn't sure how it happened, but one minute he and Lady Katherine Bascomb were all but shouting at one another and the next he was kissing her as if halting would make his heart stop.

He'd wanted her for days—if he were honest, from the moment he saw her that day in the crowd in Westminster. The want had been there, needling him, like a sharp pebble in the bottom of his boot. Of course, he'd made a habit of suppressing the feeling, or ignoring it as best he could. Not only was she far too good for the likes of him, but she was also just the sort of woman who would make his life harder, not easier.

But all that was forgotten as soon as his lips met hers, and he was reminded just how good she'd felt in his arms when they'd been together in the folly. He knew any liaison between them would be unwise in the extreme. It would risk the career he'd only just now managed to regain. Even so, he didn't care about any of that when he felt her hands creep up his neck and into his close-cropped hair, holding him to her lest he attempt to pull away.

Her mouth was soft, and when he stroked his tongue over the seam of her lips, she welcomed him in with a soft sigh that sent a jolt of heat straight to his groin. Kate kissed exactly like she argued—without hesitation and with a determination to give as good as she got. It was unlike anything he'd ever experienced and exactly how he'd known she'd be.

He knew exactly when she came to her senses because she paused for breath and then pulled back a little. She didn't try to extricate herself completely, so he kept her in the circle of his arms.

"You can go if you wish," he said, though the words made him ache at the very idea of it. He wanted desperately to see if she was as fiery in bed as she was out of it, but if she had any hesitations, then he would honor them. "I might weep, but I'll survive."

His words had the intended effect and she laughed softly, her gray eyes glancing up at his before she lowered her lashes to look at his mouth. "I would like to stay if you don't mind." The movement of her throat as she swallowed was the only betrayal of any nerves on her part. "I have to admit to a certain...curiosity about how it will be between us."

He raised a brow. "You know how that ended up for the cat, my dear."

"If I'm going to be killed," she said seriously, "I'd rather it be with pleasure than pain."

The reminder, even in metaphor, of the ever-present specter of mortality made him kiss her again. As if he needed to remind both of them that they were still very much alive.

"Then come with me." He reached down to take her hand and led her toward the bed.

With more haste than finesse, he unbuttoned the row of impossibly tiny buttons down the back of her gown, unable to keep from dropping a kiss on the vee of skin exposed above the line of her corset. She'd stepped out of the silk and stood in only her corset and crinoline when he turned her, drinking his fill of the sight of her breasts pressed high above the line of the steel stays lifting them impossibly high.

"Lovely," he said, and she shivered under his gaze. The corset was laced in front and he pulled the string of the knot settled just between her breasts, loosening the tight clasp of the garment. He didn't miss the little exhale of pleasure at the release, and as he removed the corset, he noticed the angry red lines where her skin had been pinched by it for hours, and he couldn't stop himself from leaning down to kiss her there. "Poor darling."

She slipped her hands into his hair as he licked and kissed

his way around her breasts and finally took her nipple in his mouth, pulling on it just enough to make her gasp.

The bed was just behind her, and he gently pressed her back against it until they were both sprawled atop the coverlet. Quickly, he got rid of her crinoline, and when he pushed himself up on his hands, the sight of her in nothing but lace drawers and silk stockings was enough to make his mouth water.

"Why am I almost naked, but you haven't removed so much as your neck cloth?" she asked with a raised brow. Perhaps as incentive, she lifted her hands to her breasts, but that only made him want to cover her with his body more.

Still, he knew when he'd been given an order. In far less time than he'd spent removing her garments, he untied, unbuttoned, unlaced, and undid his own clothes until he was standing naked before her. Her eyes gleamed in appreciation as he crawled over to her and untied her drawers and pulled them off in one fluid motion.

When she moved to unfasten her garters, he said roughly, "Keep the stockings on."

The first skin-to-skin contact when he finally lowered himself onto her took his breath away. Their kiss now was wetter, deeper, more carnal. There was no longer any pretense that it was anything but a prelude to the most intimate act, and there was a freedom in that, which gave them both leave to touch each other without hesitation.

Kissing his way down her neck, Andrew found a place just below her ear that made her gasp with pleasure, and while he gave that spot the attention it so richly deserved, he lowered one hand to stroke a thumb over her breast while the other curved down over the soft roundness of her belly. He felt the tension in her hips as she made a restless motion, and teasing her with his touch, he caressed softly over the patch of curls at the apex of her thighs and dipped down to feel the wetness there.

Her gasp told him all he needed to know about her readiness, but he had to indulge himself—and in the process, her—with a taste first.

Sliding down her body, feeling the friction of skin on skin before lifting first one leg, then the other, over his shoulders, he took in the sight of her open to his gaze. At the first touch of his mouth on her, Kate let out a gasp, and when she would have bucked against him, he held her still. With his tongue and his lips, he brought her to the edge of climax, then just when she needed it most, he added his fingers to the mix and sent her over the edge into ecstasy.

When her frenzy had died down, he'd already repositioned himself over her, his hands shaking slightly as he gripped her hips and held himself poised at her entrance. Somehow he knew that once they did this, there would be no going back for either of them. But he was beyond the ability to care about anything but the need coursing through his veins.

"Now," she said in a voice hoarse with wanting, "come to me."

And with one sure thrust, he seated himself fully inside her.

It had been a long time since she'd been with a man and never one as well proportioned as Andrew. But the slight stretch and fullness were pleasurable in a way Kate hadn't thought possible.

"All right?" he asked in a slightly strangled voice as he held still inside her.

She kissed him and told him with a clench of her body just how all right it was. When he still didn't move, she breathed out, "Yes, move, please."

And with a sigh of pure pleasure, he did as she asked, withdrawing slowly with a control that made her want to weep. But soon enough he was stroking back into her, and he set a pace that had them both breathless. Her hands were gripping the bedclothes, but he paused to lift them up to the headboard behind her, and raised himself so that he could see where they were joined.

"More, please." She was unable to say more but needed to let him know she was not a fragile flower.

As if her words had unleashed some last vestige of control in him, he began to thrust harder, and Kate clung to the headboard as her hips rose to meet him move for move. Her body clasped him with each withdrawal, and every time he came back, she nearly cried with relief.

Her every sense was consumed by the moment: the weight of his body, the texture of his chest hair against her sensitive breasts, the scent of his sandalwood and pine cologne mixed with that elemental scent that was simply him. It all coalesced into an experience she knew she'd never forget as long as she lived.

When her release finally came, it was unexpected and all

the more shaking because of it. No longer able to keep from touching him, she dropped her arms from the headboard and clasped him by his firm buttocks, clinging to him as if she were in danger of flying away if she let go. Then with a jolt, she felt herself clench around him, and though she remained firmly beneath him, some part of her did break into pieces and scatter, the pleasure coursing through her with the pulse of a heartbeat. She heard a cry and knew it was hers but was too caught up to feel anything but euphoria.

When his movements became more erratic, and his breathing more ragged, she held him to her as she felt him give one last strong thrust and empty himself with a cry of his own.

Closing her eyes, she surrendered to the haze of contentment that sheltered them from the outside world.

Chapter Sixteen

When Kate entered the breakfast room the next morning, she was grateful to find only Caro there, likely due to the late hour.

Just as dawn was breaking, she'd reluctantly left Eversham's bed to return to her own room. It wouldn't do to be seen wandering the halls in last evening's gown. She didn't much care about the potential damage to her reputation, but Eversham was working hard to free Clark and regain his standing at the Yard, and she didn't want to undo that.

Then there was the very real risk to her heart.

Last night had been different from any of her previous liaisons, which had, admittedly, been brief. And yet, that single night in Eversham's arms had felt more significant, more emotional, than any of those other encounters.

Was it because she felt a connection to Eversham—Andrew—on an intellectual level as well as a physical one? She was unsure. She had no prior experiences to compare this to.

Instinctively she knew that this level of intimacy could lead to heartbreak later.

And yet, she was also so invigorated and—in spite of the darkness that had drawn them together—happy, that it was easy to ignore all those fears.

He'd been sleeping when she left him, and in repose, his too serious face seemed younger, as she imagined he'd have looked when he was a boy, before he began to take on the weight of the world.

She could still feel the echoes of his touch on her body, and every so often, a flash of memory intruded on her attempt to present an unruffled facade to those who might guess where she'd spent the bulk of last night.

Just such a recollection had made her cheeks color inconveniently as she met Caro's shrewd gaze on the other side of the breakfast table.

"You're flushed," her friend said with what Kate knew was feigned innocence. "I trust your, um, headache hasn't returned?"

Taking advantage of the opportunity to escape the other woman's eyes for a moment, Kate spooned eggs onto her plate, then added a rasher of bacon. Then, on second thought, added one more because really she was quite hungry this morning.

Her features schooled again into what she hoped was an expression of innocence, she took her seat at the table and allowed the hovering maid to pour her a cup of tea. "I'm quite well, thank you. An early night was just the thing I needed to take care of it."

"I'm sure it was." Caro sipped her tea thoughtfully. "Though I should have thought you'd stayed up all night reading the journal you retrieved from Green's study, headache or no. It's a shame you couldn't have handed it off to Eversham so that he could take a look. Or perhaps you already have?"

Kate sighed. "Fine. You've guessed, I suppose. Though how, I have no idea. You're like a detective, but at deducing who has been kissing whom."

"It's really not that hard." Caro shrugged. "You forget that I know you. And it's been obvious since I first saw you together that there was a certain electricity between you."

"I hope for his sake it wasn't obvious to everyone else as well. It wouldn't do for the household and the village to suspect him of impropriety." She'd done enough damage to his reputation already.

"Oh, I think they're far too focused on the fact that two of their own have been murdered in the space of a week."

"If he's able to figure out who the culprit is, I suppose they won't care how he behaves," Kate said wryly.

Caro nodded. "That is true. Though I think we'd better expect some of the ruder representatives of Fleet Street to start arriving soon."

Unfortunately, she was very likely correct. Caro had rushed here on hearing the news of the first murder, but the fact that two people had now been killed in the same manner that the Commandments Killer had employed would soon have the crime reporters of London flooding Lewiston and the surrounding villages looking for salacious stories to recount to a reading public hungry for sensation.

"I'm still unresolved as to how we can best continue our column while remaining true to ourselves," Kate confessed to her friend.

"Of course." Caro frowned. "I'd assumed at the very least we would avoid these further murders of the Commandments Killer—and I just cannot imagine it's anyone else at this point—because you found one of the bodies. My goodness, Kate, I am eager to write our next feature for *A Lady's Guide*, but I'm not willing to force you to relive that terrible moment to do it."

Kate reached out to squeeze her friend's arm. "I know. I didn't mean you would. I just wanted to make sure we were agreed."

"Of course." Caro smiled sympathetically.

Then frowning, she added, "Though I have little doubt that there will be far more coverage of these killings than we can imagine. Not only is it murder in a location that doesn't normally have such crimes, but it's also the continuation of a series of killings the public thought were solved. It's the kind of story newspapers dream about."

"You don't have to tell me." Kate shook her head. "I really do hate this part of the business. But I do want the paper to stay profitable, and I can't deny that these kinds of stories keep us in ink. At least we try to ensure our stories are factual."

"I suppose we will have to hope that not all of the journalists who travel here from the city are the sort to invent tales out of whole cloth or overly embellish," Caro said wryly. "Though I would not care to wager on it."

They were making plans to find an empty parlor so that they could examine Delia Hale's diary—which, to Kate's embarrassment, she'd forgotten to show Eversham last night—when Valentine strode into the room.

"Kate, there's a—" he began, then broke off, staring at her for a moment.

"What is it?" she asked, puzzled by his odd behavior.

Blinking, he shook his head a little, as if clearing cobwebs from his ears. "Sorry, I just remembered something I'd forgotten to take care of."

Clearing his throat, he began again. "Miss Green, the sister of the stationer, is here to see you. She says it's important. I had Austen put her in the parlor."

The mention of Miss Green made Kate toss her napkin down and rise from the table. "I wonder what she could want."

"She didn't say." Val avoided making eye contact with her, then abruptly left the room.

"That was strange," Kate said, looking after him. "Did you see that?" Not waiting for Caro to answer, she rose. "I'll go see what Miss Green wants. I won't be long."

Before she could leave, however, Caro stopped her with a hand on her arm. Wordlessly, she removed the shawl she'd been wearing and wrapped it around Kate's shoulders, arranging it just so.

"What are you doing? I'm not going to take a chill walking from the breakfast room to the parlor."

"You have a love bite just below your ear," said Caro in a low voice. "I suspect that was why Valentine looked as if he'd seen a duck walking backward."

Kate gasped and touched her neck. She closed her eyes in mortification.

Caro gave her a quick hug. "Don't let Val make you feel bad. I daresay he's given his share of them in his day. And what's good for the gander is good for the goose."

"Besides," she added, "we can rely upon his discretion, I'm sure."

What a coil. If Kate had hoped to keep her affair with Eversham a secret, she'd been wrong twice over already in the first two hours of the day.

"Now, go see what Miss Green wants." Caro gave her a little push toward the door.

Kate had nearly forgotten her visitor. "I'll find you in the other parlor once we're finished."

Caro nodded and sent her on her way.

Really, Kate thought grimly. If this was the sort of thing she'd have to expect from her reasoning skills after an encounter with Eversham, she would do well to avoid him in the future.

Though that, she knew, given the way her breasts ached at the thought of him, was easier said than done.

When she found Miss Green, the lady was pacing before the fire in the little room that had likely been set aside for calls from less elevated visitors. It was a pretty enough room, with a comfortable-looking settee covered in a dark blue moiré fabric and a wooden bench that, while beautifully crafted, Kate suspected was dreadfully uncomfortable.

"Lady Katherine," the older woman said as she entered. "Thank goodness. I was beginning to lose my courage and was just about to leave."

The woman was quite agitated, more than she had been last evening when she'd just learned of her brother's murder. Though it understandably took some time for the shock to wear off after hearing such news.

"Please, Miss Green, do sit down." Kate gestured for her to take the settee. "I'll just ring for some refreshments."

Once she'd tugged the bellpull, she perched on the bench, which was just as hard as she'd imagined, and asked, "What has happened to alarm you?"

Miss Green twisted a handkerchief, as if she needed something to occupy her hands. "I was not altogether honest with you and Mr. Eversham yesterday." Her brow furrowed.

"I'm sure whatever it is you failed to tell us will still be helpful today," Kate said kindly. She knew that, at times like this, it was often a family member's first instinct to hold back any information that might reflect poorly on the deceased. No one liked to speak ill of the dead—especially after they'd been so brutally removed from the land of the living.

"I hope so," she said, her mouth tight. "It's just that I

thought she must be Josiah's…that is to say…when she walked out of his study as bold as you please, I thought she must have been given permission. And he'd only do that with someone he—"

One of the maids arrived with the tea tray then, and Kate was grateful for the interruption. Hopefully, tea, which was for the English a cure for all manner of ills, would have a calming effect on her visitor. Because Kate very much wanted to hear more about this mystery woman, but she was doubtful that would happen while Miss Green was unable to complete a sentence.

"Here." She handed the other woman a cup and saucer and one of Cook's excellent seed cakes. "Drink some of that and gather your thoughts for a moment. We're in no rush."

Of course, what she actually wished to say was that she was in a great rush and wanted to know exactly what Miss Green was referring to, but that would do neither of them any good.

Fortunately, the sugar and warmth soon did the trick, and Miss Green was looking much more relaxed.

"I apologize for coming to you in such a state, Lady Katherine." She frowned. "But I only just recalled the incident, and in the context of what happened to my brother, it took on an entirely different meaning."

Relieved that her guest appeared to be feeling better, Kate said, "Why don't you start at the beginning?"

"First, I wish you to know that I never made it my habit to intrude on my brother's affairs," Miss Green began. "I don't know if you are aware of what it's like to be an unmarried lady of a certain age who is forced by circumstance to live on the generosity of relatives."

"I can imagine," Kate said softly. She knew all too well how hard the plight of so-called "redundant women" could be.

Her mouth tightened. "I was engaged to be married years ago, and my fiancé died. I lived for a time with my sister and her family, but they moved last year to America and I wasn't ready for that. When I applied to Josiah for help, he agreed to let me come live with his family. The house is large and I was quite happy with the arrangement for a time."

"But something changed?" Kate guessed.

"About six months ago, I noticed that Josiah and Marianne were often at odds. I overheard them arguing one evening, and she accused him of having a—well, she thought he had a fancy woman." Miss Green blushed as she spoke.

It was a fact of life in many marriages, Kate knew, for the husband to seek his pleasure from those women from whom he might request earthier acts than one could expect from a wife. For a man like Green, a prosperous merchant with aspirations to raise his social status, a mistress would have not only afforded him pleasure, but also established him—even if only in his own mind—as a man-about-town and let other men know that he was rich enough to afford such a luxury.

"And did he?" Kate asked.

"He said he didn't." Miss Green shrugged. "But I don't think she believed him. And I admit that I would not have been shocked if it were true. Perhaps because of the way my father encouraged him to think of himself as better than a mere butcher's grandson, Josiah was always putting on airs. He didn't think of himself as a shopkeeper in a tiny village, but on the same level as the owner of Harrods. Which, to my mind, was foolish, but I was nothing but a poor relation, so it was none of my business really."

Not for the first time, Kate thanked the heavens above that when Bascomb died, he'd left her with fortune enough to ensure that she'd never be in the position of having to beg for her room and board from a resentful relative who saw her only as a burden.

Aloud she said, "So you, along with your sister-in-law, believed he had a mistress. What happened then?"

"Nothing," Miss Green said. "I didn't hear them discuss it again, and my brother certainly never said anything to me." She took another sip of tea, as if to gather her thoughts.

"Then two weeks ago, while Josiah was at the shop and Marianne was in the village paying calls, I was having a lie-down and I heard a crash from the other end of the hallway. Thinking the maid had dropped something while tidying up, I went to see what had happened. And as soon as I stepped out into the hall, I saw a woman dressed all in black hurrying around the corner and down the stairs."

"Who was she?" Kate asked, sitting up straighter in her seat.

"I don't know," Miss Green said. "I was unable to catch up to her, and by the time I made it downstairs, she was out the door and gone from view."

"You suspected she was your brother's mistress," Kate asked.

"I admit that I did," the older woman said firmly. "I'm

not sure why I thought it. Now it seems mad to think that such a woman would intrude in her paramour's home like that. But since that was the only explanation that presented itself in my mind, I suppose I accepted it as the truth."

"Did you ask him about it?" Kate's mind was racing with possibilities for the woman in black's identity, and none of them included Green's possible mistress.

"Of course not." Miss Green sounded as if Kate had suggested she ask her brother to name his favorite London brothel. "If she was his mistress, then merely acknowledging I'd seen her would have been improper. If she wasn't, then there was nothing to be done about it anyway because she was long gone."

There was a certain logic to Miss Green's rationale. "Did you discover what the crashing sound was?"

At this, Hettie Green's brow furrowed. "I retraced her steps and found the door to my brother's study ajar. When I looked inside, I found that trinket box that sat atop a file box had been knocked to the floor. It looked as if she'd been going through his papers."

She shook her head ruefully. "I thought she was looking for money or jewelry because he'd failed to pay her as they'd agreed."

A mistress who broke into her lover's home in search of money would find herself without protection if she made a practice of such behavior, Kate reflected. Men went to great trouble and expense to ensure that their wives and mistresses never laid eyes on one another. And once word got around that a mistress had made such a breach, she would be ostracized by any man who valued his neatly ordered life.

"But now you think differently?"

"I think she must have been there to search for the letters or the secret room." Miss Green's regret at misreading the situation was evident. "Perhaps he told her about them in a moment of passion?"

Or perhaps the woman in black hadn't been Green's mistress at all.

"What do you remember about her?" Kate would need to give Eversham as many details as possible about the intruder if they were to find her.

"I only glimpsed her for a moment." Miss Green's mouth turned downward.

"Anything," Kate encouraged her. "What color was her hair? How was it dressed?"

"Light brown, and it was put up with a cascade of curls in the back." This was said firmly. "And her gown was rather fine. I remember because I noticed it was more fashionable than anything to be had in Lewiston."

"Very good. And what about her hat?"

"It was wide brimmed," Miss Green said. "It was old-fashioned, which looked odd with her gown, now that I think on it. And though I couldn't see her face, I did see that there was black netting over the top, as if she were wearing a veil."

So, the hat had been chosen because it would help conceal her identity. Which could either mean she was in danger of being recognized by someone in Lewiston or she didn't want to be described by someone later. Either way, this woman possessed skills that one would not expect from a "fancy woman," as Miss Green had called her.

"I'm sorry I didn't tell you yesterday, Lady Katherine." Hettie looked much more relaxed now that she'd unburdened herself. "I didn't even remember it until this morning and then I realized that she wasn't what I thought her to be at all."

Kate moved forward to pat the other woman on the shoulder. "You had a very difficult time of it, and I daresay you were in no position to remember anything, much less a strange encounter from weeks ago."

"Do you think she may have had something to do with Josiah's murder?"

There was such a note of hope in Miss Green's voice that Kate felt guilty to offer her anything else. However, it was not her place to say one way or the other.

"I don't know, and that's the truth. But I will tell your story to Inspector Eversham, and I feel sure he'll appreciate this information as he tries to uncover who killed your brother and Mr. Jones."

The mention of Eversham gave Miss Green pause. "You don't suppose he'll be angry I brought this to you instead of him, do you? It's just that I found him rather intimidating, and I could never have told him about Josiah's fancy woman. I'd have died of shame."

Thinking back to her own shame earlier that morning—thanks to Eversham, no less—Kate rushed to reassure her. "I don't think he's quick to anger. And I will let him know that you were more comfortable speaking with me. I'm sure he'll understand."

Wishing Eversham hadn't gone into the village, Kate hurried to find Caro.

Not only did they have a new clue, but it was one that had the potential to change everything.

Could the Commandments Killer be a woman?

Chapter Seventeen

E versham had arrived back at the Hall that afternoon after a mostly fruitless day spent going over every piece of paper in first the office of the stationery shop, then Green's study at the man's cottage.

He was tired, frustrated, and suffering the consequences of too little sleep the night before.

Though if given the chance to do it over again, he'd make the same decision.

He hadn't expected to find Katherine in his bedchamber when he returned from Lewiston. And it hadn't been his intent to rip up at her like he had. But it had been a long day, and he was tired and miserable and still angry about her reckless decision to go to Green's house while there was a murderer at large.

What happened after the argument—or as a result of the

argument, he wasn't sure which—had been as passionate and emotional as it had been intense.

Kate had been every bit as delectable as he'd imagined she'd be, but there had been something else, some vulnerability there that he hadn't expected in a woman who was so self-assured outside the bedchamber.

She was one of the most remarkable women he'd ever met. And though she had been born into the nobility, he could see now that his prejudices about her background were no more valid than if she'd harbored similar thoughts about him for being of a lower class.

He wondered what she was doing right now and if it would be possible to—

With a laugh, he cut off that thought.

One night and he was already thinking about her like a lovesick schoolboy.

He'd just got himself under control again when he stepped through the front door and Austen informed him that Lady Katherine had asked for him. Eversham found himself grinning from ear to ear at the news.

He was not a man who grinned.

This was bad. Very bad indeed.

Still, he managed to tell the fellow in a reasonably calm voice to inform Lady Katherine he'd see her as soon as he changed.

Then, with as much haste as he could manage without doing himself an injury, he all but sprinted to his rooms, washed, shaved, and changed into a clean suit of clothes.

He was on his way downstairs to the parlor, where Katherine had asked to meet him, when he was waylaid by

Valentine, who stopped him in mid-stride with a hand in the middle of his chest.

"Just a moment, if you please, Eversham. I'd like a word."

The usually affable gentleman with a wide smile and easygoing manner had been replaced by a steely-eyed stranger.

He knew. Eversham wasn't sure how, but Valentine knew Kate had spent last night in his bed.

Still, she was a widow and not some simpering miss who needed to be protected from untoward advances. If anything, she'd been the one making the advances, though he wasn't so foolish as to tell Valentine that.

Bracing himself for a lecture at the very least, he followed the other man into his study and had just turned to face the door when Val drove a fist square into his jaw.

Eversham stopped himself from crying out in surprise, but only just.

He didn't bother punching back because, on a certain level, despite his earlier rationalization, he supposed he deserved it.

"Feel better?" he asked, gingerly touching his jaw while he watched Valentine surreptitiously shake out his hand. It reminded him of Kate shaking out her hand in the folly, and his face must have revealed his thoughts, because Val snorted.

"What?"

"You have no shame, do you?"

While his host moved to the sideboard to pour them both a glass of whiskey, Eversham tried to decide how to answer the question. Finally, he decided on the truth. "I don't, as it happens."

"Well, at least you're honest." Val handed him a glass. "Sorry about that, but it had to be done."

"But did it?"

Dropping into one of the leather chairs before the fire, Val indicated that Eversham should take the one opposite. "She has no one to look after her, really. Her father is dead. Her husband's family ceased to think of her once he died, which is a blessing really, since they're damned awful."

"So, you stepped into the breach?"

"I told you she was like a sister to me. Well, if I'd suspected you of leaving a love bite on my sister's neck, I'd have done the same thing."

"What?" Eversham's voice got embarrassingly high.

Val stifled a laugh. "Didn't realize it, eh?"

Not answering, Eversham covered his eyes with his hand.

Good God. Was he fifteen? Come to think of it, he wasn't even sure if he'd done such a thing as a teenager.

"She must be mortified," he said. Katherine was so poised and proud. She would hate to be visibly marked in such a way so that others could see.

"I don't think she realized it," Val assured him. "And I feel sure Caro would have alerted her by now. She might be difficult, but she is a good friend, and I know she wouldn't allow Kate to be exposed to talk."

That was a relief at least.

"So, do I need to ask your intentions?" Val looked at him with a deceptively casual gaze. He might not be poised to fight now, but there was no less threat of force in him. Eversham knew that if he did anything to hurt Katherine, he'd have this man to answer to.

Still, he wasn't going to be rushed into anything. No matter how ferocious Katherine's honorary brother might be.

"It's a bit early for that, don't you think?"

Val sighed. "I suppose so. But just so you know, I have a great number of friends in the sporting world, and I need only say the word for you to be thrashed within an inch of your life."

"It's not a good idea to threaten a policeman, old fellow," said Eversham companionably. "But because we're friends, I'll pretend I didn't hear that."

"Are we friends?" Valentine sounded surprised. "I suppose we are, come to think of it."

"You've got to have some respectable ones in your merry band. If only to come to your aid when your disreputable friends get you into trouble with the law."

"You would do that?"

Eversham was amused at the other man's gratitude. "Well, I have it on good authority that you are Lady Katherine's oldest friend. And I don't think she'd be very happy with me if I left her oldest friend to rot away in jail without assistance. Especially me being with the Yard and all."

"That's true, isn't it? I'm almost sorry I punched you now."

"You're not bad with your fists." Eversham tested his jaw for soreness again.

"I've spent the better part of my life since age fifteen at boxing matches," Valentine said. "One's bound to pick up a few things about form after all that time. Also I'm working on Jim's life story right now, and we just finished the part where he gives his own philosophy of fighting."

The clock on the mantel chimed the hour, and Eversham set down his glass with a curse.

"What is it?" Valentine asked, not bothering to get up.

"I was supposed to go to Katherine once I got back, but I went up to change and then—"

"And then I punched you and forced you to drink my whiskey," Valentine finished for him.

He didn't bother saying goodbye.

Eversham figured his new friend Val would understand.

After her conversation with Miss Green, Kate had spent the better part of the day immersed in the diary of Miss Delia Hale, a young lady of eighteen who had lived with her parents in the village of Crossmere some thirty miles from Lewiston.

The journal, it appeared, had been a gift from Sebastian Philbrick, who had met her on a visit to Crossmere, and, according to Delia at least, had fallen head over ears in love with her. She appeared to return the sentiment, but it was also clear from comments Delia made about her home life that she had a very good incentive to remove herself from her vicar father's household as soon as possible. So, Kate thought it was strongly possible that Delia would have fallen in love with the devil himself if he'd offered a way to remove her from Crossmere.

Over the course of a month, she chronicled secret meetings and, in nonspecific terms, a sexual relationship that had led to her becoming pregnant. Though Kate had

some not very kind thoughts about the honor of a man who engaged a girl some twenty years his junior in a clandestine affair, Philbrick, in this instance, did the right thing and demanded they marry at once. Of course, Delia was happy to do so. Her father, however, refused to honor Philbrick's suit because he wasn't, to the vicar's mind, a suitable match owing to his licentious history. There was also the matter of a very well-publicized betrothal be-tween Philbrick and Miss Jane Hubbard, a young lady of good family in Lewiston. Presumably, Philbrick had made the situation plain to the vicar in a private meeting, but rather than consenting to the match—as any man of sense who did not wish to bring the shame of illegiti-macy down on his family—Vicar Simeon Hale had instead condemned his daughter and ejected Philbrick from his house.

It was clear from Delia's writings that not only was Hale the sort of Christian who believed women to be either virgins or whores, and erred on the side of whore just to make sure he didn't unduly let some guilty woman get away with unpunished sin, but he was also quite likely a strong candidate for Bedlam. He preferred to punish Delia and her unborn child with a life of censure and unhappi-ness because he perceived Philbrick not pure enough a candidate for her hand. And very likely—though Kate had no notion if she was correct in this—would use her as an example to hold up to his followers as the picture of sin.

Though she had thought Delia a silly girl at first, as Kate read her outpourings of emotions on the page, she began to feel a great deal of sympathy for her. Kate had been young and foolish once. And though she hadn't fallen in love against her family's wishes, she had been utterly under her parents' control, and had been pushed into accepting marriage to a man some twenty years her senior because they'd been in need of the funds the marriage would bring to them.

She'd never been subjected to the sort of cruelty Delia had endured, however—even from George Bascomb at his worst. It would be nice to think Hale's backward views were rare, but the misogyny underlying them was all too common still. His was simply an extreme example of how much harm they could do.

Thus it was with some relief that she read Delia's plans for an elopement, and when she saw that the marriage was a fait accompli, she'd given a little cheer.

The conclusion, which had arrived only two-thirds of the way into the notebook, had left her with more questions than answers, however. Because the journal ended before the birth of Delia's child, there was no way of knowing whether it had lived. And it was clear from the dates of the expected birth and Philbrick's death that he'd never come back to remove Delia from her father's house. Nor was it clear why he'd left her there. And what had happened to Delia? Why did she stop writing?

Kate had a sinking suspicion that Delia had died in childbirth, or not long after.

Her heart ached for the girl whose short life had been marked by so few joyful moments.

Even with the remaining question, Delia's journal had

been illuminating on several points that had been un-
clear from the moment they'd learned about the Philbrick
letters.

First of all, she was now convinced that if Delia's child
was alive, he or she was the "rightful" heir Fenwick Jones
had spoken of. A look at the map revealed that Crossmere
was not as far as the crow flies from Lewiston. Had Jones
met Delia's child by chance in the neighborhood? Though
it was possible there was another connection between them,
the geographical nearness could not be discounted.

There was also a good chance that if the letters Jones had
asked about were between Philbrick and Delia, they were
love letters. Since part of Philbrick's legacy relied heavily
on the tragic tale of his early death and his mourning sweetheart, the news that he'd married a girl young enough to
be his daughter in a secret wedding, then abandoned her
to her fate, the revelations in the letters would make them
more valuable. At least to Kate's mind. She was no expert
on the valuation of memorabilia, but these letters had the
potential to change the way the world viewed Sebastian
Philbrick. She didn't see how that wouldn't make them
more sought after.

If Green's father, as Philbrick's valet, had been aware of
the marriage, then he'd have known the letters, whether
he'd stolen them or been gifted them, were a veritable
gold mine.

Was Delia's child the woman whom Hettie Green had
encountered in her brother's study?

That remained to be seen. And the possibility changed
everything they knew about this killer. Caro had just joined

her for tea when there was a brisk knock on the door and Eversham entered the room.

Though it was clear from his damp hair and clean shirt that he'd washed up before coming to them, there were dark smudges beneath his eyes, and it was obvious he'd had a long, frustrating day. Even so, his eyes met hers for the barest moment and seemed to tell her wordlessly that he'd not forgotten what had happened between them last night.

He lowered his tall frame into an armchair and gladly accepted a cup of tea from Kate.

"I hope you were able to make progress in the village today," Kate said once they'd exchanged greetings, grateful she was able to maintain some semblance of calm. She'd have liked to give him a more effusive welcome, but Caro's presence, and her own misgivings about the nature of their relationship, had made the decision for her.

"Not as much as I'd have liked. There was no sign of any more of Philbrick's letters among Green's belongings." He accepted the cup of tea she offered, their fingers brushing for the space of a moment.

"Kate's had an eventful enough day to put that to shame." Caro bit into a macaroon. Then looking abashed, she added, "But of course, I'll let her tell you."

Caro very often had enthusiasm enough for the both of them. But in this instance, Kate was bursting to tell Eversham her news.

Quickly, she informed him of Miss Green's visit that morning and the mysterious woman in black who had been riffling through Green's study.

"And she has no notion of who the woman was?" he asked, his earlier fatigue replaced with alertness.

"No, aside from mistaking her for her brother's mistress at first," Kate said, "she didn't recognize her or know of anyone who would have had permission to enter the house unannounced."

A line appeared between Eversham's brows. "Why didn't Miss Green tell me this when I saw her in Lewiston this morning? I saw her when I was at the Green cottage and she said nothing."

Kate, who had never had any trouble with diplomacy, found herself reluctant to tell him the older woman had found him intimidating. She knew, of course, that he was much warmer than he at first seemed. But he did have a certain aura of seriousness that could be off-putting for those who didn't know him.

Caro, however, had no such reticence. "You're not precisely as cuddly as a stuffed toy, are you, Eversham?"

"I'm not as bad as all that," he said defensively. "I'm very good with witnesses. They call for me when there's a particularly reluctant child we need to get information from."

"Are you sure it's not because you put the fear of God in them?" Caro asked baldly.

Taking pity on him, Kate interjected, "I'm sure you're very good with witnesses, Andrew. Miss Green, however, seems a bit uncomfortable around men."

Which wasn't a lie. The other lady had seemed relaxed among the village women who were in Green's parlor. And from what she'd said about her father, and her brother, she hadn't had very good relationships with the men in her life. It would be difficult for her to trust a man with the knowledge that she'd mistaken the situation with the mystery woman.

That seemed to mollify Eversham somewhat. "I suppose that's possible."

Kate gave Caro a speaking look, and her friend made a face, but admitted, "I may have been overly harsh when I said you aren't cuddly."

This seemed to alarm Eversham even more. "Thank you?"

Brushing biscuit crumbs from her skirt, Caro stood. "Now, I shall leave the two of you to discuss the case. I've promised Ludwig a turn around the gardens."

Once the door shut behind her, Kate gave Eversham a glance from beneath her lashes. "Oh, look," she said in feigned innocence, "this seat beside me on the settee is empty." She didn't have to say it twice.

Chapter Eighteen

Eversham gathered her against him and kissed her tenderly, reveling in the now-familiar scent of lilac and Kate.

After a few moments, he reluctantly pulled away and leaned his forehead down to meet hers. "That was a very nice greeting," he said in a low voice. "I missed you this morning."

He hadn't realized how much he'd been looking forward to waking up with her in his arms until she hadn't been there.

"I couldn't risk being caught out." She sighed, then lay her head against his shoulder. "I've already done enough to damage your reputation."

"You let me worry about my reputation." Which reminded him. Pulling back a little, he moved the shawl she'd wrapped around her neck, so that he could find the mark he'd left.

There, just below her left ear, he saw it. A rosy patch of skin that he remembered paying particular attention to, since it had elicited a sound from her that made him hard as a post.

"How did you know?" she asked, holding still while he gingerly touched the bruise. Then she spat out, "Val."

"Don't be angry." He wouldn't have imagined it when he'd seen the other man with her on his first day here, but Eversham had come to realize that Valentine wasn't lying when he said they were like brother and sister. Though he questioned the sanity of any man who didn't burn with lust for the woman in his arms, he couldn't say he was disappointed that there was nothing but friendship between them. "He cares about you and wanted to be sure that I know you aren't without friends."

"I do not need protecting." Her rosy lips pursed in frustration. "I'm well above the age of majority, and what's more, I've been married and widowed. I manage my own affairs and I own and manage a bloody newspaper."

He wasn't sure what the newspaper had to do with it, but chose not to mention it.

"Of course you don't," he soothed, rubbing her back absently. "And I told him that. But in truth, I think it's good that you have friends who care about you."

"I suppose." The admission was grudging. "I just wish he trusted me to make my own decisions. I'm not a child."

"No." And he was very glad of it.

She looked up at him then, and her eyes narrowed as they settled on his jaw.

"What happened?" Just as he'd done with her bruise a

moment ago, she touched the place where Valentine's fist had connected with his face.

"I hit it on a cabinet at Green's," he lied. "It's not so bad."

She pulled back a little and looked him in the eye. "You're lying. If Val hit you, I'm going to box his fool ears."

"It's settled, little hellcat. You have no need to defend me to Lord Valentine." He was touched that she was ready to go to battle for him. But he wasn't angry. Valentine had only done what Eversham himself would have done if their roles were reversed and he suspected the other man of taking liberties with his own sister.

"What do you mean, 'It's settled'? He hit you." Her expression was fierce.

"Katherine, you cannot be ignorant of the fact that at times men settle their disagreements with their fists." Eversham knew it made little sense logically, but there was a primal instinct to protect that sometimes expressed itself with violence. He didn't condone it in extremes, but one blow was not something he could fault Valentine for.

Katherine, however, was not so easily mollified. "Of course I'm not. That doesn't mean I think it's a sensible way to make one's point."

"Are you or are you not the same lady who just moments ago threatened to 'box his fool ears'?" Her impulse to come to his defense warmed him in ways he hadn't expected. He was so used, as a policeman, to the role of protector.

She shook her head. "I was speaking metaphorically."

He kissed her. "I'm sorry this has distressed you so."

Her eyes softened and she lay her head on his shoulder.

"Of course I'm distressed. I quite like your strong jaw, and now he's made it swollen and I won't be able to kiss you with the same degree of abandon I'd hoped to tonight."

That pronouncement sent a thrill down his spine. And to other parts. "Tonight, eh?"

"That is, if you haven't been frightened off by my terrifying watchdog," she said with a small frown as she smoothed the fabric of his coat.

"What do you think?" Eversham had never been a reckless man, but he certainly liked a challenge.

She must have seen the heat in his eyes because she lowered her lashes, then softly kissed his jaw, taking care not to press too hard.

Then, reluctantly, she pulled away. He felt the loss of her like an ache.

"I think we'd better take a look at Delia Hale's journal before we are caught in a compromising position and Val takes it into his head to call you out."

"He won't do that." Eversham stretched out his legs as he watched her get settled. "We're friends now."

She looked up from where she was paging through the journal. "He hit you in the face, and now you're friends?"

When he nodded, she looked heavenward and sighed. "I will never understand men for as long as I live."

"We are odd creatures," he agreed. Though he secretly thought that it was sometimes a more straightforward way to settle a disagreement.

Holding up the diary, Katherine spoke. "I believe I now know the content of the letters Jones was demanding from Mr. Green."

"Don't keep me in suspense," Eversham said when she paused after that dramatic pronouncement.

"This is the diary of Miss Delia Hale, who later became Mrs. Sebastian Philbrick. And I believe the letters were between the two of them."

"But Philbrick never married." Eversham frowned. "Wasn't there a grieving fiancée?"

"Miss Jane Hubbard," Katherine confirmed. "She married not long after Philbrick's death and faded into obscurity."

"So, what about the actual Mrs. Philbrick?" he asked. A wife would definitely be angry to learn that a cache of her late husband's belongings had been stolen and were in the possession of the thief's son.

Katherine nodded. "According to the journal, they eloped in early summer of 1844, and by that winter, Philbrick had been forced by debts and his failing health to retire to the Continent."

"And she went with him?"

"No," Katherine said, a glimmer of excitement in her eyes. "She couldn't travel because by that winter she was heavy with child and they didn't wish to risk the journey."

"There's proof of a child then," Eversham breathed. "So, our theory was correct."

"Yes. And I have a fair idea of where we might go to find more information about where Delia and the child might be now."

She told him about the girl's father in Crossmere and how the man had used cruelty and religion to control her.

"And Philbrick died in Italy, leaving his wife to remain

in the cruel grip of this charlatan?" He had seen what could happen to the vulnerable in the care of men like that.

"Philbrick did die there," Katherine said. "But I don't know where Delia was when it happened. The diary ends before the child is born. It's possible Philbrick sent for her after the child was born. But I'd wager not, since no one knew of the marriage. It's likely he didn't wish her to be alone with an infant in an unfamiliar place."

"Better alone in Italy than in the home of her cruel father," Eversham said with feeling.

Katherine tipped her head to look at him. "You're quite angry with the Reverend Hale, aren't you?"

"Shouldn't I be?"

"Of course," she said. "I suppose I hadn't expected you to be so vehement about it."

Feeling suddenly tired, he ran a hand over his hair. "My father is a country vicar. He's not that sort of minister at all. In fact, he despises the sort of man you describe. Though, because he's a man of God, he makes an effort to hate the sin and not the sinner."

She didn't press, just waited for him to speak in his own time. And he was glad of it.

Eversham was suddenly grateful he'd chosen to sit beside her on the sofa, deciding he'd rather have this conversation where he didn't have to look her in the eye.

Wordlessly, she slipped her hand into his.

"In my work with the Yard, I've had occasion to investigate a few so-called 'men of God' who had more in common with the Reverend Hale than my father," he began. "One of them was the Reverend Bill Lamb."

He could still remember the day he'd been sent to the Lamb household because the man's sister-in-law had reported that her sister, the man's wife, had not been seen for more than a week. The house had been well kept, with clean windows and a tidy front garden. His knock had been answered by a maid whose eyes had flashed fear when he asked about Mrs. Lamb, but just as quickly returned to the bland expression she'd shown when she first greeted him.

"I knew she had information," he explained to Katherine. "She knew where her mistress was. But before I could question her, Lamb came from where he'd been listening in the door off the entry hall."

"What was he like?" Katherine asked, squeezing his hand.

"I'm ashamed to admit I was taken in by him." Afterward, Eversham had picked apart every moment of that first meeting, trying to understand how he'd been fooled. He'd learned later that there were men—and women, too—who had the uncanny ability to mask their inner evil with the most innocent, even personable, exteriors. "He explained that his wife had gone to visit her friend in Sussex who'd been feeling poorly. He went on about how concerned she'd been and how he'd suggested, nay insisted, that she travel there to reassure herself.

"He was charming," Eversham admitted. "I found myself laughing along with him when he made a joke, and when he offered me refreshment, it was brought in by the same maid. And I recalled that flash of fear."

"What did you do?"

"I knew I had to be cautious." He remembered how he'd

been careful not to show that he'd seen through the man's facade. "With someone like that, I knew I couldn't demand to search the house to look for his wife. So, I told him I'd been thinking about buying a house in the area and asked if I might have a tour. Fortunately, the square was fairly new and they'd all been built by the same company, so they were similar in layout."

"Clever," Kate said.

"You may not think so in a moment." He laughed bitterly. "He was more than happy to give me a tour, but it became obvious as we went from room to room that he was avoiding a door at the end of the hall where the family bedchambers were housed. Finally, I lost my patience and asked him what was in that room.

"He said it was just a storage closet and that his wife would die of mortification if he let me see the disarray inside."

"And?"

"And I pushed past him and threw open the door myself."

"Was his wife there?" Katherine asked, her voice breathy with fear. "Was she dead?"

"She wasn't dead." Eversham rubbed the back of her hand with his thumb. "She was there, however, and she'd been beaten black and blue by the man who'd spent the better part of an hour trying to convince me that he was a jolly good fellow."

"I hope you arrested him on the spot."

"I couldn't," Eversham said with barely suppressed anger. "It's not against the law for a man to discipline his wife. And even if it were, she wouldn't admit that he'd done it. She said she'd taken a fall down the cellar stairs."

Kate used a word that was not acceptable in polite company.

"My sentiments exactly," he said with feeling.

"How did you finally catch him?" That she didn't doubt he *had* caught the man made his heart swell.

"I had to find another way," he said simply. "It occurred to me that a man who would entertain a detective from Scotland Yard for the better part of an hour while his wife was imprisoned in another room might be brazenly criminal in other areas of his life."

"It took me the better part of a year to uncover his theft of funds from his own church," he continued. "And I was afraid the whole time that he'd kill his wife before I found the proof. But finally I discovered the documentation I needed. The day I clapped the irons on Bill Lamb was one of the proudest moments of my career."

"You saved her, Andrew." Katherine took his hand in hers.

"And their daughters as well," he said. In the end, it was the children that made him break down. They'd been such quiet little things. Four girls who had lived in fear for all of their lives.

"What happened to them?"

"They moved to live with Mrs. Lamb's sister, the same one who'd asked us to find their mother."

"You're a good man, Mr. Eversham," Katherine said softly.

At that, he turned to face her. "Don't put me on a pedestal, Katherine. I'm just a man. I did my job. Nothing more."

She kissed him one last time, then stood. "You don't like praise, so I won't embarrass you further."

He got to his feet and followed her to the door.

"I think I was more comfortable when you were questioning my abilities." He had always felt as if celebrating his good deeds was tempting fate in some way. That as soon as he became too vain about something, he'd fail spectacularly.

She gave a husky laugh, and he was suddenly reminded of what it felt like to have her naked beneath him. "Perhaps not all of my abilities," he amended.

Before they stepped into the hallway, she said, "I will find out from Val how far it is to Crossmere from here. If it's on the rail line, we should be able to go there and return in a day's time."

He nodded, but if Hale was as unpleasant as his daughter said, Eversham had no intention of exposing Katherine to his particular brand of vitriol.

It was even possible the man was the Commandments Killer himself.

She might think she was invincible, but he'd seen the damage this killer could do with a knife.

"I'll need to go back to the village to meet with the constable, so I won't see you at dinner," he said.

He'd expected some sort of protest, but she nodded. "Perhaps it would be better if we sleep in our own beds tonight?"

"That's probably sensible." It was the truth, but that didn't mean he hadn't felt a pang of disappointment at her words.

"You can't solve a murder on too little sleep."

Eversham bit back a smile. Ever the practical one, his Katherine.

"Besides," she said over her shoulder as she opened the door and stepped into the hallway. "We'll need to be well rested for the trip to Crossmere."

She was going to be furious when she found he'd gone without her, Eversham reflected as he watched her walk away.

But he had a job to do, and at least here at Thornfield, he'd know she'd be safe.

Chapter Nineteen

Kate wasn't surprised that conversation at dinner that evening revolved around the murder of Mr. Green.

The murder of an acquaintance would upset anyone, but when the deed had occurred mere hours after you'd seen the person, there was an added layer of alarm.

"I suppose this means the order I discussed with him won't be possible now," said Barton pettishly as he dug into his soup.

Well, for some people it was alarming, Kate thought wryly.

"Somehow I don't think Green's shop will be back to regular business this week, Barton." It was unlikely the American recognized the hint of mockery in Valentine's tone. The man was oblivious to conversational subtlety, Kate had found.

"When will that beastly detective allow us to leave?" demanded Lady Eggleston. "We're going to be murdered in our beds! It's perfectly obvious none of us is the killer. It's insulting to suggest otherwise."

"I've engaged extra security for the house," Val assured the countess. "Though I don't believe there is any risk to us, I do want to ensure that you all feel safe while you are here."

Miss Barton looked visibly relieved. "You do not know how much I appreciate your kindness, Lord Valentine."

Genevieve, who was seated to Kate's right, said in an undertone, "They needn't worry. I believe the killer is long gone. It would be mad to remain here when every able-bodied man in the county is looking for him."

Before Kate could respond, Mr. Thompson, who was seated on her other side, spoke up. "I don't know, Lady Genevieve. Perhaps hiding in plain sight would be the better choice."

"There's a thought," Genevieve said approvingly. "If I were writing the story, I would definitely give that notion serious consideration. After all, he would be able to stay one step ahead of the investigation. Depending on his reasons for killing, he might even lay a false trail to lead the police astray."

"This isn't an amusement, Lady Genevieve," chided Lord Eggleston. "This fiend has killed twice."

"But surely, my lord," Caro said from her seat across the table, "when we speak of things like this, it takes a bit of the killer's power away from him."

The earl made a noise of skepticism.

"I should have expected such a sentiment from the author of *A Lady's Guide*," Lady Eggleston said dismissively.

"You treat murder as if it were a game. And discuss topics that no lady of proper upbringing would ever deign to raise in polite conversation."

Kate forbore from pointing out that she was discussing such a topic right now.

"I'd almost forgotten we have experts with us." Mr. Thompson turned to Kate. "Perhaps you could tell us your thoughts, Lady Katherine and Miss Hardcastle. You interviewed the witness who saw the murderer, didn't you? What have you to say about the matter?"

"I wouldn't say one conversation with a witness makes us any more qualified to discuss the case than anyone else." Kate met Caro's eyes across the table. "While it is true that we have followed the case from the beginning, our impressions are likely no different than the next person's."

"And what are those impressions?" Thompson seemed genuinely interested.

Caro, who had been listening to the whole exchange, spoke up before Kate could find her words. "The ugly truth is this: At any moment, any one of us could have our life snuffed out. It's as simple as that."

Jim Hyde, Valentine's prizefighter, had been listening to the conversation silently while he ate his dinner, but now he set down his wineglass with a laugh. "The lady isn't wrong."

"But it's not polite to discuss it," Lady Eggleston said, frustration ringing in her voice.

Kate had endured enough London parties with ladies like the countess, who thought it was their mission in life to police the world around them, enforcing the rules that they believed governed polite society. Before her fall from grace, a word from Miss Frampton, as she was known then, could see a rival excluded from all the best parties or even ruined entirely. Now, though she was the one who'd been shunned, she still seemed to prize the proprieties. It was rather like following the regulations of a club from which one had been blackballed.

"Perhaps we should change the subject," Kate said in an effort to keep further strife from Valentine's dinner table. "Is anyone familiar with the village of Crossmere?"

Valentine gave her a silent nod of thanks for diverting the conversation. "A bit. It's twenty miles or so from Lewiston. Charming but remote. Unfortunately, it was one of the villages bypassed by the railway, so it's a bit isolated."

"Are you considering a visit?" Caro asked, her eyebrows raised.

"Of course, that's impossible." Lady Eggleston didn't bother to hide the smugness in her tone. "Lady Katherine is confined to Thornfield just like the rest of us."

"Unless Inspector Eversham has given her some special dispensation," Mr. Thompson said in a teasing voice.

Perhaps they hadn't been as discreet as Kate had thought. She would need to keep her distance from Andrew for the next few days.

Or at the very least have Caro put it about that she was ill with a headache tomorrow while she was gone to Crossmere with him.

"Of course not. I was reading about the"—she searched her mind for some reason Crossmere might be referenced in a book—"historic church." Since the English countryside was littered with picturesque houses of worship, it stood to reason there was one in Crossmere. "I find something so charming about a country churchyard."

"Sebastian Philbrick has a poem about such a churchyard," Miss Barton said. "There were a few of his books in my bedchamber and I've quite enjoyed them. I wonder why he never achieved the same degree of fame as his mentor, Mr. Wordsworth."

For all that she'd spent the past few days thinking of Philbrick, Kate hadn't thought to read the man's verse.

"I've always suspected if he'd lived longer, his poetry would have become more popular," Genevieve said thoughtfully.

"Keats died young," Caro argued, "but he gained a following."

"I think Philbrick's day has yet to come." Mr. Thompson's voice held a surety that made Kate turn to look at him.

At her scrutiny, color rose on his cheekbones.

"I do not speak with any authority," he said hastily. "Just that of an admirer of the man's work."

The rest of the meal passed without incident, but Kate couldn't stop thinking she was missing something by ignoring Philbrick's writings. What if the man had written about Delia in his work?

She knew some of his poems had been published posthumously. It was entirely possible that there might be some clue as to where his wife and child may have settled after his death there.

Once the household had retired for the night, still dressed, she crept down the hall to the library.

Fortunately, it was a separate chamber from Valentine's study. She hadn't spoken to him privately since learning he'd struck Eversham. And she was still too angry with him to do so.

She appreciated that he looked out for her well-being, but that didn't mean she wanted him to ride to her rescue whenever he considered her to be at risk.

What had happened between her and Eversham was no one's affair but their own. And she didn't appreciate Valentine assaulting her lover, no matter how justified he might think his actions.

When she stepped into the book room, she was relieved to find it empty. Given that the guests were confined to the house for the time being, it would not have been surprising to find they'd sought out entertainment.

The only light in the room was from the lamp she'd brought with her and the fire in the hearth. The rest of the chamber was bathed in shadows.

Kate wasn't normally given to flights of fancy, but perhaps because of the discussion of murder at dinner, she felt a shiver run through her as she contemplated the dark corners of the library.

"Don't be foolish," she told herself. Her pragmatism was something that had stood her in good stead, and she wasn't about to let a little darkness frighten her.

Squaring her shoulders, she made her way to the shelves where she recalled seeing the Philbrick books on an earlier visit to the room. Soon enough, she found them. And not only were there books of his own poetry, but she noted there was also a full shelf of books written about him.

Pleased by her find, she set down her lamp on a nearby table and began gathering an armful of volumes.

So engrossed was she in her task that she didn't hear the footsteps behind her.

When the blow came, she fell against the bookcase from the force of it. She grabbed the sturdily built shelf, which had been secured to the wall, to break her fall, but the pain soon had her knees buckling.

As the books fell to the ground, so did she.

Eversham made a concerted effort to concentrate on the investigation for the rest of the day, and not let himself get distracted by the memory of Lady Katherine Bascomb in his arms.

He had a job to do, and despite their easy rapport, he needed to focus. Lives were at stake. And given his current disillusionment toward the Yard, this case might be the last case he'd be working as a member of the Metropolitan Police Force.

She would be angry with him once he left for Crossmere in the morning without her, in any event.

So, he'd met with Constable Miller and once more gone over the inventory of the items that had been removed from Green's secret closet. To his disappointment, there had been no sign of letters between Philbrick and Delia Hale. Nor had there been any indication where Philbrick's wife had gone after his death in Italy.

This meant that the trip to Crossmere was more important than ever.

It was late when he returned to Thornfield, but to his surprise, the first few stories were aglow with light.

What the devil was going on?

He was greeted at the door not by Austen but by Valentine, who looked grim.

Eversham's stomach dropped. Something had happened to Katherine.

"She's all right," Valentine said in a soothing tone. "She took a blow to the head, but she's awake and—"

"Where is she?" he interrupted.

No sooner had the word "library" escaped the other man's lips than Eversham was pushing past him and all but taking the stairs two at a time toward the second floor.

Not bothering to knock, he pushed his way into the room to find Katherine trying to stand up and Caro, despite her smaller stature, managing to keep her in a reclining position on the settee.

At the sound of the door, Miss Hardcastle turned and gave a sigh of relief. "Good, perhaps you can convince her to remain here until the doctor comes."

"I'm perfectly able to stand on my own, Caro," Katherine said in an aggrieved tone. "I have a headache, nothing more. And I wish to go to my rooms, where I can be comfortable."

The sound of her voice, annoyed as it was, made Eversham close his eyes in relief.

When he'd seen Valentine's face downstairs, he'd imagined the worst. And though Val had assured him that she was in no danger, he'd needed to lay eyes on her before he believed it.

Even so, when Caro stepped back, he took her place and, without saying a word, lifted Katherine into his arms.

"Oh!" She didn't fight him, which told him in a way that her voice had not that she was indeed in pain.

"I'll take her to her room, Miss Hardcastle," he told Caro as he walked past her. "Please have the physician sent there."

"I don't need a doctor." But the way she sagged against his chest said otherwise.

He carried her toward the door. "I'm sure you don't. But why not see him for Caro and Valentine's sakes? They're concerned, I'm sure."

That seemed to convince her.

"Very well, but, Caro, don't forget my books."

"I'll bring them along in a little while," Miss Hardcastle said from behind them.

Now that he was assured she hadn't been permanently injured, Eversham asked, "What happened?"

"Not here," she said in a low voice.

They passed the rest of the way to her bedchamber in silence, where they found her maid, Bess, waiting for her. The bed was turned down and a nightgown that made Eversham's pulse quicken lay across it.

"I'll leave you to undress," he said once he'd gently deposited her on the counterpane.

"Do not go far," she ordered. "I must speak to you tonight."

If Bess thought it a scandal that her mistress had just asked a man who was not her husband to wait upon her at this late hour, while she was in a state of undress, she didn't say so.

"Of course." He was a policeman, he reminded himself. The girl very likely assumed, correctly, that it was related to the investigation.

He didn't cool his heels in the hallway for long and was soon back in Katherine's bedchamber.

She was propped against the pillows. From what he could see of her above the bedclothes, she was now wearing the nightdress, but it was modestly covered by a dressing gown.

"My dear, you gave me a fright." He leaned down to kiss her gently on the lips. "What happened?"

She gripped his hand and pulled him to sit facing her on the bedside. "I went to the library after everyone had gone to bed. The conversation at dinner reminded me that I hadn't read any of Philbrick's poetry, and I thought perhaps there might be a clue to where Delia may have gone after his death."

"It was a good thought." He'd been so focused on the items in Green's closet, it hadn't occurred to him that Philbrick's poetry might mention places to which his wife may have fled.

"I also found a few books that had been written after his death about his poetry and life," she continued. "I had a stack of books in my arms when I heard something behind me."

"Someone struck you?" he demanded through clenched teeth. He'd thought her injury must have been an accident. "Who was it?"

He had never thought himself capable of murder, but the flash of anger that ran through him said otherwise.

"I don't know," she said in a soothing voice. "Sit down."

His fists were clenched, but he allowed her to pull him back to a sitting position on the bed.

"I'm not badly injured. I didn't lose consciousness. I fell, and by the time I got back to my feet, he was gone."

"Are you certain it was a man? Did you get a glimpse of him?" He knew Valentine had hired guards to protect the house. And there were so many servants, it would be difficult for a stranger to wander in.

Could her attacker have been someone in the house?

"No." She sighed. "I wish I had. But by the time I turned around, there was no one there."

"It must be because you've been involved in the investigation." There was anger in his voice, but it was all directed at himself. He had been too cavalier with her safety. Though he'd been planning to go to Crossmere without her tomorrow, that was too little, too late. Now she was at risk in Thornfield Hall.

"You'll return to London tomorrow," he said firmly. "There's no reason for you to remain here. I won't have you putting yourself at risk."

She had been stroking his hand, but at his declaration, she pulled away and stared at him as if he'd grown horns. "You don't get to make that decision. I believe I was targeted tonight because I've come close to learning who the killer is."

That's just what he was afraid of. "Which is all the more reason for you to leave. This man is dangerous, Katherine. Tonight he coshed you on the head, but what's to stop him from killing you the next time?"

Something of his anguish must have shown in his eyes because she put her arms around him. He held her tightly, grateful to feel the beating of her heart against his.

"I won't be reckless, Andrew." She tucked her head against his chest. "I'm not foolhardy. And I like being alive too much to risk giving it up."

"I like you being alive, too," he said finally.

Stroking a hand down her back, he closed his eyes, the idea of what might have happened tonight too dreadful to contemplate.

Pulling away, he looked at her, unable to keep the emotion from his voice. "If something were to happen to you, I don't know what I'd—"

A knock at the door made him pull away, as if they'd been caught *in flagrante*.

When the door opened to reveal Valentine accompanied by the doctor from the village, Eversham was seated in the chair beside the bed.

He rose. "I'll leave you now, Lady Katherine. Thank you for answering my questions regarding your assault."

Valentine gave a speaking look as he shook hands with the doctor and stepped out into the hallway.

When the two men were alone, Eversham turned to Valentine.

"I thought you had guards outside the house. How could someone have gotten inside?" Eversham tried to keep the blame from his voice, but he was still reeling.

Valentine's mouth was grim. "I don't know. I've spent the past few hours questioning every man who was on watch, but none of them saw anything out of the ordinary."

"Could it have been done by someone inside the house? One of the guests? A servant?" Eversham demanded.

"I honestly don't know," the other man said. "But I can't imagine any of my guests would have reason to assault Kate like that. I know she's had differences with Barton, but this doesn't seem like his style. And the others don't seem the type."

That had been Eversham's assessment as well. "She isn't going to like it, but I want a guard with Katherine at all times."

"Already done." Valentine lifted his chin to indicate Eversham should turn around.

He hadn't noticed before, but a tall muscular footman sat in an armchair at the far end of the hall. The man lifted his beefy hand in a salute.

"You trust him?" Eversham wished he had some of his own men from Scotland Yard here.

Valentine nodded. "With my life. He's been with me for years. You know how I feel about Kate. I wouldn't let just anyone have this job."

Reassured the man was to be trusted, Eversham went on. "Is he up to the task of reining her in? She may be cowed at the moment, but I predict she'll be attempting to slip through the net first thing tomorrow."

"He's not just a pretty face," Valentine said with confidence. "She's clever, but I don't doubt he's up to the challenge."

That settled, the detective said, "I'll be away for most of tomorrow. I leave her to your care."

The other man clapped him on the shoulder. "You have

my word. That she was harmed in my home makes me furious."

Eversham would let his own anger fuel his investigation.

And once he'd caught the man who dared touch Katherine, he'd unleash it.

Chapter Twenty

As Kate had known he would, the physician assured her that the wound on her head was superficial, and aside from a headache, she should suffer no lasting ill effects from it.

Once he was gone, she rang for Bess and relaxed against the pillows, thinking.

Andrew had been white as a sheet when he burst into the library earlier.

She wondered what Val had told him. She'd hoped her friend would have broken the news without alarming him too much. But she supposed there was no way to hear that someone you—she struggled to find a word for what lay between them—cared for, she settled on, had been attacked.

Were their positions reversed, she knew she'd have been distraught.

And angry. So very angry.

She would not, however, have ordered that he return to London at once to protect himself from further danger.

While she understood his impulse to keep her safe—indeed, she, too, had concerns for her safety now—she did not agree that he had the right to order her about as if he were her lord and master.

She had no intention of going back to London before they'd found the killer. And contrary to what Andrew might think, she also had a plan to keep herself safe.

She would stick as closely to him as she could. Which meant she would accompany him to Crossmere tomorrow.

Bess arrived then with a cup of tea and a sleeping draught the doctor had left. "One of the footmen is seated in a chair out in the hall, my lady. I believe Mr. Eversham has set him out there to keep watch over you."

Kate wanted to be annoyed, but she was perversely grateful to know she'd be able to sleep without fear of her attacker trying again. Though she'd rather have had her detective himself watching over her from inside her bedchamber, if it came to that.

She took the tea but refused the potion. "Bess, I need you to do a little investigating below stairs for me."

"If it's to learn about Mr. Eversham's plans for tomorrow, my lady"—the maid grinned—"I've already found out for you."

Bess had been with Kate long enough to guess the direction of her thoughts, especially when it came to matters of subterfuge.

"Lord Valentine gave orders that Harry is to have the cart

ready at dawn to take Mr. Eversham to the train station so he can travel to Crossmere."

She knew it! The wretch was planning to go interview Reverend Hale without her.

"Good work. Now, I need you to pack an overnight bag, and wake me early enough to get to the station before Mr. Eversham. I'll need you to arrange it with Harry to get me there first." Andrew would get the surprise of his life when he found her waiting on the train when he boarded.

It would serve him right, too.

"Not a problem, my lady. I've made a friend of Harry, and he'll do anything I ask of him."

Bess was a pretty girl and wasn't above using her looks for the greater good when necessary.

"Excellent." That settled, Kate felt the previous night's lack of sleep combine with the excitement of tonight envelop her in a blanket of fatigue.

"Rest well, my lady," Bess said as she put out the light. "You leave it to me. You'll be well on the way to Crossmere in the morning."

As it happened, Kate was far more tired the next morning than she'd expected, but she was determined to make the journey to Crossmere regardless.

She allowed Bess to dress her in a traveling gown of crimson silk, and donned her favorite straw hat, which was festooned with a sprig of cherries. It was an ensemble that made her feel feminine but confident. This was precisely the sort of strength she needed to project today.

Fortunately for her escape plans, the first footman had been replaced sometime in the night by another, and he, too, was beguiled by Bess's charms, so Kate was able to slip past him into the servants' hall without being seen by any other members of the household.

Harry drove her to the train station and purchased two first-class tickets to Crossmere for her, promising to give the other to Eversham later.

Fortunately, the train had remained in the station overnight and she was able to board long before it was scheduled to depart.

Once she was secreted in the private carriage, she removed one of the books of Philbrick's poetry she'd retrieved from the library last night and began to read.

It was little more than an hour later, after she'd nodded off, that the door to the carriage opened and she heard a muffled curse.

Her eyes flew open, but it was only Eversham, who was looking more resigned than cross.

"I should have known that bit about Valentine insisting on a first-class ticket was a ruse." He sighed.

Closing the door behind him, he stalked toward her and stood there for a moment, their eyes meeting in a contest of wills.

"Well, aren't you going to sit down?" she asked, not bothering to hide her defiance. He should have known better than to try to tell her what to do.

"I suppose I am." He did just that and leaned back against the plush velvet seat. Glancing around the compartment, he said, "I've never actually ridden in a first-class carriage before. I suppose this is a common thing for you?" There was another question embedded in that one, but Kate decided to ignore it for the time being. They hadn't really discussed the class differences between them. To Kate's mind, they were immaterial. But she'd known it was something he struggled with.

"This isn't quite so lavish as some I've seen. And I didn't think you'd approve of me in the more public car, given your fears for my safety."

"Oh, I hadn't realized you'd noticed that," he said wryly. "I'd assumed, since you refused to return to London, as I asked, and then allowed one of Valentine's servants to drive you to the train station, where you boarded an empty train compartment to wait for me, for God knows how long, that you had entirely disregarded my wishes."

"Pouting doesn't become you." Kate reached out to take his hand in hers. "There was no way I could let you meet with Delia's father without me. And I'm annoyed you even considered it."

"I was trying to protect you." He lifted his eyes heavenward. "Clearly that was a misguided notion on my part."

"I think you underestimate your own ability to keep me safe, Andrew."

He sighed. "It's unfair of you to use my given name as a way to disarm me during an argument."

"But did it?" she asked pertly.

"You know it did," he groused. "Infernal woman."

She leaned her head against his shoulder. "Don't be angry with me. I would have gone mad locked away in the Hall waiting for you to come back from Crossmere with news."

"I'm not angry." He lifted their joined hands to kiss the back of hers. "But I don't know what I'm going to do with you and that's the truth."

"Who says you have to do anything with me? Why can't you just let me be me?"

"I'm beginning to understand that I don't have a choice." Eversham didn't sound too alarmed by it, however.

"You truly don't," she agreed. "It's good you've figured it out."

He barked out a laugh.

They sat in companionable silence for a short while before Kate asked, "What is our strategy for questioning Hale? Shall I try to play him up sweet while you stand sternly beside me making him fear you'll tear him limb from limb?

"Or," she continued, "perhaps I should be the stern one? It sounds as if he doesn't like women very much. He probably had a difficult relationship with his mother. You can be his friend while I order him around."

"What goes on in that imagination of yours?" he asked, sounding both aghast and impressed at the same time.

"I've read a great many sensation novels." She shrugged.

"This is real life," he told her patiently. "And why don't we be ourselves? I'll ask him questions in my capacity as a policeman."

"Should I tell him I'm a journalist?" She was being

serious now. "I have a feeling he will not be a regular reader of *A Lady's Guide*, and even if he were, he wouldn't approve."

"I suspect you're right."

"Why don't I just pretend to be your wife?" she asked. "It's a simple enough explanation. You're making inquiries about Delia Hale, and I insisted on accompanying you because…"

"Because we're newlyweds and you won't let me out of your sight?"

The smolder in his eyes made her think of exactly what she'd rather be doing as a newlywed other than conducting a police investigation.

"Do you think we'll be convincing enough?" she whispered, her eyes darting to his lips.

"Oh, I believe we can be quite credible," he said softly, his breath fanning over her lips. "But we'll need to practice a little."

It was a two-mile walk from the train station to the village of Crossmere, which had taken its name from the small lake nearby.

The town itself was quaint enough, with an attractive, shop-lined high street, boasting a bustling inn at one end and a stone church at the other. Before the railway, Eversham imagined, it would have felt remote to a young girl like Delia Hale, whose journal had shown her to be aching for adventure. Philbrick would have seemed like the answer to a prayer, albeit not the kind her father would have had her make.

They stopped at the inn for refreshment and to make discreet inquiries about Delia Hale.

"We don't get many visitors this time of year, sir," said the owner's wife, who served them in the taproom. "What brings you?"

Before Eversham could speak, Katherine took the reins of the conversation. "I had a friend years ago who came from Crossmere. We're at a house party in Lewiston and decided to come to see if we could find her."

"And who might that be, Mrs. Eversham?" It was odd to hear Katherine addressed by anything other than "my lady," but there was something that felt right about it, though Eversham would never say so out loud. Not yet anyway.

"Delia Hale."

A shadow crossed Mrs. Stringer's face. "Oh, you won't have heard then? She died some twenty years ago, the poor thing."

"Oh no. How dreadful." Katherine's dismay wasn't feigned.

Taking his role as comforting husband seriously, Eversham handed her his handkerchief. "I'm sorry, my dear. I know you looked forward to seeing her."

She took his hand in one of hers, and dabbed at her eyes with the other. "What happened, Mrs. Stringer? Do you know?"

The older woman wiped her hands on her apron. "It's no great secret, missus. The poor thing died bringing her babies into the world."

Death in childbirth was common enough, Eversham reflected. Even with medical advances, there were still any number of things that could and did go wrong during the process. Still, her words brought him up short. "Did you say 'babies'?"

"Oh yes, sir. A boy and a girl." He waited for her to go on, but she seemed reluctant to continue. Had something happened to the children as well?

Katherine must have thought the same. "They died, too?" she asked, looking as disappointed as he felt. Not only was Delia Hale dead and gone, but if her children were dead as well, that meant they'd need to search elsewhere for the heir Jones spoke of. Or it was entirely possible he'd been lying about the existence of a rightful owner at all.

Mrs. Stringer shook her head, as if throwing off cobwebs. "Oh no, I'm sorry. I didn't mean to give that impression. They lived. Grew up right here in the village with their grandparents."

Eversham's relief was palpable. "So, they would be twenty now."

"Yes."

There was something about the twins that Mrs. Stringer was reluctant to speak of, and he was trying to figure out how best to broach the question forming in his mind when Katherine spoke up. "Do they still live in the area? I should like to pay them a visit and give them my condolences about their mother."

"They left these parts a little under a year ago, Mrs. Eversham." Her mouth tightened. "I don't wish to speak ill of them when they've borne so much in their young lives, but it's for the best that they're gone. Once their grandmother died, there was nothing left here for them. And I don't mind saying I feared young Bastian would do his grandfather a serious injury one day."

"His grandfather?" Katherine asked, her eyes darting to meet Eversham's. "Is Reverend Hale still living, then?"

"Oh yes," Mrs. Stringer said. "He's no longer the vicar, of course, but lives in a little cottage not far from the church."

In a low voice, she added, "Between ourselves, I was never that fond of the man. He's a cold one. And I thought he was too hard on those children. They couldn't help where they came from after all."

"What do you mean?" Katherine had asked the question, but Eversham knew exactly what the innkeeper's wife meant.

"Well," Mrs. Stringer colored, "that they were not...that is to say...their parents weren't..."

"My dear," Eversham said, patting Katherine's hand, "what I believe Mrs. Stringer is trying to say is that your friend was not married to the children's father."

Katherine gave an audible gasp. "But that's—"

Before she could finish her sentence, revealing that they knew the truth about Delia Hale's marriage to Philbrick, he cut her off. "I know, it's terribly sad, isn't it? But it's the way of the world."

"The poor girl was convinced that she actually had married the father, you know," Mrs. Stringer said. "It was the saddest thing. She was mad, I'm afraid. Her father wouldn't let her out of the house, of course, because of the shame. My sister Elsie was a maid up at the vicarage and said that she talked about her husband coming for her as soon as he was well enough. But the vicar assured her it was just a fantasy. You couldn't help but feel sorry for the girl. I suppose it was easier to believe that rather than that he'd left her high and dry in the family way."

Katherine was visibly shaken by the news, so Eversham said, "What a sad tale. For poor Delia and the children. It's no wonder they left Crossmere. I suppose it would be better to go someplace where their history wasn't known."

"Yes, it was a lonely existence for them, I fear," Mrs. Stringer said. "The vicar, as I said, was quite hard on them. And you know how village folk can be. They kept to themselves."

"I would like to pay a call on Reverend Hale." Katherine set down her glass with a thump. "Do you think he'll see us?"

"I don't see why not." Their hostess shrugged. "He doesn't get much company these days, so I imagine he'd enjoy a visit. He's not quite as hard, now that the children are gone."

"Thank you for your hospitality, Mrs. Stringer." Eversham rose and took Katherine's arm.

Once they were out in the street again, Katherine hissed. "That horrible man. He told the world she was a whore when she was actually married to the father of her children. He branded those children as bastards rather than accept that she'd made a marriage to a man he found unsuitable."

"Easy," Eversham said in a low voice. "We don't want to call attention to ourselves. And you definitely don't want to approach Hale with rage in your eyes. We need him to talk to us willingly, and if we go in with accusations, he's unlikely to tell us anything."

She took a deep breath. "I know. I'm sorry, I'm just so angry. That poor girl. First she fell prey to Philbrick, who, though he was probably a decent enough man, was entirely unsuitable for one so young."

"It's chilling, I admit," he responded. "Especially given how insular and judgmental small communities like this can be. Those children didn't have a chance for a normal life. Their grandfather made sure of that before they were even born. And for what?"

"So that he could have someone to control," Katherine bit out. "First Delia, then when she died, that left him with two infants to dominate."

"It sounds as if their grandmother offered them some comfort, though." He was trying to find a silver lining where there were few options.

"If Delia's diary is anything to go by, her mother was just as persecuted by Hale as she was."

Eversham's chest squeezed at her degree of upset over these people she'd never even met before. For someone who hailed from the upper class, Katherine Bascomb had a depth of empathy for others that he'd rarely seen. It should have been clear to him from the moment he met her, but then he'd been too caught up in blaming her for his career troubles. Now that he'd had the opportunity to spend days in her company, he could see that it wasn't an act. It was genuine.

And it made him want to wrap her in his arms and protect

her from these strong feelings that made her grieve for the lost childhood of Delia Hale's children.

They were walking in the direction of the church, but when the opportunity arose, he took her hand and led her into a narrow alley between two shops.

Once they were hidden from sight, he pulled her into his arms and kissed her.

Chapter Twenty-One

E versham, we'll be seen," Katherine hissed once she was able to get her breath back.

"No one can see us here. And besides, in case you have forgotten, we're married now." Andrew's eyes crinkled at the edges, giving him a youthful appearance.

"Mr. Eversham, this is highly shocking to my delicate sensibilities."

He smiled, but there was something serious in his expression.

"What is it?" she asked.

"I just didn't like seeing you so upset," he confessed. "Especially not because of the man we're on our way to see."

Her eyes stung with tears. It had been a very long time since someone besides Caro had cared about her feelings.

"He's not worth it." Andrew wiped away a tear that had escaped. "I haven't met him yet, but I know his type."

"So do I," she said emphatically. "Which is why he makes me so angry. It's difficult enough to be a woman in this world without having one's father deliberately set out to make you seem like a lunatic."

"Or to be a child without one's grandfather telling everyone that you're illegitimate and shaming you in front of the only world you've ever known."

He understood, she thought. This dear man, who might have told her to stop being such a sentimental fool, was just as angry as she was, and she loved him for it.

"I want to confront him," she admitted. "I know you don't want me to because we need him to talk. And I promise I won't, but I so wish that I could."

Andrew kissed her nose and pulled away from her. "Let's see what happens when we get there. We may find he's a broken man and you won't want to bully him."

As it happened, however, the man who greeted them in the parlor of the tidy cottage on the far side of the Crossmere churchyard was still robust-looking at sixty years or so.

Eversham had introduced himself in his official capacity, since he wagered that someone like Hale would respect authority more than the mere husband of his late daughter's friend.

"What can I do for you, Inspector?" Reverend Hale asked once they'd seated themselves in his austere parlor.

He addressed Eversham and seemed ready to ignore Kate's presence altogether. Except when they'd first introduced themselves and the man's eyes had lingered on her bosom. Old goat.

"I'm looking into an incident in Lewiston, Mr. Hale," Eversham said coolly. His demeanor was calm, and there was no trace of the anger he'd shown earlier regarding the man's treatment of his daughter and grandchildren. To do his job effectively, Kate supposed, he would need to be able to hide his true feelings about the situations he investigated.

And that he'd trusted her enough to let that mask drop gave her a warm glow.

"I'd heard about that." Hale frowned. "The stationer, wasn't it? A bad business. There's far too many out there who've lost their way and disobey God's laws."

He paused, as if waiting for Eversham to agree with him, but Andrew only watched the man with those piercing eyes that Kate knew from her own experience could be unsettling.

"It was the stationer, Mr. Green," Eversham said, "and another man, Fenwick Jones, the steward at Thornfield Hall near Lewiston."

"How would I know anything about it?" Hale finally demanded, a little pettishly.

"I believe your daughter, Delia, was married to the poet who once owned that estate. A man named Philbrick?"

At the mention of Delia, the vicar's expression turned dark. "What about it?"

"It's true then?" Kate asked, unable to stop herself. "She was married to Sebastian Philbrick?"

He turned cold eyes toward her, and she felt a chill run

through her body. "Yes, she was married to that scoundrel. Much good it did her."

"What do you mean?" Still, Eversham kept that calm tone.

"I mean that she got nothing out of it but a pair of brats who killed her coming into this world and did nothing but cause me misery until the day they left here."

Well, that was plain speaking, Kate thought.

"They were twins?" Kate wanted him to say their names.

"A boy and a girl. Emily for my wife and Sebastian after his fool father. She lived long enough for that."

"Why did you dislike Sebastian Philbrick so much?" Kate couldn't help but ask. The vitriol seemed outsized if it was only because the man had had the temerity to want to marry Hale's daughter against his wishes.

"Because he was a seducer. The man was known far and wide for his womanizing and bad behavior. Not at all the sort of God-fearing man for a daughter of mine."

"But he did marry her, did he not? That doesn't seem to be the act of a man without scruples." Eversham's tone was mild, but he may as well have shouted it because Hale took the words as an insult.

"He stole her away like a thief in the night. He may have married her—I saw the marriage lines myself—but he abandoned her here not a few months later and left for the Continent without a backward glance."

"I was given to understand you told the village she didn't marry him." Kate tried but didn't quite manage to ape Eversham's calm manner.

"And what right have you to say anything?" the old man demanded, turning his venom on Kate. "I don't like having my business talked about by strangers, and that's what comes of letting a woman get involved in men's affairs."

"I'd watch myself if I were you, Vicar," Eversham said softly. There was a menace in his tone, and Kate watched as Hale realized his mistake.

"Sorry," he mumbled in a chastened tone so different from the strident one he'd used a moment ago.

"But is it true?" Eversham's voice was firm, betraying a little of his frustration. "Did you lie to the village about whether your daughter had been married to Philbrick?"

"I didn't tell those busybodies anything," Hale snapped, his anger getting the better of him again. "It was none of their affair. I wasn't going to proudly declare my daughter had run away with a whoring poet. And when he abandoned her here, I just let them believe what they wanted."

Kate shook her head. "Surely the twins told them the truth of who their father was once they were old enough?"

Then she remembered what the innkeeper's wife had told them: the way he'd put it about that Delia was mad and believed herself to be married when it wasn't actually true. What was to stop him from lying to his own grandchildren as well?

"You never told them," she said baldly.

"It wouldn't have done them any good. It wasn't as if he was a father to be proud of."

"What happened when they found out?"

Kate turned a surprised gaze on Eversham.

"They left." Hale scowled. "The girl, Emily, was poking her nose where it didn't belong and found her mother's marriage lines."

Eversham asked, "Do you know where they've gone?"

"I don't know and I don't care," Hale said firmly. "There was nothing of their mother in them."

It was ironic that he faulted Delia's children for not being enough like her, when Hale hadn't cared for her in the least when she'd been alive.

"How long ago was this?" Eversham asked.

"Last July," Hale said.

Kate's heart stopped. The first Commandments killing had been in August.

"Did they have something to do with the killing of that man Green in Lewiston?" For the first time, Hale's voice wavered. Whether it was because he feared for his own safety or if his grandchildren had been involved, Kate couldn't guess.

"I don't know," Eversham told him, rising to his feet. "But if your relationship with them was as rancorous as you say, you might wish to ensure you keep your doors locked. It sounds as if you've not endeared yourself to them."

Kate slipped her arm through his and allowed Eversham to lead her from the house, Hale staring silently after them.

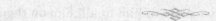

As if by mutual agreement, they didn't talk about the interview with Reverend Hale until they were safely alone in the private carriage of the train back to Lewiston.

Once the door closed on them, however, Katherine burst out, "All this time, we thought the Commandments Killer was one person, but it's been two all along."

If the subject weren't so deadly serious, Eversham would have laughed at the annoyance in her tone. "We don't know that yet," he cautioned. "All we really know is that two mistreated children grew up and left the home of their abuser for London. We don't have anything connecting them to the first four murders except their grandfather's word that they were bound for there. There's a bit more to tie them to the Lewiston killings, but would they really kill two men over stolen property?"

Katherine was not ready to be dissuaded from her theory.

"Tell me you've had better suspects in the months since you began investigating this case," Katherine countered. "They grew up isolated and alone with only Hale and his wife for companionship. If his conversation with us—or their mother's diary, for that matter—is any indication, he was harsh and made sure to remind them every day of their young lives that they were the product of sin. They leave the notes as a sort of mockery of him and all he believes."

"If that's the case," Eversham asked, "then why didn't they kill Hale? He's the one responsible for their misery."

"Perhaps they wanted to punish him by showing him what he'd driven them to?" Katherine's brow furrowed. "Or maybe they were still too afraid of him to kill him on their own? But how angry they must have been when they found those marriage lines. Not only were they punished for their mother's sin their entire lives, but it was all a lie."

He'd seen less dramatic betrayals that had led to murder, Eversham thought.

When he'd issued that warning to Hale when they'd left him, he'd been goaded to it in part because of his own anger toward the minister. But now that he had some distance, he rather thought it had been sensible. He'd always thought the killings had been a cry for attention. What if they were meant to gain the attention of the man in the killer's life who had been the most intent on eradicating sin?

Aloud, he mused, "It was a lie that he'd used to make an example of them. What if that's what they've been doing with the killings? Making examples of the victims?"

Katherine's eyes widened. "Of course. The notes were to warn others away from the sins written on the notes. They were only doing the same thing that had been done to them."

"Except they weren't murdered," Eversham said wryly.

"Well, no," Katherine agreed impatiently. "But perhaps they saw what Hale had done to them as—oh, I don't know—murdering who they could have been. They were robbed of their rightful name, their legacy as the legitimate children of one of England's foremost poets, and their inheritance."

"Why not come forward and declare themselves?" He shook his head with disbelief. He'd been investigating crime for over ten years, and he still could not understand what made someone decide to forgo the sensible option and instead take justice into their own hands. "It's not as if these were murders in the heat of the moment. They were planned. Meticulously calculated. They had the opportunity to do the right thing and made the decision to do the exact opposite."

"We won't know until we speak to them," Katherine said. "Perhaps they don't even know themselves."

Her words brought him up short. "You aren't going anywhere near them. They've murdered six people, Katherine."

"You seem once again to have forgotten that I'm an adult who makes my own decisions, Eversham." Her eyes flashed with temper. "You are not my husband, nor are you likely to be, so stop behaving like one."

That brought him up short. "What do you mean, nor am I likely to be?"

"Just that," she said. "I don't intend to remarry, and merely because we've enjoyed one another, it doesn't mean that I intend to lose what's left of my mind and let you make an honest woman of me."

That brought him up short. He only just realized it, but he'd somehow assumed they were working their way toward marriage.

This was a shock even to him. He hadn't considered marriage since a long-ago courtship, which had ended badly when the lady in question had asked him to leave the police force. That he considered it now, with a woman who objected not to his profession but to the institution of marriage itself, was frustrating, to say the least.

"Why not?" he demanded. Moving to sit beside her on the opposite bench, he took her hand in his. "What's so bad about the idea of marriage to me?"

She frowned down at their joined hands, but when she looked up, she must have seen the intensity in his gaze because her eyes softened. "It's not you, Andrew. I care for you. I truly do."

"Then why not?" he asked again. "We make a good team, wouldn't you say?"

Katherine lifted a hand to touch his cheek. "We do, but I've told you how unhappy I was in my marriage. I could never place myself under the yoke of that institution again. For one thing, everything I own would become yours. You would own *The Gazette*. You could decide to turn it into an entirely different sort of publication, and I would have no say in it."

"I would never do that." He was insulted she'd even suggest it. Did she really think so little of him?

"You say that now." She pulled her hand away. "But what if *The Gazette* somehow interfered with your job? Or your superiors pressured you to take over because they didn't like what the paper had been printing about them? Is that so very different than the Home Office pressuring Darrow to find someone to arrest?"

"I know what the damn law says, Katherine." Andrew thrust a hand into his hair in agitation. "I know that it's weighted heavily in favor of the husband when it comes to all manner of things in this country. But you must know that I would never behave in the way you're describing. For one thing, I don't know the first thing about the newspaper business and wouldn't be so foolish as to tell you how to run *The Gazette*. And I don't want your money either. How can you even think it?"

"I don't believe you want it now." She shrugged. "But the very fact that you could take it is enough to make me hesitate. I have known both freedom and the lack of it. And I would prefer to not give it up."

He had known she had very strong views of marriage. Though they hadn't discussed it, he understood that her first marriage had given her good reason to fear the institution. But somehow he'd assumed that if she loved him enough, she would reconsider.

"What if you are with child?" It had been a possibility that had weighed on him since their night together. He'd assumed that if there were consequences, she would tell him and they'd marry. Now it would appear that she might not do so. "Would you allow our child to grow up as the Philbrick twins did? Believing she's the consequence of sin?"

"It won't be an issue." She waved her hand. "I never conceived during my marriage. It's unlikely that I will now."

"But you know of no medical reason why you could not?" he pressed.

She colored. "No, I don't. And I give you my word that if a miracle occurs, I will inform you. And will reconsider my notions on marriage. I wouldn't let my child grow up to endure that sort of stigma. Though neither would I let them anywhere near a church like Hale's, where they might hear such filth."

That was a relief at least. "Thank you."

"I'm not saying this to hurt you," she said quietly. "I do genuinely care for you. But I won't give up my freedom. Not even for you."

"Even if I love you?"

Katherine gasped. She turned to look at him, her gray eyes intent as she tried to determine the veracity of his words. "Do you?"

A few hours ago, he might have given her a different answer. But her outright rejection of the very idea of marrying him had made him realize that his feelings for her—which he'd known included admiration and genuine liking—were far more serious than he'd acknowledged.

He was in love with her.

"I do," he said, reaching out to touch her face.

Her eyes welled. "I love you, too."

Unable to stop himself, he pulled her to him and kissed her with all the sweet intensity of a man who loved and was loved in return.

Chapter Twenty-Two

They spent the rest of the train ride back to Lewiston in an uneasy silence.

Kate, whose head had begun to ache, pretended to sleep. She knew her refusal to marry didn't make sense to Eversham. He was an honorable man and didn't understand why she would deny them both if only because of a law that would grant him rights of which he would never take advantage.

He said he loved her, but look at what had happened to poor Delia Hale. She'd loved Philbrick and he'd claimed to care likewise for her, but she'd ended up back in her father's house to endure more punishment at his hands. According to the diary, it had been because he feared travel would harm their unborn child, but that seemed a weak reason.

Of course, it was unfair to compare their situations. She was a widow of means, Eversham was in perfect health, and, as far as she knew, he had no desire to visit Italy ever, much less repair there for his health.

The point was, that no matter how much she and Andrew loved one another—and she did love him—sometimes love wasn't enough.

Eversham might be a hundred times the man Bascomb had been, but he was still a man and, in law, would hold all the cards in their relationship.

When they finally arrived back at Thornfield, Austen greeted them at the door with a dour expression even for him.

"Lord Valentine would like to see you in the study, Mr. Eversham," he said with uncustomary coolness.

To Kate, he smiled sadly. "Miss Hardcastle is waiting for you in her sitting room."

"Thank you, Austen." Kate exchanged a puzzled look with Eversham.

They walked to the staircase together, and under her breath, she said, "Is it me, or was Austen behaving oddly?"

"It's not just you." Eversham, who had taken her arm as they ascended the stairs, kept his own voice low as well.

She had never known Austen to be rude to a guest in all the years she'd known him. Something was going on, and she wanted to find out what.

At the landing, when she should have turned right to go to the sitting room to find Caro, she instead turned to walk alongside Eversham.

When he looked at her askance, she said, "I'm coming with you to see Val. Whatever is going on, he's the one who will have answers."

"And you're suspicious because Austen sent you to Caro as if he were fobbing you off with ladies' business."

Eversham was nothing if not a good detective.

"Something must have happened while we were gone, and I want to know what." She nodded. "And while I can get the story from Caro, I want to get it from Val first."

"Why do I get the feeling Valentine won't be so sanguine about you barging in on his meeting?"

"He knows better than to try to manage me." Kate grinned. "Besides, I'll have you there to protect me."

When they reached the door of the study and their knock was answered with an invitation to enter, Kate stepped inside first and was startled to see the scowl on Valentine's face.

"You were supposed to go to Caro. This is between Eversham and me." He stood and looked as if he were about to bodily lift her and remove her from the room.

"You of all people should know that I do not do what I'm told, Val," she said with a lightness she didn't feel. It was as if some dark cloud hung in the room. But she was determined not to let her friend's foul mood color her own. "Whatever you have to say to Eversham, you can tell me. Especially if it's about the case."

She glanced back to where Eversham stood before the door, his own eyes narrowed as he watched Val.

What was going on?

Unbidden, her eyes went to the purple bruise on his jaw, where Val had hit him just yesterday.

"Kate," Valentine said in a gentler voice, "you don't need to hear this. Just go to Caro. Please."

Eversham stepped up beside her and took her hand. "Maybe you should go." He was still looking at Val, who was now staring daggers at him.

"No, I'm staying." She wasn't certain why she was so determined to remain, but instinct told her this was not something she wanted to hear from Caro.

"Fine," Val bit out, "if you won't leave, then I'll just tell Eversham now that his wife called while you were out."

All the air went out of her, and Kate felt her knees buckle. If Eversham hadn't been standing right beside her, she'd have fallen to the floor.

Before she even knew what was happening, she was in his arms and being carried to the sofa on the far side of the room. When he made to put her down in a reclining position, she shook her head and sat up, despite the spinning of her head.

"I hope you're happy, damn you," said Val, pushing Eversham out of the way to take Kate's hand. "Kate, are you all right?"

"I don't have a wife," Eversham insisted from just behind the other man. "Katherine, you know this. You've followed the accounts of me in the paper for years. There has never been mention of a wife."

She tried to concentrate. He was right. There had been no mention of a wife in any of the articles she'd read about him.

"Well, someone had better tell the woman who came here some two hours ago," Valentine said grimly. "She seemed to know a great deal about you, Eversham."

Eversham pressed a glass of brandy in her hand. "Drink this."

She took it from him and looked up into his eyes. There was no trace of guilt there.

"He's telling the truth, Val," she told her friend. "I may not have known him personally for all this time, but I've known of him. If he were married, I'd have heard about it."

Taking a sip of brandy, she sat back and closed her eyes. Once she'd regained her composure, she opened them to see two pairs of concerned male eyes staring at her.

"What? I'm fine. If you recall, I was hit quite hard on the head last night and foolishly got up before dawn so that I could outwit a stubborn detective I know."

Eversham made a noncommittal sound.

Val's gaze was speculative.

Ignoring everything they weren't saying, she changed the subject. "So, if it wasn't your wife, then who was this woman?"

"I didn't see her." Val lowered himself into the chair opposite her. "She only spoke with Austen and said you could find her at the vicarage in Lewiston when you returned. Though I daresay if she was lying about being your wife, she was also lying about that. I can't imagine Reverend Tallant going along with such a scheme."

"It has to be Emily Hale." Eversham moved to stand before the fire.

Quickly, he and Kate filled Valentine in on what they'd learned from their visit to Delia Hale's father in Crossmere.

"So, this Emily Hale is the daughter of Sebastian Philbrick and Delia Hale?" Valentine asked. "And there's a son as well?"

"Bastian," Kate confirmed. "We don't know that they're

still together, but I would be surprised if they'd separated. They've been one another's only comfort their whole lives."

"And perhaps partners in crime as well." Eversham paced. "I'm almost certain she's not at the vicarage, but I'd better go check just to make sure."

"Neither Emily nor Bastian can be fond of men of the cloth, considering what they suffered at their grandfather's hands." Kate frowned. "Do you think Reverend Tallant is in danger?"

"I don't know that," Eversham said, "but I'd rather be safe than sorry. I shouldn't be gone long."

Carefully, Kate got to her feet. When the men tried to take her arm, she shrugged them off. "I'm fine. I'll go speak to Caro. She's very likely burning you in effigy right now, Eversham, so I'd better make sure she doesn't singe Valentine's curtains."

When they hesitated, she pushed past them and walked out into the hall.

"Go," she said. "And be careful."

Valentine walked on, leaving Eversham to speak with Kate in private.

"What?" She was startled by the look in his eyes.

"Was it really just the bump on your head that made you faint?"

Her heart beat faster. "I didn't faint. I lost my balance. That's all."

He leaned down and kissed her quickly on the mouth. "We'll finish this conversation later."

He hesitated and Kate frowned. "What?"

"I'm trying to figure out how best to tell you not to leave the house in a way that will lead you to actually listen."

She groaned in exasperation. "I'm not a simpleton, Eversham. If Emily Hale is the one who called here earlier, then she knows you're looking for her."

"What's more," he said with a frown, "she deliberately called here because she wanted to drive a wedge between us."

This hadn't occurred to her, but it made a kind of sense. But only if... her breath caught.

"You think she's seen us together." It wasn't a question.

"One of them has." Eversham nodded. "And the purpose of this little prank was to hurt you. Not me. That bothers me."

"Jealous?" Her laugh rang hollow.

He ignored the jest. "I don't like that they've singled you out for their mischief. To be honest, it unnerves me. So I want your promise that you won't go out alone."

The fear in his eyes made her gut twist. "I promise," she said, touching him on the arm.

"Good." He kissed her again. "Now, I'd better go before Valentine comes looking for me."

She stood staring after him for a moment, his warning ringing in her ears, her head still a little fuzzy from earlier.

She had been telling him the truth, hadn't she? She'd lost her balance. That was all. It certainly hadn't been that the idea of Eversham having a wife had stricken her to the core.

Had it?

And now a suspected murderer had singled her out for attention.

One thing she could say for keeping company with an inspector.

It was never dull.

Rather than take the carriage, Eversham and Valentine decided to walk into the village. After spending the day mostly on the train—and given the news that their suspects had deliberately sought both him and Katherine out for their attentions—Eversham badly needed to expend some energy.

"I was ready to finish what I started with you yesterday," the other man told him candidly as they set out. "That's why I asked Kate to go to Caro. I didn't want her there when I beat you into a bloody pulp."

Eversham had guessed as much, but he could hardly say so in front of Katherine. Still. "I'd like to see you try it, Thorn. The first punch was a gift from me to you because I felt I'd earned it. Anything after that would have prompted me to defend myself."

He was hardly a small man. He outweighed the lordling by a stone and was taller by a few inches. He'd also learned how to defend himself on the streets of London, where criminals didn't play by the sporting rules Valentine set such store by.

"I was highly motivated," Valentine said baldly. "As soon as Austen brought word to me what had happened, I was ready to take the carriage to Crossmere to find you then and there. It was only Caro pointing out that Kate would have my guts for garters that I decided against it."

"She knows her friend well." Eversham laughed. One of the things he most appreciated about Katherine was her refusal to sit back and meekly let people ride roughshod over her. If she had a quarrel with someone, she'd let them know it. No games or hidden machinations for her. Only plain speaking and home truths.

This realization prompted him to change the subject. "Tell me about Bascomb."

She'd mentioned her marriage but never told him about it in more detail. And he had a feeling her fears about marrying him had their roots in what had happened before.

He wasn't so vain as to think himself irresistible. He knew damned well that while he was a decent man, he was a poor catch for a woman who could still have her pick from among the most eligible bachelors of London society.

But there was a genuine connection between them. And it wasn't just physical—though that was nothing to ignore. He'd never experienced the kind of kinship of spirit he had with her. She shared his same inquisitive nature and a determination to learn the truth, though she often went about finding her answers in a different way.

They made a good team and he was, against all odds, in love with her.

So he needed to know just what it was about her late husband that prevented her from accepting his proposal.

And if she wasn't going to tell him herself, he'd have to ask the man who'd been there to see it firsthand.

"Why do you want to know?" Valentine's eyes were narrowed with suspicion.

Eversham was famous for his patience when interrogating suspects, but when his future was on the line, he completely lost his aplomb. "Why do you think, man? I'm in love with her, and I want to know what he did to her." He ran a hand over the back of his neck.

"That was fast." Valentine glanced sideways. "Have you told her?"

Eversham was silent.

Val gave a short laugh. "Turned you down, did she?"

Eversham let out an aggrieved sigh. "Are you going to tell me or not? If not, then perhaps we can just continue our walk in silence."

"Do not fly up into the boughs, old fellow," Valentine said mildly. "I'm just giving you some difficulty in retaliation for the hours I spent today plotting your untimely demise."

"I'm not married," Eversham said through his teeth. "And attempted murder is a crime. I'm still with the Yard, you know."

"You can't arrest me," his companion said easily. "You need to get back into Kate's good books. Locking up her oldest friend would be antithetical to that."

Eversham raised his eyes heavenward. "I am trying to be patient. I truly am. But I feel sure she realizes that you can be an annoying sod and would forgive me."

"If you care to risk it," Val said.

At Eversham's growl of impatience, Val held up his hands in surrender. "Very well, I'll talk to you."

His voice lost some of its humor then. "But I warn you, it's not a pretty tale."

Eversham hadn't expected it to be. A woman as strong as Katherine would have had to endure a great deal for it to leave her still traumatized after all these years.

"I'm not sure what you know about how she came to be married to Bascomb," Valentine began. "But the long and short of it is that her father, the Marquess of Edgemont, had a bit of a gambling problem. And when I say a bit of a problem, I mean that he lost more at the tables in one night than most men see in a lifetime. So, she knew from the time she was small that she and her sisters would have to trade their excellent bloodlines for wealthy husbands."

It wasn't an uncommon tale, Eversham reflected. In a way, it was a corollary to the match Barton was trying to arrange for his own daughter. Except it was Miss Barton's wealth that would be traded for some cash-poor nobleman's title.

But his heart ached for what must have been a difficult way to grow up for a girl of Katherine's intelligence and spirit.

"When the time came for her to make her come-out, she caught the eye of Sir George Bascomb, who had made his money in the newspaper trade. He'd even been granted a life peerage for it, which seemed to soften the blow for Edgemont, who was pained at his daughter marrying so far beneath her. Never mind that he had been the one whose recklessness made it necessary in the first place."

Eversham cursed.

"Just so," agreed Valentine. "Edgemont was a miserable creature, and I daresay he'd have made her life more difficult if he'd lived much past her wedding."

He'd known Kate's parents were dead but not how or when.

"Her mother was not quite so snobbish as her father." Valentine made a noise of disdain. "Especially since once Kate was wed, she was able to fire her other daughters off on the marriage mart and they were able to marry in a manner more suited to their exalted lineage. She's quite content to spend Kate's money but doesn't like to be reminded of where it came from."

Since much of the money that had kept the aristocracy afloat over the centuries had come from the slave trade, colonial interests, and various other methods that relied upon the subjugation of other human beings, Eversham found the Marquess and Marchioness of Edgemont's distaste for their son-in-law's involvement with the newspaper trade particularly egregious.

But something in Valentine's words made him stop. "Do you mean to say that Lady Edgemont is still alive?"

"Oh yes," Valentine said with disgust. "She lives with Kate's sister, the Countess of Seaford, in the style to which she has become accustomed."

"I thought because she never spoke of them that both her parents must be dead." Of course, Eversham thought, there was more than one way to lose a parent.

"They aren't close," Valentine assured him. "Which is a good thing for you because I have little doubt that she would not approve of Kate's involvement with a policeman—even a celebrated detective from Scotland Yard."

Since Eversham wasn't entirely sure that Kate would remain involved with him, he wasn't sure her mother's opinion mattered.

"So, we've established her parents were less than ideal," he said. "What about Bascomb?"

At the mention of Katherine's late husband, Valentine scowled. "It was a disaster from the first. He was some twenty years her senior, and while he wasn't physically cruel, he was heavy-handed and controlling enough to crush the spirit of a sensitive young woman like Kate. He was more of a father to her than a husband and made sure to scrutinize every aspect of her life. He did so to such a degree that she once told me he limited her pin money because he learned she'd donated a few pounds to a charity. When a member of the board mentioned her generous donation to him, Bascomb was livid because he felt she'd kept it from him to purposely embarrass him in front of the other man. As if the other fellow gave a hang."

Eversham imagined the joy Katherine must have felt at her donation. And how her husband's scolding must have stung. He tried and failed to imagine what it would be like to have someone else wield so much control over his day-to-day life. Even as a child, he'd had more freedom than it seemed she ever had.

"He also cut her off from most of her friends," Val continued. "I didn't learn any of this until after he'd died. I thought she'd decided to cut me off, but it turned out that Bascomb was jealous and didn't allow her to see me anymore. Her only time outside the house was when he accompanied her. She was a prisoner in her own home."

Eversham clenched his jaw. "But you say he never hit her?" It was hard to believe that the man Valentine described would have refrained from raising his fists when he thought it necessary.

"She says he didn't." Valentine's voice betrayed his own suspicions about the matter as well. "And I never pressed her on it. Bad enough that he was able to control her for years. If he subjected her to other indignities, it wasn't my place to make her relive them."

And there were any number of indignities that a husband could visit upon a wife that left no marks but wounded all the same.

Eversham clenched his fists. He wished he'd had the opportunity to meet Bascomb just once. So that he might have shown the other man what it was like to feel fear.

"It took her some time to regain herself after he died," Valentine said. "But she did. I'm proud of how far Kate's come. Especially given that just five years ago, I feared the girl I'd known since childhood was gone forever."

That he'd had no notion of any of this in his interactions with her was a testament to Katherine's strong spirit. He'd known she was a lady of determination but had no inkling of just how much she'd had to overcome.

"Thank you for telling me," he told Val. He understood now why she was so vehemently against the institution of marriage. And he couldn't really blame her.

It was hard to imagine her going willingly again into the institution that had robbed her of all her liberty. She'd been unable to make any of her own choices.

She knew, he hoped, that he would never put her under such constraints. But some fears went beyond what one could explain with the rational mind.

He'd simply need to exercise some of the patience he was famous for and give her some time.

But in truth, even if she never relented, he would accept her love on whatever terms she was willing to give it.

He was just that desperate for her.

Once Eversham and Valentine had reached the village, it was a quick walk to the vicarage, where they were soon greeted by a ruddy-complexioned man who seemed the polar opposite of Simeon Hale.

"Lord Valentine," the Reverend Tallant said, welcoming the visitors into his parlor. "It's good to see you. I hope you're well."

"I am, thank you, Mr. Tallant," Val said. "And may I introduce you to Detective Inspector Andrew Eversham of Scotland Yard?"

The older man shook Eversham's hand. "I've had a visit from your lovely wife this afternoon, sir."

"That wasn't my wife." Eversham wondered who else Emily Hale had tried to cozen with this falsehood.

The vicar frowned. "I don't understand." He looked to Val as if for some explanation.

"We believe she may have something to do with the murders, Vicar," Val explained. "She could be dangerous."

This brought the reverend up short. "I can't imagine the lady I met today being involved in anything like that." He turned to Eversham. "She spoke most fondly of you, sir. She even asked if you had been working long hours while you were here."

Eversham could see that convincing the man of Emily Hale's guilt would take far longer than they could afford, so he changed the subject. "Did she ask you about anything in particular? What was her reason for calling on you?"

They were interrupted just then by a plump woman in a mobcap, whom Tallant indicated was his housekeeper. She deposited a tea tray laden with biscuits on a side table before leaving the men to speak. Once she'd gone, Tallant said, "I'm not sure what's going on, Inspector, but I'll do whatever I can to help. I should imagine you would know if you have a wife or not."

"What reason did she give for calling here at the vicarage?" Eversham repeated.

"She said she'd already been up at the Hall and you were away, so she thought she'd make some inquiries here about the poet Sebastian Philbrick. She said she was an admirer of his work. In particular, she wished to know what became of his betrothed after his death."

Eversham frowned. Why was she interested in Jane Hubbard?

"And what did you tell her?" Val asked, exchanging a look with Eversham.

"Of course, I told her about the connection to the Greens," Tallant said.

"Because Green's father was Philbrick's valet, you mean?" Valentine asked.

"Well, that, and the fact that Peter Green, Philbrick's valet, married Philbrick's fiancée after the poor poet died in Italy."

What?

"I'm sorry, Mr. Tallant." Eversham tried to remain calm in the face of such a revelation. "Are you saying that Josiah Green's mother was the former Miss Jane Hubbard?"

"Yes." Tallant looked puzzled. "I thought it was common knowledge, but you're the second visit I've had today asking after Sebastian Philbrick's betrothal. It was hardly a secret. A bit of a scandal when it happened, since she married Philbrick's valet, but I suppose that's the way love happens sometimes. Of course, as you must know, she's been dead for many years now. The pleurisy, I believe."

It was a surprise to learn that there was one more connection between Green and Philbrick, Eversham thought, but he couldn't see how it pertained to the investigation at hand.

Indeed, the entire visit to the vicarage had yielded no useful information.

He felt a chill run through him.

"How long has it been since Miss Hale was here?" he asked the vicar.

"A few hours." Tallant frowned. "Is there something wrong?"

"Not at all," Eversham said, but his haste belied his words. "You've been most helpful."

He was almost to the door when he remembered. Retracing his steps, he found Tallant still standing where they'd left him. "Was there a young man with Miss Hale? Or did she mention a brother?"

"No." The man shook his head. "She said nothing about family aside from her husband—that is, you."

Thanking the vicar again, he strode from the vicarage with Valentine hot on his heels.

"What's going on?" Valentine asked once they were out of earshot of the house. "Why are you in such a hurry?"

"Because I think she purposely led us here on a fool's errand," Eversham bit out. "And we bloody followed without hesitation."

"But why?" Val asked.

"I don't know." Eversham had some idea, but he dare not put his fears into words just yet. "But we must get back to the Hall at once."

Chapter Twenty-Three

As it turned out, Caro wasn't surprised by Kate's revelation about the identity of Eversham's supposed wife.

"I wasn't as convinced as Valentine," she said once Kate had settled in with the hoped-for cup of tea.

Much as she hated to admit it, she was flagging a bit after the long day, and was grateful to relax for a moment.

Still, she was itching with curiosity as to why her friend had been so trusting of Eversham. "What made you doubt it?"

"For one thing, I've seen the way the man looks at you." Caro grinned.

"That's hardly proof of anything." Kate had known any number of married men who looked adoringly at women who were not their wives.

"I also have come to understand something about the man," her friend continued. "And to be frank, I don't think he has the patience to juggle more than one woman at a time."

"I'm certainly glad to hear it." It was difficult for Kate to imagine Eversham doing such a thing either, but she was interested to hear Caro's reasoning. "Do go on."

The other woman settled back in her chair, causing a slumbering Ludwig, who was draped across her lap, to let out a low yowl of frustration before he settled down again.

"I mean that it takes a certain degree of concentration to get one's stories straight when one is trying to be deceptive," Caro continued. "It's plain as the nose on your face that he devotes almost all of his concentration to his work. There is some left over for thinking about you, of course. Though that has only happened recently. And since both of you are currently working on solving this case, then he can think of both at once when you're together."

Kate wasn't sure whether to be flattered or concerned. "Should I be offended that he seems to be thinking of me at the same time as a grisly string of murders?"

"Only if you expect him to be offended that you do the same thing." Caro sipped her tea. She must have seen Kate's expression, because she shook her head. "Do not try to deny that one of the things you like best about him is that he allows you to be involved in this investigation at all."

Though she did appreciate the fact that Eversham had allowed her to have a role in investigating the murders, Kate wasn't sure that she'd say it was one of the primary reasons she found him attractive. "I feel sure I'd like him just as well if he'd forbidden me from—" she began, then broke off when she realized the absurdity of her words.

Of course she wouldn't like him nearly as well if he'd forbidden her from the investigation.

Caro smiled at her.

"Fine, one of the things I like about him is that he's allowed me to help," Kate admitted. "But what has that to do with his not having a wife?"

"Nothing." Caro shrugged. "But back to my first point. I daresay he may from time to time be required to lie as part of his profession. But that's not the same as lying in his personal life. And I just can't see him deceiving you in that way."

Kate told her the story of how he'd lied to Reverend Lamb in London in order to find the man's missing wife.

"But," Caro continued, "I don't think he could do that with you. And I certainly don't believe he'd lie to you about something so fundamental. There are men who would lie about the existence of a wife, but Inspector Andrew Eversham isn't one of them."

"I'm sure he'll be pleased at your confidence in his honor." Kate laughed.

"He should be," Caro said firmly. "Now, tell me everything about Crossmere."

Quickly, Kate outlined what they'd learned from Reverend Hale and their suspicions about the twins.

"So you believe it was Emily Hale who came here posing as Eversham's wife?" Caro's eyes were wide with shock. "Why on earth would she do that?"

"I think she must have known we were not here," Kate said thoughtfully. "Otherwise she'd have risked being discovered. And Eversham has a theory about why she'd plan such a ruse."

Though she'd been skeptical at first, the more she considered his reasoning, the more sense it seemed to make.

"He believes," she continued, "that Emily wished to sow discord. Because somehow she'd seen us together and guessed the truth of things between us."

"So she's been watching you?" Caro gave a little shiver.

"Or her brother has." Kate pulled her own shawl tighter. It was chilling to imagine that her and Eversham's movements over the past few days had been under scrutiny from the twins they now suspected of multiple murders.

"And we have no notion of what either of them look like?"

"Only what Austen told us about Emily, but dark-haired and pretty could describe anyone," Kate said.

"So they could be anywhere and we wouldn't know them."

"Austen would recognize her, of course, so I doubt she'll show her face here again," Kate said thoughtfully. "But as for Bastian, no. We wouldn't know him."

"Then I have to say, I echo Mr. Eversham's instructions for you to remain in the house. What's to stop Bastian Hale from posing as one of the grooms and approaching you as you take a turn in the garden?"

Nothing. Kate knew that, and though she was sturdier than most women, she wasn't exactly comforted by the notion. And she hadn't forgotten that someone had snuck inside to attack her.

"I won't be venturing out," she said. "But neither will I sit here like Patience upon a monument either."

"Oh Lord, when you start quoting Shakespeare, I know we're in trouble." Caro grinned. "What is our plan?"

"Nothing too outlandish." Though she'd thought her fatigue had caught up with her, the tea and conversation had reinvigorated her. "Were the rest of Philbrick's papers from the folly moved into the attics this morning, as I asked?"

"They were." A slow smile broke across Caro's face. "I take it we're headed upstairs?"

"We are indeed." Kate rose. "Since no letters between Philbrick and Delia were found with Green's things, it occurs to me that maybe he never had them in the first place."

"But you already know what happened between them. Why do you need letters, too?" Caro asked with a frown.

Kate considered her question. "Something about the way Philbrick abandoned Delia to her father doesn't make sense to me. He knew what sort of man Hale was. He took her away after all. But to leave her there after having met the man. It makes no sense."

"I agree," said Caro.

"Though I fear poor Ludwig is going to be quite put out with me for taking you away." Kate eyed the way the cat lolled in repose on his mistress's lap.

"Like every man, he will have to learn to live with the occasional disappointment." Caro lifted the Siamese and set him down in his basket. As predicted, he made his displeasure known.

But when they got to the door, instead of remaining where Caro had placed him, Ludwig darted out the door and raced down the hall.

"Oh, infernal beast," Caro muttered. "I'll have to go after

him. I fear he'll tear to shreds any servant who attempts to catch him."

"I'll help." Kate had been friends with Caro now long enough to know that Ludwig wouldn't allow himself to be captured until he was good and ready, but she also knew that Caro would appreciate the company. "Though I might go change my gown first. I need to wash the travel dirt from my face."

"No, you go on up to the attics when you're finished." Caro was already looking down the hall in the direction her cat had gone. "I'll come up as soon as I find him."

If she were honest, Kate had to admit that she would rather investigate the attics than chase after a cat who didn't wish to be caught.

"You're sure?"

"Absolutely," Caro said over her shoulder. "I'll be up in a trice."

And a half hour later when Kate reached the doorway leading to the attics, a lamp in her hand so she would be able to see her way inside, the light shining from the open door told her Caro had been right. She'd found the cat as quickly as she'd predicted.

"The beast has been tamed then?" she called, pushing open the door and stepping into the room. It was brightly lit, thanks to the lanterns hanging on hooks from the ceiling. But she didn't see Caro anywhere. "Caro? Are you here?"

The room was crowded with everything from wardrobes to chests to lamps to trunks. And on the far wall beneath the dormer windows, she recognized some of the trunks that had been stored in the folly.

Deciding that Caro must have had to leave again for some reason, she set down her own lamp and made a methodical search for Philbrick's things.

She'd just knelt down before a trunk when she heard footsteps. Some instinct told her it wasn't Caro.

Spying a walking stick lying on the floor nearby, she bent to pick it up—thinking to use it as a weapon. But just as she bent forward, she felt movement behind her.

Rolling to the floor, she got to her feet and swung. But her assailant jumped away just in time.

She gasped. "Mr. Thompson?"

Reeve Thompson smiled, but it didn't meet his eyes. "I beg you will call me by my proper name, Lady Katherine. After all, you've gone to such a lot of trouble to find me."

And suddenly, it all fell into place.

"Bastian Hale."

"I prefer my actual surname, if you please." He bowed. "Bastian Philbrick, at your service."

The two men arrived back at the manor house, some thirty minutes later, to find Caro waiting for them, her face drawn.

"Kate is gone," she blurted out before they'd even taken off their coats. "I was supposed to go with her to search the attics but I had to chase Ludwig and he didn't want to be found and it took longer than I expected and by the time I got there she was gone and it's all my fault."

It was a good thing Valentine was there because all

Eversham had heard of Caro's speech was the fact that Katherine was gone.

"Easy there," the other man said with more patience than Eversham had ever heard him use with Miss Hardcastle. "Let's go take a look at the attics and see if there are any clues, shall we?"

They began climbing the stairs, but before they could get past the first landing, they were assailed by the other guests, who began pouring from the open door of the drawing room.

"What's going on?" Lady Eggleston demanded, clutching her husband's arm. "I heard Miss Hardcastle shouting. Has there been another murder?"

Eversham was in no mood for the high-strung peeress's questions. "I want all of you to go back into the drawing room and shut the door."

"I say, Eversham, you can't—" Lord Eggleston began, but was interrupted by Valentine.

"He's from Scotland Yard, Eggleston." Val indicated with a wave of his hand that they should follow Eversham's instructions. "In this house, he can do as he likes."

The guests murmured among themselves and were turning to go back into the drawing room when Eversham thought to do a head count. "Where is Mr. Thompson?"

Miss Barton turned back. "I haven't seen him all afternoon. I thought perhaps he'd taken ill." Her cheeks colored as she spoke. It was obvious that she'd developed a tender spot for Thompson.

Eversham thanked her, and when the rest of the guests were asked, none of them could account for the missing man either.

Once they were on their way upstairs again, Valentine said, "Perhaps she got an impulse to go for a walk?"

"No." Caro's earlier agitation had calmed somewhat. "Kate was quite firm about remaining indoors because you'd asked her to, Eversham."

In this instance, Eversham thought with a sinking feeling, telling Katherine to remain at Thornfield may have put her in greater danger than if she'd left.

"What do you know about Thompson?" he asked Valentine as they neared the attics. "You said before that you met him in London?"

"Yes." Val opened the door to the upper room. "I met him at my club. He'd expressed an interest in visiting the Lakes sometime before and I thought he'd make an interesting addition to the party."

"But you don't know anything about his family?" Eversham pressed. He thought about the young man's hair, which was shot through with the same red highlights he'd seen in what remained of Reverend Hale's natural color.

"No, nothing," Val said as they stepped into the attics. "I didn't think I needed to. We were introduced by mutual friends."

"I think we may have found the missing Mr. Bastian Hale." Eversham pushed past the other two to scan the room for any trace of Katherine.

"Dear God." Caro's voice betrayed every fear that Eversham felt. "Do you really think it's him?"

"We've been wondering all day where he was." Val clenched his fists. "And this whole time he's been right here under our noses posing as Reeve Thompson."

"He helped me search for Ludwig," Caro said, coming to a stop in the middle of the attic floor. "I told him where she was. I said we were searching the attics and he disappeared."

"You couldn't have known," Val told her. "It's my fault for inviting him here in the first place. I should have known better than to invite a relative stranger into my home. And now Kate is in danger because of it."

While they talked, Eversham moved to the corner of the attic where he recognized some of the crates and trunks from the folly. His eyes lit on the trunk Kate had hurt her finger on and had to look away before the ache of the memory could assail him. He didn't have time for sentiment now. He had to think clearly so that he could find her.

"Look." Val strode forward and handed him a page. "It was attached with this to the wall."

Valentine held up a small knife. Eversham cursed.

He looked at the page and saw it was one of Philbrick's poems, *The Maze*.

"Is there a maze on this property?" he asked, his anxiety for Katherine growing by the minute.

"We saw it on our way to the folly." Caro took the note from Val before returning it. "It's mostly grown over now."

"There are ways to get in if you know where to look," Valentine said, handing the note back to Eversham. "Come, I'll take you."

This man and his sister had already killed multiple times. They'd kidnapped Katherine to set a trap for him. He had no intention of letting her, or anyone else, get hurt because of him.

"Give me the knife." When Val handed it over, Eversham asked, "Do you have any weapons of your own in the house?"

"Any number of them in the gun room for hunting," the other man answered.

They were already striding out of the attics and into the hallway when Caro called out. "Wait! I have an idea."

Biting back impatience, Eversham turned, gesturing for her to hurry up.

"Bastian isn't stupid," Caro said. "The entire time we've been searching for him, he's been right under our noses. If you go barging in demanding he hand over Kate, he'll be ready for you."

"I don't care," Eversham said. "All that matters is getting her away from him alive and in one piece."

"Think, Eversham. You need to do something to put him off balance."

"What do you have in mind, Caro?" Val asked, his expression grave but curious.

"It may not work if Emily Hale has joined her brother," she warned, "but we haven't got much choice. If we arrive and see her there, we'll have to adjust accordingly."

Eversham bit back a groan of impatience.

"The short version is that I'll put on a veil and pretend to be Emily Hale," Caro said. "Then, once we see she's not there, one of you will lead me out—I'll be wearing the veil to hide my face. We'll offer to trade me—that is, Emily—for Kate. And instead of actually giving me to him, you'll get Kate back and capture Bastian."

Eversham blinked. It was risky. Especially if Emily Hale

did turn out to be there. Though they hadn't seen her on their way into Lewiston, it was entirely possible she'd come back to the Hall after visiting Tallant. She'd had a reason for sending Eversham away from Thornfield and into the village after all.

Still, Caro's plan would give them an option for distracting Bastian should they find him alone.

But they didn't have much time. "It might work." He nodded. "But you need to hurry. He's had Katherine for far too long as it is."

"You have hidden depths, Miss Hardcastle." The admiration in Valentine's voice was not as grudging as it might once have been.

"Wait until it works before you give me too much praise." She frowned.

Then she went upstairs to retrieve her veil.

"We'll get her back," Val told Eversham as they hurried downstairs to the gun room.

Eversham couldn't speak past the lump in his throat.

The alternative didn't bear thinking of.

Chapter Twenty-Four

The middle of the Thornfield Hall maze wasn't as overgrown as Kate would have imagined from the outside. Yes, the shrubs were leggy and showed only a vague resemblance to what once must have been precisely trimmed, squared-off walls of greenery. But the paths she and Bastian had followed once they'd pressed into the narrow corner opening were easy enough to see. And Kate only occasionally felt the prickly drag of branches against her bare arms, which her captor had bound behind her back with a silk stocking. She'd lost her shawl somewhere along the way, and the chill of the early evening air was already beginning to bring gooseflesh up on her exposed skin.

Again and again she struggled with the knot around her wrists, grateful Bastian couldn't see her hands from where he stood.

From her seated position on the scrolled ironwork bench

in the center of the open-air room, she wondered whether the others had found Bastian's message on the wall. She hadn't been able to see what it was—it looked like a poem—but surely it contained a clue as to where she'd been taken. Andrew was clever. Whatever it was, he'd figure out what it meant and come to her.

He had to.

She had things she needed to say.

If he asked her now, her answer to his marriage proposal would be entirely different than it had been earlier.

There was nothing like imminent danger that made one reassess one's priorities. "Where is your sweetheart, Lady Katherine?" Bastian said through clenched teeth from where he paced around the enclosure. "I cannot imagine little Caro hasn't sounded the alarm by now."

"Perhaps he and Lord Valentine are still in the village searching for your sister." Kate hoped to make him as fearful as he'd made her. "Did you know she came to Thornfield today? That was taking quite a risk, don't you think?"

But if she'd hoped to rile him, she was going to need to be more forceful than that. "They won't find her." Bastian smiled slyly. "She's far too clever for the likes of Inspector Eversham. We've been ahead of him every step of the way."

As if remembering something, he raised one finger in the air in a dramatic gesture. "I almost forgot to thank you, Lady Katherine. Your interview with Lizzie Grainger really was a stroke of luck for us. Not only did it encourage Eversham's superiors to take him off the case, but Lizzie's description gave old Wargrove somebody to arrest.

"Of course," he said with a smile, "it matched me, too. But I was too smart to let them catch me."

Kate gasped. She'd been so busy worrying, she hadn't even thought about Lizzie's description. Of course it had been Bastian she'd seen.

"Don't feel too bad, dear lady," her captor continued. "I doubt he'd have been able to find us even if he had remained on the case. We learned subterfuge from the cradle, after all. Impossible not to in that house."

"Yes, we met your grandfather today." Kate thought that perhaps if she could keep him talking long enough, she'd be able to loosen her bonds. "He was quite unpleasant."

She'd expected him to scowl, but to her surprise, the young man laughed, albeit bitterly. "Unpleasant, you say. It's as if you're talking about a visitor to afternoon tea who wouldn't stop eating all the biscuits."

"Hardly that." Kate tried to infuse her voice with sympathy. "I thought he was horrible. And the way he treated you, your sister, and your mother was unconscionable."

He made a sound of disgust. "He made our lives a misery. And for what? When Emily found the marriage lines, I thought it must be some sort of trick. I could never have imagined he could hate us enough to present us to the world as bastards when we were just as legitimate as any other poor fool in his congregation. I'd even absorbed enough of his Bible thumping to believe that we maybe even deserved his cruelty. But those lines told us everything we needed to know about the Reverend Simeon Hale."

"Why didn't you kill him?" As long as they were here and Bastian seemed willing to talk, Kate decided to ask the question that had been bothering her ever since they'd laid eyes on the twins' grandfather that morning. "I should have thought that he would be the first you'd punish. Not strangers in London who'd never done you any harm."

She shifted in her seat as the hard iron of the bench was beginning to make her back ache. As she moved, her hand caught on a sharp bit of scrollwork and she only just kept from showing her surprised pain to her captor.

But her question had distracted him enough that he didn't notice the change in her expression. "I did consider it," he said thoughtfully. "We both did. But once we'd thought a little, we realized that it would harm him more to see how we'd perverted his precious Commandments. So, we stole the purse he kept hidden away in his study and left that day for London."

His expression darkened. "I was foolish enough to think that all we needed was to show the marriage lines in town and we'd be welcomed as the long-lost children of the great Sebastian Philbrick. But no one believed us. And a little research told me he'd died penniless. So we changed our plans. If we couldn't go back to Crossmere triumphant as our true selves, we'd have to make sure that Grandfather saw tidings of our new lives in the newspaper."

While he spoke, Kate had worked her hands in such a way that she was able to lift the coiled stocking around her wrists over the protruding piece of iron on the back of the bench. So slowly that her movements couldn't be detected, she rubbed the binding across the iron in a sawing motion.

"How could he know that you were the ones responsible

for the killings?" she asked, making a show of attention to his story, lest he figure out the reason for her distraction.

"He drilled the Ten Commandments into us from the moment we learned to speak." Bastian's smile was gleeful like a child's, and Kate felt the chill right down to her bones. "I told him to look for us in the papers. I would have sent him a letter saying as much, of course, but that old brute would have given our names to the police without a backward glance."

Kate knew intuitively that he had enjoyed sending messages to his sadistic grandfather with the bodies of his victims, but it was a testament to the insularity of Bastian's thinking that he and Emily had assumed that Hale would be able to recognize their handiwork just from the use of the Ten Commandments, which were known the world over as tenets of the Christian faith.

"You were in London for the better part of a year. What made you decide to come to Lewiston?" She'd felt the stocking begin to give a little and had to keep him talking long enough for her to free her hands.

Now that he'd begun to tell his story, Bastian seemed in no hurry to stop. "That's an interesting tale. You see, while we were in London, I spent every moment I could spare from my position as a clerk looking for information about my father. I was in the British Library one day and one of the librarians with whom I'd become acquainted told me he'd found a letter my father had written to his publisher."

His eyes gleaming with excitement, he continued, "It wasn't the content of the letter that was interesting. But where it had come from. You see, the library had acquired it from a collector, who bequeathed it to them upon his death. I learned from his family that he'd purchased it from a dealer. And where do you think he got it?"

"He'd bought it from Josiah Green." She stilled while the man's gaze was on her.

"Very good, Lady Katherine." Bastian nodded approvingly. "I begin to understand why poor Eversham is so fond of you. You're almost as clever as my sister."

Ignoring his praise, she pressed him. "So you came to Lewiston in search of Green?"

"It stood to reason that if he had one letter, he might have more. And after a little more investigation, I learned that his father had been my father's valet and, well, we simply had to make the journey here."

"But why as Reeve Thompson?"

"We could hardly come to town telling everyone we were the long-lost Philbrick heirs, could we?"

"And Valentine?" Kate leaned forward as if on the edge of her seat to hear his answer, but she was really just dragging the stocking over the ironwork.

"We needed to get into Thornfield Hall, obviously, just to ensure that none of our father's things were still here. After all, we're his rightful heirs, and all of his belongings are ours now."

Kate decided it wasn't the right time to explain English inheritance law in cases where the descendant's estate had been sold to pay off debts.

"I made some inquiries as to the new owner, and it was easy enough to attend a few sporting matches and strike up an acquaintance with Lord Valentine. When he mentioned he was getting up a house party, it was impossible to find a reason why I should turn him down."

The stocking was beginning to tear now, and Kate schooled her features not to reveal her relief.

"My sister, of course, could hardly join me as a guest," Bastian continued. "I had introduced myself as a single man, so I couldn't invent a wife at this late date. And just in case someone from our old life recognized us, we couldn't present ourselves as brother and sister either. So I came to Thornfield and she stayed in a neighboring village, coming to Lewiston from time to time, of course, when necessary. For a chance encounter with poor Mr. Jones, for instance."

"What sort of chance encounter?" Kate asked, wanting to keep him talking.

"Oh, come now, Lady Katherine," Bastian chided. "You're a woman of the world. You know precisely what sort it was."

Of course, Kate thought. She'd seduced the man into going to Green for them. It had been a neat trick. Not only had Jones's inquiry of Green let them know that there were more letters, but having Jones act as go-between had kept their presence in the village a secret.

"Which of you killed Jones?" she asked, just as the last bit of cloth broke apart. It took every bit of muscle control Kate had to keep her hands from flying apart as the bindings tore.

"Emily." Bastian shrugged. "Jones had proved useful, but he was no longer needed. And my sister doesn't have patience for men for very long after they've outlasted their usefulness."

His tone became apologetic now, however. "I am sorry you were the one to find him. I had hoped Barton would be the one to stumble upon the body. But I hadn't counted on your needing to flee from him. I should have, given how he's leered at you from the moment he first saw you."

Mr. Jones was seemingly more deserving of an apology, but Kate wasn't quite sure that would be the thing to say to her captor at that moment.

She was trying to work some circulation back into her hands so that she could use them to aid in her escape when the sounds of footsteps and thrashing in the bushes came toward them.

"Ah, excellent," Bastian said, for all the world, as if he were a host about to greet his guests. "Your policeman has arrived."

Chapter Twenty-Five

Eversham could see lamplight shining through the thick boxwood as he walked on one side of Caro, his hand clasped around her upper arm. Valentine, on the other side, did the same.

He had to admit that when Caro had explained her idea, he'd thought it mad, but once she'd donned the black gown and hat with the black veil covering her face, he was quite sure her own mother wouldn't be able to recognize her. Since Emily Hale had donned a similar disguise when she'd broken into the Green house, she might conceivably have other reasons for wearing it again.

Of course, Bastian might very well know where his sister was, in which case this ruse would be an abject failure.

But it gave them a way in. And would possibly be enough distraction to help them get Kate away from him before he could do her more harm.

"Come in, come in," said Bastian Hale as the trio rounded the last corner and came into the square center of the overgrown maze. "I wondered if you'd get my—"

He broke off as soon as he spied Caro and began to rush forward. Prepared for such an eventuality, Eversham pulled Caro roughly before him and placed the dagger Bastian had used to secure the poem in the attics to her throat. "Don't come any closer."

With a curse, Hale came to a halt. "You're a dead man, Eversham. I thought I'd make it quick for your lady's sake, but now I'm going to play with you for a while. After I kill her first and make you watch."

Even if the man had a pistol on him, he couldn't risk shooting Eversham without harming his sister. Which was precisely what they'd counted on.

"You say the nicest things," Eversham said coldly. "Now, come over here away from Lady Katherine and hand me your gun."

Valentine stepped forward and pulled a pistol from his pocket and pointed it at Hale's chest. "Over to the bench," he said, prodding his captive.

While the two men walked, Eversham looked at Katherine, trying to determine whether she'd been harmed or not. She had just stood and taken a step toward him when he noticed her eyes widen.

"Eversham!"

Without the warning, he'd have gone down like a load of

bricks. As it was, however, the glancing blow did stun him, and though he turned to strike back at his attacker, Caro got there first.

"Get off me!" screeched Emily Hale as Caro leapt onto her back like a monkey.

The two women went to the ground in a tangle of arms and legs and skirts.

Valentine, who had been about to tie Bastian to the bench, saw that Caro was in trouble and handed the pistol to Kate.

"He's your prisoner now," he told her before sprinting toward the brawling women.

Perhaps thinking this was his opportunity for escape, Bastian tried to wrestle the gun away from Katherine. He wasn't, however, expecting her knee, which she used to render him ineffective for anything but writhing on the ground in pain while the others restrained his sister.

Eversham hurried to where Katherine stood over Hale and, after hauling the man to his feet, tied him securely to the bench arms, which wouldn't allow him to escape as Kate had. "Are you all right? Did he hurt you?"

"Only my pride," Katherine said with a laugh. "I thought I was far too clever to be caught out unawares like that. I should have guessed it was Thompson all along."

His task completed, Eversham pulled her into his arms and kissed her thoroughly. "I thought I'd lost you." He pulled her against him, desperate to feel for himself that she was alive and safe.

"I thought the same thing." She buried her face in his

neck before leaning back to look him in the eyes. "I'm so sorry I refused you. I don't know what I was thinking."

"You were afraid," he said. "And I wasn't hearing you. I'm sorry. However long you need, I'll wait. If you never want to marry at all, that's all right, too. However you'll have me in your life, Katherine, I'll take it."

"I think I'm going to be sick," Bastian Hale said from behind them.

"Be quiet or we'll gag you," Kate said over her shoulder.

To Eversham, she said, "I love you. And if you want to be married, then I trust you enough to risk it."

"I hate to interrupt your happy reunion," Valentine called from the other side of the clearing, where he and Caro were struggling to control Emily Hale between them, "but we could use some help."

"Kate, I was in a fight and I think I won!" Caro shouted.

"We'd better go," Eversham said. There would be time enough for sweet words and plans later.

For now he was happy to have her safe and out of harm's way.

It was some hours later when Eversham finally slipped into Katherine's bedchamber, having transported Bastian and Emily Hale, with Valentine and Jim Hyde's help, to the jail in the nearby village of Kendal. He liked Constable Miller well enough, but he didn't trust the man to be able to keep a pair like the Hale twins locked up for longer than an hour at most.

Once they'd realized they wouldn't be able to talk their way out of this, the pair had become sullen. And the last he saw them, they'd been sitting in separate cells staring straight ahead in eerily similar poses.

"You're back." Kate, who had been curled up in the chair beside her bed, rose and pulled him into her arms.

"Let me change." He laughed softly. "I smell of the road and God knows what else."

"I don't mind." But she pulled him toward the dressing room, and showed him the wash basin; brought him soap, a cloth, and a towel; and left him to his ablutions.

Once he'd cleaned himself up, he stripped down to his drawers, folded his clothes neatly, and left them on a chair.

Back in her bedchamber, he found Katherine sitting up against the pillows, her skin bathed in lamplight and looking like everything he'd never known he needed.

"Come to bed." She reached out her hand to him. And though he'd meant to let her rest, once Eversham slid between the sheets that had been warmed by her body, he couldn't have kept from pulling her to him if his life had depended on it.

Later, as they were lying entwined, Katherine's head resting on his chest, she asked, "What will become of them?"

He didn't need to ask of whom she was speaking.

"They killed a half-dozen people," he said grimly. "Though they were badly done by their grandfather, I don't see how they'll escape the hangman's noose."

She nodded, then tucked her head beneath his chin. "And what of the man who was arrested for their crimes before? Clark."

"I sent a messenger to London to let Darrow know," Eversham said. Ensuring that the man who'd been wrongfully accused was set free had been his first priority after clapping irons on the twins. Once he returned to London, he would do what he could to see that Darrow and Dolph Wargrove were punished for their misdeeds as well. "Barring some administrative delay, he should be with his family within the week."

He felt her let out a breath.

"Didn't you think I'd take care of it?" he asked curiously.

"Of course." The degree of trust in her voice humbled him. "But," Katherine continued, "I wasn't sure how soon you'd be able to get word to London. I still feel so bad about the role our interview played in his arrest in the first place."

Eversham smoothed a hand over her back. "If anyone should feel guilt, it's Wargrove and Darrow. Though I doubt either of them will lose much sleep over it."

They were quiet for some moments before he spoke again. "I'll sign whatever you want me to. To ensure that the newspaper doesn't belong to me when we marry."

She rose up a little to look at him. "You would do that for me?"

"What do I know about running a newspaper?" he asked wryly. More seriously he added, "I want you to know I heard what you said about fearing that someday my superiors at the Met might try to pressure me into taking it from you. Or shutting it down. I don't ever want that fear to come between us."

He saw her eyes glisten with unshed tears. "Thank you."

Wrapping her arms around his neck, she leaned forward and kissed him.

"There is one thing, however," he said once she'd pulled away. "I must insist that you change the name of your column."

At that, her smile disappeared. "What?"

"It's just that it's no longer appropriate to call it *A Lady's Guide to Mischief and Mayhem* when it's obvious to anyone that neither you nor Caro is involved in either mischief or mayhem."

At his light tone, her shoulders relaxed. "What do you suggest we call it then?"

"Why not *A Lady's Guide to Law and Order*?"

Kate stifled a laugh. "That's a terrible name."

"Why?" He was a little insulted. It was his profession after all. "What do you suggest then?"

"How about," she asked, slipping her arms around his neck, "*A Lady's Guide to Love and Happiness*?"

"It's a difficult task, but I suppose I'll just have to make sure you have plenty of both so you'll have something to write about."

Eversham was sure he was up to the challenge.

Acknowledgments

As with every book, this one wouldn't have been possible without the hard work of so many people working behind the scenes. Thanks to my always supportive rock star of an agent, Holly Root, whose calm guidance, enthusiasm, and (where appropriate) pragmatism, have talked me down from about a dozen instances of "the historical romance is dead" crises. *#TeamRoot* Thanks to my legendary editor at Forever, Amy Pierpont, whose sharp editorial eye and patience as a literal pandemic raged around us ushered this book into being. Big thanks also go out to the always gracious Sam Brody, editorial assistance extraordinaire, who never chides me when I forget to reply all and loves some of the same books I do. Thanks to Jodi Rosoff, director of marketing and publicity at Forever, whose excitement about this book is contagious. And, of course, thanks to the production team, including production editor Luria Rittenberg and my amazing copy editor, Joan Matthews. I don't know their names, but I know the sales team has been hard at work adjusting their work to the new way we do business. Thanks to you all.

Finally, thanks to Karen and Georgia of the *My Favorite Murder* podcast have been a long time coming. I stumbled upon their show at a time when I was in desperate need of distraction, commiseration, and hope. And they've kept me sane through the last four years with their humor, their shared horror at the harm we can do to one another, and their open acknowledgment that none of us can get through this life without help. SSDGM

Any errors, mistakes, or flubs are my own.

While investigating a disappearance, Miss Caroline Hardcastle is caught between disdain and desire for the man who broke her heart—Lord Valentine Thorn.

DON'T MISS THEIR STORY IN AUTUMN 2021.

About the Author

Manda Collins grew up on a combination of Nancy Drew books and Jane Austen novels, and her own brand of historical romantic suspense is the result. A former academic librarian, she holds master's degrees in English and Library & Information Studies. Her novel *Duke with Benefits* was named a *Kirkus* Best Romance of 2017. She lives on the Gulf Coast with two lazy cats, a very spoiled Shih Tzu, and more books than are strictly necessary.

Do you love historical fiction?

Want the chance to hear news about your favourite authors (and the chance to win free books)?

Suzanne Allain
Mary Balogh
Lenora Bell
Charlotte Betts
Manda Collins
Joanna Courtney
Grace Burrowes
Evie Dunmore
Lynne Francis
Pamela Hart
Elizabeth Hoyt
Eloisa James
Lisa Kleypas
Jayne Ann Krentz
Sarah MacLean
Terri Nixon
Julia Quinn

Then visit the Piatkus website
www.yourswithlove.co.uk

And follow us on Facebook and Instagram
www.facebook.com/yourswithlovex | @yourswithlovex

PIATKUS